CW00839711

Song of the Skald

Song
of the
Skald

Ann Neve

Matador
9 De Montfort Mews
Leicester LE1 7FW, UK
Tel: (+44) 116 255 9311 / 9312
Email: books@troubador.co.uk
Web: www.troubador.co.uk/matador

ISBN 978-1906510-503

A Cataloguing-in-Publication (CIP) catalogue record for this book
is available from the British Library.

Mixed Sources
Product group from well-managed
forests and other controlled sources
www.fsc.org Cert no. TT-COC-2082
© 1996 Forest Stewardship Council

Typeset in 11pt Garamond by Troubador Publishing Ltd, Leicester, UK
Printed in the UK by The Cromwell Press Ltd, Trowbridge, Wilts, UK

Matador is an imprint of Troubador Publishing Ltd

For my children, Helen and Russell

Contents

PART FOUR

PART ONE

I

Escape from the mountain fortress

The mountainous region we now know as Switzerland had, by the second half of the seventh century, been overrun by successive waves of invaders. First the Celts settled the land; then the Roman legions came, eager to safeguard the route from Italy to Gaul. Once they had brought the whole area under Roman rule it became, until the fifth century, a buffer state between the Roman Empire and the barbarian hordes of northern and eastern Europe. Finally, the Teutonic tribes broke through: the Alemannians conquering the north and east; the Burgundians the south and west. The latter were fewer in number and were soon absorbed by the Romanized Celts. They adopted their way of life and their language: a form of provincial Latin called French. The Alemannian tribes, however, were strong and many in number. They kept their German tongue and way of life, and extended their territory far into central Switzerland. But in their turn, both the Burgundians and the Alemannians were conquered by Clovis, King of the Franks, and their lands annexed to his empire. According to custom, when Clovis died his realm was divided and distributed amongst his relatives. His successors were neither powerful nor able and the Alemannians seized the opportunity to re-assert their independence. Their great landowners chose to ignore their weak Frankish overlord and to rule their country themselves as true tribal chiefs. They guarded their possessions jealously; they attacked their neighbours at the slightest provocation and maintained private armies for that purpose. Once more, warlords ruled the land.

The Lord Bardolph charged up the hillside at the head of his hunting party, his face aglow with the victory of the kill. He galloped through the gates of his stronghold scattering men, women, children and livestock in all directions. Once this had been a Roman fortress, strategically placed at the head of a high alpine valley where none could journey unobserved to the mountain pass above. In those days it had been manned by a large garrison. Necessity had demanded that Bardolph make modifications to the original structure so that it might be successfully defended by a much smaller band of men. This he had done by sealing up three of the four gateways with stone from the mountain, leaving only the main gateway which faced down the valley towards the plain. The large area of ground inside the battlements, where once Roman soldiers had pitched their tents, now provided winter pasture for Bardolph's cattle and a place of shelter for his many tenants and their families when danger threatened. Against the inside of the massive stone walls, wooden structures had been erected: storehouses, workshops, stables, barracks for the soldiers who guarded the fortress and shacks for its workers – a self-contained world whose inhabitants owed total allegiance to the man who rode so recklessly through their midst.

Bardolph raced ahead towards his own living quarters which he had built at the highest point inside his stronghold. He had surrounded them with a wooden palisade as a second line of defence in the unlikely event that his enemies should succeed in breaching the outer stone perimeter. The jubilant hunters threw the freshly-slaughtered game outside the door of the kitchens – a lean-to which rested against the side of the main building. The men dismounted noisily, Bardolph himself requiring the assistance of a servant. Many years before, his right thigh had been bared to the bone by his old adversary, Raoulbrun the Burgundian. Since then he had walked with a limp and prolonged riding had given him much pain. He had been forced to come to an arrangement with his younger brother, the Lord Gustavus, that the latter should take over the command of both armies and be responsible for the defence of Bardolph's many scattered estates as well as his own; in return, Bardolph administered Gustavus's lands, his peoples and their affairs. The arrangement had worked very well for years: one brother ruling the estates and dependants, the other brother indulging the art which he had perfected – the art of war.

Bardolph's injured leg did not prevent him from enjoying the pleasures of hunting and hawking. He liked nothing better than to be roused at first light and ride out with his nobles. They would eat their first meal of the day together in the forest, entertaining one another with bawdy tales of the previous night's exploits. When the sun was well-risen they would return to the fortress, proudly bearing the rewards of their sport.

Bardolph stood in the courtyard, his face a picture of contentment and well-being. He was a stocky, heavily built man with an enormous growth of black beard. He was subject to violent rages and equally violent bursts of good humour. Today, he had been forced to return home earlier than usual but this had not spoiled his enjoyment. The winter snows were melting fast and there was the promise of months of such expeditions before Nature once more curtailed his activities.

Suddenly, Bardolph sensed he was being watched. He looked up to a small window above him. A tiny solemn white face with huge eyes was coolly surveying him. At once, Bardolph's equanimity left him. His black bushy eyebrows drew together and a scowl spread over his face. Abruptly, limping badly, he made for the front of the building. His men, seeing the change in his mood, followed him anxiously – except for one who lingered behind. Bardolph crashed through the main doors, strode the length of the Great Hall, his leg throbbing badly now, passed the fireplace in the centre of the chamber to the table at the far end and his own chair. Dogs scurried for cover; servants ran to bring him wine to drink and water to wash away the stains and smell of the hunt. The people crowded against the walls, who had waited patiently for his return, shivered when they saw his dark and angry countenance. This was the day he sat in judgment on them and they feared his judgment would not be kind.

Thorkell waited until the Lord Bardolph and his nobles had turned the corner of the building and were out of sight, before looking up at the small window. He made a theatrical bow and whilst still bending low, blew a kiss in the direction of the white face. The little girl beamed with delight and blew a kiss back. Thorkell, a slim agile man in his mid-thirties, straightened and with a mischievous look in his eyes and using his fingers dramatically, he indicated that he would go around the back of the building and climb to the first floor to meet her. The child nodded her head happily and left the window.

Thorkell hurried around the back of the Great Hall to where the chapel had been built along the side of the main building in much the same way that the kitchens huddled against its opposite wall. He slipped quietly through the chapel doors and ascended the small staircase to the upper floor balcony, two steps at a time. At that moment, the inner door to the balcony opened and the little girl ran eagerly to meet him.

'Thorkell, I am so pleased to see you. Have you come to tell me more tales of your Norse homeland? I like the stories about the brave shield-maidens best.'

'I know that you do, little one, but I have not come to tell you heroic stories but, I regret, to bid you farewell.'

'No, Thorkell! Not so soon. Not yet.'

'The snows have melted; the spring offensive can begin. Your uncle, the Lord Gustavus, demands that I attend him. As his skald – his warrior poet – I must be in the thick of the fighting. How else can I record the brave deeds of the combatants and sing of them afterwards? I am held in such high esteem by our Lord General that battle cannot commence without me.'

'But I do not want you to go, Thorkell. You are my dear friend.'

'And you are my dear friend – my little shield-maiden. I shall miss you but when I return – when the winter snows halt the fighting – I shall have many more tales to tell you. Now I must leave. I have much to do and many people to see before I depart. I came to you first, my little Lady Matilda, because you are a most important person and the only lady who has ever won my heart.'

Bowing low, Thorkell kissed the little girl's hand before dashing down the narrow staircase and across the chapel to the door. There he paused and gave an exaggerated farewell salute. She waved back and called out, 'Take great care, Thorkell,' as the door closed behind the skald. She sat down on the bench which ran the length of the balcony, beaming at the skald's compliments, but then a look of sadness spread across her small face and tears came into her eyes. She brushed them aside and slowly descended the staircase. She wandered around the empty chapel, passing between the benches where the servants and the other members of the household made their devotions. Then she went behind the altar to a curtained alcove which was the home of her tutor, Father Almeric. She half expected to find the old man asleep, just as her mother and her nurse were asleep in the room she had just left, but the priest's cot was empty; no-one was in the tiny bare room. Then she remembered: on court days her father, the Lord Bardolph, having few scholars amongst his followers, insisted that Father Almeric sit by him to record his judgments and in particular, the fines he imposed. These were the only occasions upon which the old man could be induced to enter the Great Hall. He much preferred the sanctuary of the chapel and the silence of his room which he had often told the Lady Matilda reminded him of the monk's cell he had occupied in the happy days of his youth.

The child was about to leave when she noticed that the small door which had been cut in the outside wall of the priest's abode had been left ajar. She thought that perhaps Father Almeric had been pleased to smell the fresh spring air. She moved closer and peeped through the opening. The yard outside was always a busy place but on court days the activity increased. Men came from far and wide, bringing their families and their dues – the grain and the livestock which they owed the Lord Bardolph as rent in kind. As the child watched a cart trundled by, children running beside it, laughing and chattering. A second wagon followed, with only the driver and his wife aboard. She made a momentous decision. She darted from her hiding place, pulling the hood of her gown well down over her face, and ran around to the far side of the vehicle. She prayed that the cart would provide sufficient cover as she danced along, one hand resting upon the framework.

They left the Great Hall behind and reached the gateway which separated the inner courtyard from the outer enclosure without incident. Soon they were crossing the large expanse of the bailey towards the battlements. The area was alive with people but no-one noticed her. She held her breath as the wagon approached the main gateway. She could see down the valley now and her excitement grew. Would the couple in the cart look round and discover her? Would the guards challenge her? The driver slowed down as they passed through the gates. She feared all was lost. She bent her head even lower and stumbled on. They crossed the wooden drawbridge which spanned the deep trench surrounding the stronghold but not until the cart suddenly gathered speed did she look up. She was outside the fortress. She let go of the wagon, turned and dashed back across the drawbridge, seeking the shelter of the huge Roman wall.

She stood shielded from view by a buttress, her thin body pressed hard against the stonework, her heart pounding. She waited for the cry of the guards; none came. Her feeling of panic began to subside. More vehicles left through the gateway and more arrived. No-one paid any attention to her. She looked up and alarm gripped her again when she saw two sentries standing together on the parapet above her head. They talked for a few moments until one chanced to glance down, straight at her. She was frozen to the spot but the man, assuming she was playing some game with other children, merely smiled and put his finger to his lips, indicating that he would not reveal her hiding place. Somehow, the child managed to smile back. Once more her panic abated; the sense of relief was overwhelming; she felt weak and drained of strength. Then realization dawned: she had left the fortress without being challenged. She had escaped; she was free. Joy flooded her soul. Without a backward glance, she gathered up her skirts and ran along the ramparts until she felt it was safe to leave the protection of the wall. Then she climbed down into the ditch, scrambled up the other side, raced across the open pasture and disappeared into the trees.

II

The deception begins

The child did not dare to stop running until she was sure the fortress must be far below her. Then she collapsed against a tree trunk, exhausted by the uphill climb but still elated by the success of her escape. She had seldom left the confines of her father's stronghold and on those very rare occasions when she had been permitted to do so, she had always been in the company of her uncle, the Lord Gustavus. For a while she sat contentedly, revelling in thoughts of her new found freedom, but later more urgent considerations crowded her reflections. She had run away, but where was she going and to whom was she fleeing? Was it to her uncle, the Lord Gustavus? He would not welcome a little girl on the battlefield, even supposing that she could find him. Who else would care for her? In her short life she had never had to care for herself. What would she eat? Where would she sleep? The decision to escape had been made so suddenly there had been no time to consider its consequences. She had felt hot after her exertions but now she shivered. She looked around. The forest was all about her, dark and sinister. The warm spring sunshine scarcely penetrated the interlocking branches above her head.

She stood up, panic beginning to rise within her yet again. Suddenly, the bushes in front of her moved. A dead twig snapped as it was trodden underfoot. A moment later the beast appeared. It stood still, surprised to see the child, but then out of curiosity it ambled up to her. She backed against the tree, arms outstretched, fingers digging into the bark. The beast lowered its head to rummage in the undergrowth where she had been sitting and in so doing, its horns almost touched her. She was paralysed with fear. Only when the animal raised its head again and looked her full in the face did she find her voice. She opened her mouth and screamed. The effect was immediate: the goat fled for its life and as it disappeared from view its keeper came running through the trees to ascertain the cause of the uproar. The child, still clinging to the tree trunk, found herself once more confronted by curious eyes. This time they belonged to a young boy about four years her senior. For a few moments he stood scrutinizing the frightened child; then he stretched out his arm, took her trembling hand in his and led her down through the trees again to a clearing where goats were grazing. The child hesitated when she saw the herd.

The boy said quietly, 'They are only goats. The one you scared will have warned the others to keep away from you.' He pointed to a tree stump where she should sit and squatted down on the grass beside her. He said nothing more and after a while the child felt she should break the silence.

'I am sorry I upset your goat,' she ventured.

The boy shrugged his shoulders. 'You are only a little girl,' he replied disparagingly. The child blushed and could think of no suitable retort. There was another uncomfortable silence until the boy said slowly, 'You do not live in this forest. What are you doing here?'

Once more she was at a loss for words; she could produce no clever answer so she admitted simply, 'I am running away.'

The boy pondered this reply for a while then inquired, 'Do they beat you?'

At first, the child did not comprehend the question. When the significance of it dawned on her she answered, 'No!' in a startled voice.

'Do they starve you?' was the boy's next thought.

'No!' she said vehemently.

'Then why are you running away?' demanded the boy, making no effort to hide his amazement.

She hesitated then responded with equal candour, 'I am lonely.' She could see from the boy's reaction that he found this an incredible reason for leaving a home where there was plenty of food and an absence of beatings. On reflection, the child shared his opinion. As they had sat together she had felt increasingly foolish and had begun to regret her hasty action.

Suddenly, the boy sprang to his feet. 'You will be from the fortress. Come, perhaps you have not been missed.' So saying, the young goatherd grabbed her by the wrist and started off down the hillside at a fast pace. She made a half-hearted attempt to struggle free from the boy's grasp but, in fact, she was grateful to him for making the decision which pride would not have allowed her to make for herself. Almost immediately they were out of the trees and crossing the meadow above the fortress. As they drew close to the Roman wall, the boy stopped and faced her. 'For the next few weeks,' he began hesitantly, 'I shall let the goats feed here on the lower slopes or just inside the trees where we were today.' He looked down at his feet and shuffled them awkwardly. There was no need for him to say more – the little girl understood at once that he was extending the hand of friendship.

On impulse she declared, 'I am Tilly.'

The boy looked up and was astounded at the transformation. The white solemn face was radiant; the sad eyes aglow with happiness. 'I am Conrad,' he responded. The pair stood beaming at one another for a moment until the little girl pulled her hand gently away and ran towards the gates. She turned and waved to the goatherd before disappearing from view.

Thorkell, standing on the battlements being clapped on the back in farewell by the sentries, watched in amazement as the two children stood together on the meadow below him. As the little girl neared the gates, he left his friends, climbed down the steps and followed her as she crossed the bailey.

She made no attempt to conceal herself: her new friend had pushed all thoughts of caution from her head. The gate area and the bailey were packed with people and vehicles. As usual, the court had ended well before sundown to enable as many as possible of those who had attended to reach the safety of their homes before nightfall. The happy child was oblivious to the hurrying crowd as she picked her way lightly through its midst. Only when she reached the gateway to the inner courtyard did she come to her senses, pause and pull her hood over her long fair hair. At that moment, the doors to the Great Hall were thrown open and the people who had witnessed the last of the trials rushed out in a noisy jostling mass, headed for the gate to the bailey. Tilly shrank back against the palisade in horror, realising she could be trampled underfoot.

Thorkell, seeing the danger, hurried to her side. 'Come, little one, I will carry you. Keep your face buried in my shoulder; your arms around my neck. Hang on tightly.' Holding Tilly close to him, Thorkell elbowed his way against the tide of the crowd, struggled to the side of the Great Hall and deposited her gently on the steps of the chapel.

'Oh, Thorkell! Thank you! Thank you!' cried Tilly.

'What were you doing outside the fortress, little one?'

'I was running away,' replied the child, shamefaced.

Thorkell smiled as he wiped away her tears. 'And where were you running to?' he asked gently.

'I do not know. I had not thought about that.'

'So the goatherd found you and brought you back to the fortress?'

Tilly nodded. 'Yes. He could not understand why I was running away.'

'Did you tell him who you are?' asked the skald anxiously.

'No. He assumed I was a servant.'

Thorkell laughed. 'Well, you *are* dressed like a servant.'

'My mother, the Lady Isolda, insists I be dressed modestly to encourage a state of humility in me,' replied Tilly seriously.

Thorkell looked at the solemn face with great affection. 'My dear little shield-maiden, humble is one thing you will never be, but thanks to your pious mother, you are safe. Had you told the boy you are the Lord Bardolph's only surviving heir ... I do not wish to frighten you, little Lady Matilda, but your father has many enemies who would stoop to nothing ... It is as well you did not tell the goatherd who you are. And now you must promise me that this will never happen again.'

Tilly looked away and considered her words carefully before she replied. 'I promise I will not run away again.'

'That is good, little shield-maiden. Hurry inside before anyone realizes you are missing. I will see you when the snows return.' As Thorkell opened the door of the chapel for her to enter Tilly, tearful again, darted forward and hugged the skald. He returned the embrace before pushing her gently into the chapel and closing the door behind her.

The curtain was drawn across the priest's alcove. Tilly tidied her hair and her gown before coughing politely. Father Almeric, a small white-haired old man, came to the entrance and drew back the curtain. 'Come in, child. I have not had time yet to read what you have written today: I have only just returned from attending upon your father, the Lord Bardolph.'

'Mother sent me to ask you for some more work to do, Father Almeric,' said Tilly sweetly.

'Your dear mother,' replied the priest fondly, 'so anxious that you should grow up as virtuous as she herself.' Tilly's face coloured and she looked away from Father Almeric's warm gaze. The old man misinterpreted her reaction as modesty. He took her small hand in his. He could not have loved her or her mother more dearly had they been his own children. 'Such a modest child ... The Lady Isolda must have been about your age when her father summoned me to be her tutor. He had just been widowed as I recall, and had invited the ladies Adela and Gertrude, the children of his distant cousins, to share his only daughter's upbringing. And so I had three pupils instead of one and Bertha the Nurse had three little girls to fuss over. How happy we all were ... But then there was a lull in the fighting and your maternal grandfather, Lord Raoulbrun the Burgundian, decided to seal the truce with the marriage of his daughter to the Lord Bardolph. The four of us, and our physician, accompanied the Lady Isolda to this Alemannian fortress and we have been here ever since – even though the truce was soon over. But I must not be sad: we have been allowed to stay together and you, Lady Matilda, are now as dear to us as your mother.'

The priest picked up some manuscripts from his table and handed them to Tilly. 'I think you have done enough work for today. Take these to occupy you and when the Lady Isolda awakes perhaps you can recite some holy passages to her.'

'Thank you, Father,' murmured Tilly, head bowed. She could not bring herself to look at the kindly, wrinkled face. She departed quickly, embarrassed by her tutor's unquestioning trust in her. She hastened up the narrow staircase to the balcony in the chapel roof, passed the bench where she sat for morning prayers with her nurse and her mother's ladies, to the internal door to her dormitory. There she paused and listened intently. She could hear no voices so she ventured inside. The room was empty. She crossed quickly and quietly to the door at the far end and opened it slightly. The servants downstairs in the Great Hall were clearing the mess left behind by the crowd. She heard them sweeping the floor; spreading fresh straw and dragging the trestles and benches back to their usual positions around the central fireplace, ready for the evening meal. Across the landing, Tilly could also hear Lady Adela and Lady Gertrude talking in excited voices to her mother. She knew they would be relating all they could remember of the events they had witnessed at the court that day. Tilly closed the door quietly and sat down on the little stool beside her bed.

A few minutes later, the ladies left the Lady Isolda and entered their dormitory. They found the child intent upon her books and assumed she had been similarly engaged all afternoon. Lady Adela praised her at once. 'How quiet you have been, Lady Matilda. Your mother thanks you for being so considerate. She has rested well and feels much better. She would like you to go to her.'

Tilly rose obediently, gathered up her books and smiled at the two ladies as she passed them. Lady Gertrude, the plumper and more cheerful of the two women, patted her arm. 'When you are a little older we shall ask the Lord Bardolph if you too can attend the court. It was so interesting – and so many people!'

'The child is far too young to witness such proceedings,' interrupted Lady Adela.

'I did not mean at the present time, cousin,' protested Lady Gertrude.

Tilly left them to their argument, crossed the landing to her mother's room, knocked and entered.

The curtains around the Lady Isolda's large canopied bed had been drawn back and she held her arms out to her daughter. The child ran to her, climbed onto the bed and nestled against her thin frail mother. 'You have been a very generous girl, Tilly, and let me sleep all afternoon. Now we shall spend the time until nightfall together. I have already sent Bertha to the kitchens to order your favourite dish – a reward for being so kind.'

Once more, Tilly felt ashamed. How could she, even for a moment, have considered deserting her mother? She thanked God that the boy, Conrad, had made her return. She reached up and stroked her mother's long fair hair. 'I shall never ever leave you,' she whispered earnestly.

Tilly lay in her bed listening to the sounds which drifted up from the chamber below. Her father and his men were enjoying themselves with their usual abandon. The singing and dancing seemed louder tonight. Then Tilly remembered that some of the participants at the day's hearings would be from the more distant estates. They would have requested and been granted, a night's shelter.

Lady Adela and Lady Gertrude returned through the door from the chapel, their evening prayers over. They both leant over Tilly's bed inquiring kindly if she were well and bidding her a fond goodnight. They extinguished the lights and went to their own beds which were situated on either side of Tilly's bed. Soon the child heard both ladies snoring but she herself lay awake. Downstairs, she heard the tables and benches being pushed aside: the company below was also preparing for sleep. Voices were raised in argument. The nights were still cold and Tilly knew the men would be squabbling over the warmest positions around the central hearth. She snuggled down under her own fur covers and as the household grew quieter she allowed her thoughts to dwell on the wonderful events of the afternoon. She had left the fortress and returned undetected; best of all she had found the friend she craved. The child finally fell into a fitful dream-filled sleep in which she was pursued over mountains and through forests by all manner of beasts, and was defended at every turn by a tall handsome boy with eyes as blue as the summer sky.

III

A dream confided

Tilly awoke next day feeling refreshed in spite of her restless night. She found it difficult to concentrate on her lessons that morning, the prospect of another meeting with her new friend being uppermost in her mind. When at last Father Almeric dismissed her, she rushed from the chapel back to the dormitory and applied herself intently to the work her tutor had set her for her afternoon's studies. She had just completed this when she heard the servants bring the midday meal to her mother's room. Seconds later, she was called to join the ladies. It was the custom of Bertha, Lady Adela and Lady Gertrude to spend the morning with their mistress while Tilly was engaged in the chapel. They had always delighted in one another's company and they chattered together happily all through the meal. Tilly, lost in her own thoughts, barely listened to their conversation.

The problem of how to escape from Lady Adela and Lady Gertrude that afternoon seemed insurmountable. There was no court downstairs to occupy them and Tilly feared that they would, as usual, turn their attention towards her whilst her mother and Bertha rested. So absorbed was she in searching for a solution that she did not realize at first that the ladies were discussing that very matter. Lady Gertrude proposed that as the weather was fine and the Lady Matilda had had no fresh air for so long, that she might be allowed to take her books outside for an hour or two. They would sit in their usual spot: a small corner of the inner courtyard behind the Great Hall which was screened from prying eyes. The two ladies would occupy themselves with their needlework whilst their young charge applied herself to her studies. Tilly normally welcomed any relief from the routine which confined her to the dark and stuffy dormitory, but today her face registered alarm. Worse was to come when Lady Isolda expressed her concern at her daughter's withdrawn behaviour throughout the meal and inquired whether she felt ill. At once, the child was inundated with questions from all the ladies concerning possible symptoms. In spite of her vigorous denials it was concluded that she might have caught a fever. Bertha was dispatched immediately to summon the Lady Isolda's physician, whilst Tilly was put to bed by Lady Adela and Lady Gertrude.

The physician arrived without delay. It had rarely been necessary for him to attend Tilly who was a strong and hardy child in spite of her thin and pale appearance. He was most dismayed to note her heightened colour, her restlessness, her quickened pulse and watering eyes. Gravely, he confirmed the ladies' worst suspicions. 'I fear there is an imbalance of the body's ruling humours. Watch the Lady Matilda very carefully and if the fever increases, send for me at once and I shall endeavour to restore the balance by bleeding and purging.'

Tilly wanted to cry out, 'I am not ill! I am just angry!' but she did not dare. Instead of rushing up the hillside to meet the goatherd she spent a frustrating afternoon in bed, the worried ladies watching her every movement and expression like hawks. At last, Tilly resigned herself to her fate and making a great effort to control her temper, she turned her thoughts to devising plans of escape for the future. Firstly, she vowed she would never repeat the mistakes she had made that day: nothing in her manner must betray her inner excitement and anticipation; she must always appear composed yet alert and interested; she must never ever give vent to her irritation should her plans be thwarted. Secondly, Tilly concluded she must be as careful in her conversations with Conrad as with her mother and the ladies. Just as the latter would instantly condemn the relationship if they discovered its existence, so the boy would never dare to meet her again if he knew she was the Lord Bardolph's daughter.

Next, she let her mind dwell on the problem of how to avoid detection by any of the hundreds of people who lived and worked in her father's stronghold. She considered how many could positively identify her and realized thankfully that outside her mother's small retinue, there were few who had ever met her face to face. There were, of course, the servants who cleaned the upper rooms and brought the food. She knew that they spent their lives almost entirely in the vicinity of the inner courtyard working, eating and sleeping in the kitchens. She was convinced that she had little to fear from them. The same servants, together with other household workers, filled the chapel for Father Almeric's services but few ever thought to glance up at the balcony where she sat with her mother's ladies, and the building was anyway very dark. As for those who lived and worked in the outer bailey, she had already proved that to them she was just another child. But what about her father's other dependants: his close band of noble followers on whom he relied for companionship as well as service? Tilly recalled them to mind one by one. Their faces were familiar to her since she had often watched them from her mother's small window. On reflection, she was certain that none of them would recognise her – with the exception of Gareth the Bailiff.

Tilly thought about Gareth. Yes, he posed a threat for he was the only one of her father's men with whom she had any contact. A tall handsome man with greying hair, he had a serious manner and smiled only rarely. Tilly had never heard him laugh. Yes, he was quite unlike any other of her father's retainers. She knew he was the most powerful man in the domain, second only to her father himself. His duties were many and varied; there was no aspect of the daily life of the tribes with which he was not concerned. He had control over all of her father and uncle's land-stewards who ran the individual estates, and because he was the only man her father trusted implicitly, he was the only man permitted to trade with merchants on behalf of the community. In this capacity he would visit the Lady Isolda, always observing proper decorum by announcing his proposed visit well in advance. Tilly's mother always spoke of him with respect and gratitude – he was her link with the outside world.

The interviews always followed the same pattern: Gareth would inquire what purchases he should make for the Lady Isolda and her household, he would solemnly add them to his list and then, as though aware that the ladies, fearing Lord Bardolph's wrath, would not dare to ask for more than bare essentials, would courteously suggest other possible requirements. His official business completed, Gareth would linger to pass on any interesting news which he had gleaned on his travels around the vast estates. When the bailiff returned after a few days, Tilly always contrived to be present. She knew there would be other purchases beside those her mother had ordered – and something special for her also. Gareth never failed to say that these gifts came from the Lord Bardolph, and never failed to apologise on his master's behalf for the fact that urgent matters prevented him from presenting his gifts personally. Tilly, nevertheless, felt a little afraid of Gareth. She was convinced that God must have a face like Gareth's – all seeing, all knowing with a steady gaze which penetrated her soul seeking out her innermost thoughts. She decided she must be on her guard against the bailiff at all times; then she fell into a deep sleep.

The next morning, Tilly put aside her bitter disappointment of the previous afternoon and with her usual optimism, looked forward to a better day. Her hopes were to be fulfilled. The physician and all the ladies were amazed at Tilly's miraculous recovery from her fever and when Father Almeric said Mass for Lady Isolda that morning, he included prayers of thanksgiving. Tilly forced herself to eat normally and to take part in the conversation at the midday meal. When her mother and Bertha settled down for their rest and Tilly and the other two ladies had withdrawn to their own dormitory, the opportunity she had wished for presented itself: Lady Adela and Lady Gertrude both began to yawn. So great was their devotion and concern for Tilly that they had taken turns throughout the night to sit by the child's bed in case her condition suddenly worsened. The long vigil had taken its toll. Tilly at once proposed that they should sleep while she sat quietly with her books. The ladies were so grateful for her consideration that she felt quite ashamed but when both were peacefully snoring, she pushed aside her qualms.

Tilly made her departure as before, through the chapel. Father Almeric was asleep too, the remains of his meal on the table. The child placed the book she had brought with her – a precautionary measure to explain her presence – beside the dishes and listened at the open side-door before venturing forth. All the sounds that she could hear came from the other side of the main building – from the area of the kitchens. Tilly hurried through the gateway of the wooden palisade as though intent upon some errand. Though her hood was pulled well down, she felt much safer once she had left the inner courtyard behind and could mingle with the mass of busy people in the outer enclosure. She contrived to leave the main gates at the same time as a group of children. Very soon she was climbing eagerly up the hillside, looking frantically around for some sign of the goatherd. If he were not there after all the trouble she had had, she felt sure she would die of frustration. Suddenly, she spied him with his beasts just inside the trees. She ran across to him and dropped to her knees beside him. Her small face mirrored her joy at seeing him again, but he scarcely managed a smile in return. He looked away from her shining eyes and continued whittling a small piece of wood.

'Conrad,' Tilly whispered, 'are you not pleased to see me?' The boy merely nodded in reply and went on with his carving. Tilly was hurt and bewildered. Had she misunderstood? Perhaps he did not want her for a friend after all.

'You did not come yesterday,' the boy remarked quietly, interrupting her deliberations.

Tilly was so relieved that her fear was unfounded that she hastened to reassure him. 'Oh! I tried, Conrad. I tried very hard. I even managed to finish my day's work by midday but it was no use; I could not get away. Today, the ladies fell asleep so I was able to make my escape. I dare not be absent too long. I promised to continue my work quietly so as not to disturb them but if they should wake and find me gone I fear I should never be allowed to meet you again.'

Conrad's face was at once full of concern. 'I am sorry, Tilly. I did not understand. I thought you had changed your mind and did not wish to be my friend.'

'Conrad, I want to be your friend forever,' Tilly declared with innocent enthusiasm. 'There will be many days when I cannot come to visit you but you may be certain that I have tried my hardest.'

'Do not try too hard,' Conrad said anxiously. 'I do not wish you to get into trouble and your mistresses to punish you.'

Tilly smiled to herself but remembering Thorkell's warning, she said nothing to correct the boy's assumptions. Then an idea occurred to Tilly and she voiced it without thinking. 'On the afternoon I was running away, I hid for a while against a buttress near the entrance to the fortress. My hand dislodged some loose material. We could leave one another messages there, in the cavity, and secure them with a tight-fitting stone.' Conrad looked puzzled so Tilly continued enthusiastically. 'I mean that on the days when I cannot meet you I might be able to slip away just long enough to leave you a message.' She beamed at the goatherd, pleased with herself for having thought of such a plan.

Conrad continued to stare at her. At last he asked, 'What do you mean by "messages"?'

'Why, I mean I shall write to you and tell you if I cannot join you,' Tilly replied, laughing.

'Write,' pondered the boy. 'You mean write in a book as I have seen the bailiff do in the village?'

At once Tilly understood. How stupid she had been. 'Conrad, I am so sorry. I should have known that you do not read or write.'

'Me!' scoffed the boy. 'What use would reading and writing be to me? That is for bailiffs. I have all the skills I need.'

Tilly cursed herself. What a bad beginning she had made to this new relationship: in her eagerness she had wounded her friend's pride. He confirmed this by moving slightly away from her and applying himself with renewed vigour to his woodcarving. Tilly considered another aspect of this revelation: if her friend possessed not even the rudiments of learning, how would they spend their time together? How could she discuss with him theology, philosophy, history, mathematics, or any of the subjects which filled her day? She made up her mind there and then that she would have to teach him to read and write. The problem which then confronted her was how she could persuade him to allow her to do this without offending him further. As soon as she had arrived at a possible solution she began again, tentatively and warily, choosing her words carefully this time.

'Conrad, I have thought a great deal about you since we met. You must know everything there is to know about farming the land and caring for animals. I know nothing of these matters and had hoped you would teach me.' Tilly waited, not daring to look at the boy. Would her design succeed?

Conrad put down his handiwork and replied solemnly, 'Yes, it would be fitting for you to learn of such matters. Many a woman has been widowed with her sons still young. One day you may have to till the soil and tend your livestock alone, without a man to help you.'

Delighted at the boy's reaction, Tilly pressed home her victory. 'If you teach me these things I must repay you. I have nothing to give you except the learning which is inside me. Please, Conrad, let us exchange one skill for another.'

She looked at him with such pleading that he could not refuse. 'Very well, little Tilly, it is a bargain,' he agreed in a tone which implied that he was merely humouring a child. 'I shall teach you all I know and in return, you shall teach me to read and write.'

Conrad decided there was no time to waste; he began immediately to explain to Tilly the essential facts of rearing goats. Words did not come easily to him but he persevered. Tilly found there was a great deal more to the beasts than she had imagined and Conrad found her incredibly ignorant of even the simplest facts.

Tilly did not dare to stay long and as he walked with her down the hillside, Conrad asked the question she had feared he would ask. 'How is it that you have learned to read and write?'

The child had her answer ready. 'The Lord Bardolph has an only daughter. I share her lessons.'

Conrad nodded. 'I have heard that sometimes a servant's child might become a companion to a rich man's child.'

To prevent him from questioning her further, Tilly said, 'If you learn to read and write, Conrad, you may be a bailiff yourself when you are a man.'

This remark had an astonishing effect: the boy was suddenly fired with enthusiasm. 'Oh no, Tilly, I do not wish to be a bailiff. I know what I shall be when I am a man. Last year I chanced to pass this fortress just as the Lord Gustavus was leaving with his men. I stood and watched them, Tilly, as they rode by. I knew then that I must be a soldier too and ride at the Lord Gustavus's side.'

'That is a noble ambition, Conrad. You will make a fine brave soldier, I am sure.' Then, seizing her opportunity, Tilly added, 'But I am certain that all who ride in the company of the Lord Gustavus would be learned men. It is as well that we have made our bargain.'

IV

The secret language

In the weeks that followed, Tilly found many opportunities to visit Conrad. She had the fine spring weather to thank for that. During the long winter months there had been few travellers on the roads but now people were able to go about their business once more. Many strangers came to Bardolph's stronghold, some seeking shelter before embarking on the most hazardous part of their journey over the mountains, others selling merchandise or their own particular skills. All were welcome at Bardolph's table and Lady Adela and Lady Gertrude accepted every invitation to sit with the visitors. Both ladies detested the company of Bardolph himself but they overcame their aversion when there were strangers present so that they might indulge their highly inquisitive natures. Lady Isolda encouraged them in this in the knowledge that their detailed observations would brighten the long tedious hours of her irksome existence.

The ladies assumed that Bardolph requested their company because they brought an air of refinement and gentility to the gathering which was otherwise missing. They were partly correct in this assumption: Bardolph was convinced that their elegant manner and cultured speech – qualities he normally abhorred in his female companions – must impress his guests favourably. And, although no longer young, both ladies still retained some hints of beauty. But Bardolph had another reason for requesting the ladies' presence: the fiendish pleasure he derived from observing their reactions to the vulgar antics and coarse language of his more uncouth henchmen. As he watched the horrified expressions on their prim faces his delight would increase. When he tired of his game, he would have someone divert his guests and then summon to his table a particularly scurrilous fellow whose obscene behaviour would appall the ladies. The two cousins would then make a hasty retreat upstairs to report the offensive conduct to their mistress.

Fortunately for Tilly, the ladies' curiosity was strong enough to overcome the hurt to their pride. When Bardolph's servant again informed them of the presence of a newcomer in the Great Hall, they would forget their previous humiliation and descend to the chamber below, their enthusiasm barely contained. Tilly would meekly agree to continue her studies in her mother's room but as soon as the Lady Isolda and Bertha fell asleep she would be off to meet her new friend. There were times when she came close to being caught: the ladies would leave the Great Hall sooner than she had expected and find her missing. If they met her coming up the chapel staircase she would merely say she had been to Father Almeric with her books. If they found her entering the chapel door she would pretend she had been enjoying the sunshine in the courtyard outside.

From time to time, Tilly felt pangs of conscience but she always convinced herself that the deception and subterfuge were necessary. She came from a long line of Alemannian chieftains who had survived numerous plots and assassination attempts through their superior cunning and, before long, she found herself relishing the excitement of the intrigue. Father Almeric posed the biggest problem. It had been instilled in her that she must never lie to the priest for in so doing, she was lying to God. The solution, she found, was to develop an ambiguous form of speech in the knowledge that the guileless old man believed she could do no wrong and would interpret her confessions generously. She made her peace with God privately, explaining to Him that her intentions were good and not evil. As for everyone else, including Conrad, her tiny stature, big eyes and sweet smile gave an impression of a small child, much younger than she actually was, who was innocence personified.

Throughout the spring and early summer, Tilly and Conrad were able to meet frequently. At first, the little girl regarded the knowledge the boy had to impart as irrelevant and a waste of precious time, but in order to achieve her own ends she indulged him by feigning interest. Soon the pretence became unnecessary and she found herself enthralled by all he told her. He conveyed to her the wonder he felt in all growing and living things and Tilly came to understand and share his love of the countryside. Before long, she could find and identify a flower or plant as easily as Conrad; she could catch fish in the stream; she could even milk a goat.

Conrad, for his part, had taken Tilly's words to heart. He truly believed he must be an educated man to be a soldier in the Lord Gustavus's own bodyguard. Tilly gave much thought as to how to teach her friend and she spent many hours surreptitiously compiling simple manuscripts for this purpose. She was relieved to find that he was quick and intelligent. Within weeks, he was capable of composing easy sentences in fairly legible writing on the scraps of parchment she brought him. He was also able to read the little tales she had meticulously copied out for him in her neat hand – manuscripts which she had smuggled out of the fortress concealed inside her gown.

One day, Tilly and Conrad were engrossed in their studies when they were startled by the sound of suppressed laughter behind them. Two young cowherds, whose charges grazed alongside Conrad's on the meadowland, were hiding in the bushes. The boy chased them away then resumed his work with his usual good humour, adding, 'I know those two. They mean no harm.'

Tilly could not dismiss the incident so lightly. 'Conrad, it would not be wise for the other herdsmen to discover that you are learning to read and write. They would be suspicious and, fearing you had evil intentions, might report our meetings to the Lord Bardolph in the hope of some reward. Who knows what punishment we might suffer?'

'That may be so,' Conrad agreed anxiously. 'I do not want you to come to any harm, little Tilly. We had better cease these studies.'

'No! Conrad,' cried Tilly. 'I want you to realize your dreams – and you are doing so well. You are such a quick learner. The danger lies in our conversations being overheard but, if we speak in a foreign tongue, no one creeping upon us would be any the wiser.' Conrad did not agree: he felt that strange words would arouse rather than allay a listener's suspicions. Tilly, having made up her mind, would not be dissuaded. 'If we speak the language I speak with my mother – the language of her homeland – no one from this valley will understand what we are saying. Our secrets would be safe.'

'I am having enough difficulty mastering my own language,' Conrad insisted. 'That is enough learning.'

Tilly would not admit defeat. 'It would be a simple matter for someone such as you to master another tongue. There is no need to learn to read and write in this language; only to speak it. You have such a keen ear for sounds, Conrad. You can identify so many birds by their song and you know which animal is hiding in the undergrowth by the noises it makes. I will teach you the sounds of the words and their meaning and in no time at all, we shall be conversing in our own secret language.' For good measure, the child concluded her entreaty by turning the full force of her radiant smile upon the boy. He was soon won over – by the flattery and the smile!

As Tilly had predicted, Conrad did not find his new task too arduous since he did indeed have a keen ear. Time passed so quickly for the children that mid-summer arrived without warning. Tilly went to meet her friend one afternoon and was distressed to find him preparing to leave. Conrad explained that the lower slopes had to be left to recuperate from the devastation they had suffered from all the cattle which had fed on them since the snows had melted.

'All the herds – cows and goats – must move up through the tree-line to the high alp for the rest of the summer. Their keepers must go also, Tilly.'

'But I shall be so sad without you,' cried Tilly, adopting the same "tiny child" guise she normally reserved for Thorkell the Skald.

'I shall miss you, Tilly, but I am taking the books you made for me with me – see, hidden inside my shirt,' said the boy. Then he continued enthusiastically. 'But I doubt I shall have much time for reading because we must make the most of the short summer. There will be crops to sow and harvest; winter feed to set aside for the cattle. And I must ensure that my herd leaves the lusher pastures for the others – goats are less particular about what they will eat. I must take my turn also at sentry duty. We could be invaded by men and beasts from another valley seeking to graze upon our choice pastures. And there are robbers who watch and wait for a chance to steal our animals – either for fresh meat or to sell at the markets on the plains below. The most feared of all are the Raetians, the warlike tribes who inhabit the heart of the mountains. They attack us and drive off our herds to replenish their own stocks.'

Tilly was alarmed. 'Conrad, I am afraid for you. You will be in great danger. Do not go.'

Conrad laughed. 'I look forward all year to these weeks on the high alp. The hard labour gives me much satisfaction but it is the fighting and the thrill of living with danger that I love most of all. I can recall my mother telling me only one thing about my father: that he was a soldier. I want to be the kind of boy any soldier would be proud to own as his son. So do not worry about me, little Tilly, and mind you take great care whilst I am gone. I shall see you again before autumn.'

Tilly knew she must not attempt to visit Conrad on the mountain for she would be absent from the fortress for so long that discovery would be certain. Already she had seen a shadow of suspicion cross Lady Adela's face once or twice when she had lied to cover her whereabouts. Although she hated the thought of being parted from her friend Tilly was, nevertheless, relieved to be spared the necessity of evasion for a few weeks. But time hung heavy and there was no prospect of a happy afternoon meeting to look forward to when boredom engulfed her. There were occasions when boredom gave way to gloom. One day, after the midday meal, only quick thinking saved Tilly from betraying herself. She had been standing at the small window looking out towards the tree-line and the high alp, thinking of Conrad and wishing she could be there with him. Bertha the Nurse, a plump woman of cheerful disposition, was sitting beside Lady Isolda's bed. Lady Adela and Lady Gertrude were there too – all four women laughing together – when the nurse called out to Tilly.

'Come and sit with us, Lady Matilda, and hear how your mother and her cousins used to play tricks on poor old Bertha when they were children.'

'Our Lady Matilda's thoughts seem far away,' observed Lady Adela. 'Where is she, I wonder?'

Tilly blushed, turned from the window and came to her mother's bed-side. 'I miss Thorkell the Skald,' she explained – which was also true. 'He will not be back until winter.'

Lady Adela was satisfied with that explanation. 'Hah! That man fills your head with tales he should not tell a child.'

'He makes me laugh,' Tilly replied. 'He is my friend.'

'It is such a pity that you do not have other little girls your own age to spend your time with – as we did,' said Lady Gertrude, kindly.

'I have always lamented that I could make no such arrangement for you but there are no girls amongst your father's relatives or richer vassals. There may be some in *my* family but, sadly, since my family is Burgundian, they would be your father's enemies,' Lady Isolda explained.

'Do not distress yourself, Mother. I have all of you – and I have my manuscripts.'

The weeks passed; late summer gave way to early autumn. The herds left the high ground and were driven back down the mountainside by their keepers. Tilly passed them, and the men pushing handcarts laden with the last of the hay for the winter storehouses, as she ran happily up the sloping meadowland to the sound of cow-bells. She was no longer afraid of the cattle; she pushed them aside as she skipped between them looking for Conrad. Suddenly, she spied him emerging from the trees with his goats. She waved frantically until he saw her and ran eagerly to greet her.

'There, I told you I would only be gone a few weeks. See, Tilly, how the grass has grown back again on these lower slopes? There will be pasture here until the winter snows arrive.'

'And we shall be able to meet until then. I am so glad you are safe,' said Tilly warmly, taking the boy's outstretched hand.

But all too soon, autumn began to fade and winter approached. Neither Tilly nor Conrad had forgotten the lessons they had learned from each other in the spring and early summer. They had resumed their studies eagerly and by the time they had to part once more, Conrad could communicate with Tilly in their secret language with little difficulty. They were huddled together one afternoon, inside the trees, when Tilly began to shiver.

'You must not come here again,' said Conrad gently. 'Winter is coming, little Tilly, and I must return the goats to their owners before the first snows fall.'

Until that moment, Tilly had thought that Conrad always lived with the goats. Surprised, she asked, 'Where will you spend the winter?'

'Over there,' replied the boy pointing to where the trees grew densely together. 'I live in a shack in the woods with Hulda.'

'Hulda? Is that your mother's name?'

Conrad shook his head. 'Soldiers attacked our village when I was young. They ransacked the huts, taking the food and livestock, and set fire to the fields all around. My mother ran with me to the forest to hide and when the raiders had gone she told me it would be useless to return to the village because there would be no food there. We walked for many weeks, Tilly, resorting to begging and stealing to stay alive. One morning,' Conrad paused and the pain he felt showed in his eyes, 'I was unable to rouse my mother. All day I tried to warm her cold body, covering her with leaves and bracken. Just before sunset an old woman found us. She told me that my mother was dead and dragged me, in spite of my protests, to her shack.'

'Conrad,' murmured Tilly. 'I am so sorry ..., and you so young. If my mother ...' Tilly paused, unable to voice the one thing she dreaded most, and waited for Conrad to continue. Though he was normally reluctant to talk about his past, now that he had begun the words came easily to him.

'Ever since that day the old woman, Hulda, has been my only family. She cared for me when I was small and now I am repaying the debt. Some time ago she was afflicted by a sudden and strange sickness. At first she was unable to speak or move. I nursed her as best I could and eventually she was able to walk again but with a shuffling movement, dragging her left leg awkwardly. The use has never returned fully to her left arm and the left side of her face remains distorted, twisted downwards in an ugly leer. Few, but me, can understand her slurred speech. The people in the surrounding countryside had always been afraid of Hulda because of the strange powers she possesses to cure the sick; after her affliction, they became convinced that she was a witch. They stoned us, Tilly, burned down our hovel and drove us from the area. We journeyed for many days; this time, I was the one who begged and stole for our survival. When, at last, we reached this high valley, I knew that Hulda could travel no further. I managed to carry her to a safe hiding place in this forest above the fortress and there we made our home. I built another shack for Hulda and set about earning our keep by hiring my labour to anyone who would employ me.'

'I am sure you are the best goatherd that has ever been, Conrad,' said Tilly solemnly. 'But why do the goats not live with you during the winter? Why do you take them back to their owners?'

'Our shack is only big enough for the two of us. I could not provide shelter for them as well and how would I feed them? They live in the individual homes of their owners for the duration of the winter. They have the fodder to feed them.'

'But who will feed *you* through the winter?' asked Tilly anxiously.

'I am entitled to claim a little food from each of the owners whose goats I have protected, but as winter progresses the amounts get smaller. I supplement our meagre diet by hunting and trapping the smaller wildlife of the forest. Hulda too contributes to our upkeep. The villagers here have learned to overcome their fear of her and they bring her their sick animals. She has a wonderful knowledge of the healing properties of herbs and plants, Tilly. She almost always finds a cure and the people repay her with a chicken or a little grain – and so we survive.'

'What you have just told me about when you were a small boy makes me sad,' said Tilly gently, 'but I am very glad that you decided to settle here.'

'So am I, little Tilly,' agreed Conrad. The boy put his arm around Tilly's shoulder and gave her an affectionate hug. 'But it is time for you to go now. I promise I shall make good use of the long winter hours to study the more difficult books that you have so kindly made for me. You must stay safe and warm in the fortress. When the spring sunshine melts the snow we can be together again.'

V

Discovery and punishment

Tilly stood at her mother's window sorrowfully watching the snowflakes fall. Suddenly, a snowball plopped on the pane in front of her. She looked down and saw Thorkell the Skald dancing about in the snow and waving at her. He indicated in his usual dramatic way that he would meet her in the chapel. Her screams of delight startled the ladies who were sitting beside the Lady Isolda's bed sewing a tapestry.

'Thorkell is back!' Tilly cried. 'Please, Mother, let me go to him.'

'Very well, for a while,' said Lady Isolda, nodding at Lady Adela. The latter immediately put aside her needlework and took Tilly's arm.

'Come then! You have been pining for that scoundrel long enough, child.'

Moments later, Thorkell dashed up the staircase and caught Tilly as she ran along the balcony towards him. He lifted her up above his shoulders and then set her gently on her feet. 'You are heavier, little one.'

'I am so happy that you are back,' Tilly enthused. 'Did you get wounded? Are you well? Have you many tales to tell me, Thorkell?'

The skald laughed. 'I did not get wounded – very much. I am well. I have hundreds of tales to tell – enough to last the winter. But first, I have a gift for you.'

Lady Adela looked up sharply as she took her seat on the bench. 'It had better not be a weapon,' she said threateningly.

'Have no fear,' the skald replied. 'It is a gift fit for a young lady.' He put his hand inside his shirt, brought out a package and handed it to Tilly. The child unwrapped it; her face aglow with expectation. She displayed a long length of pale yellow silk and some reels of gold thread. Lady Adela leant forward, inspected the gift and sniffed disdainfully.

'Oh, thank you, thank you, Thorkell!' cried Tilly.

'And who did you steal that from?' demanded Lady Adela archly.

'The fruits of victory, my lady,' responded the skald.

'Exactly! You stole it,' Lady Adela maintained.

'Why do you hate me so, Lady Adela?' asked Thorkell. 'Most ladies find me – entertaining.'

'I do not hate *you*, Skald; I hate your way of life.'

'It will be the Lady Matilda's way of life one day.'

'I realize that and so does the Lady Isolda. Why else do you think she allows you near her daughter? She knows you are preparing the child.'

'Be comforted, my lady. If I am still in the service of the Lord Gustavus when the time comes, I shall protect her with my life.'

Thanks to the skald, the dark cold months passed pleasantly enough for Tilly. Whenever Thorkell could escape from entertaining Bardolph and his men, he would spend time with the child. Lady Adela, happy to assume the role of chaperone, was aware that the chieftain would not approve of the relationship and she ensured that the meetings did not go on too long. Much to Tilly's annoyance, Lady Adela would send the skald back to the Great Hall long before there was a chance that he would be missed. When Thorkell was not around, his gift kept the child amused. On the day that he had given it to her she had unfolded the material fully once she was alone in the dormitory; to her delight there was much more of the silk material than she had first thought. Knowing that Lady Adela's inspection of the gift had been only cursory she knew she had the opportunity to make decorative cloths publicly in front of her mother and the ladies and to make something quite different secretly, when the others were occupied in the Great Hall or asleep.

With the promise of spring on its way, the snows melted and Tilly took a tearful farewell of Thorkell before he left to join the Lord Gustavus at the start of the military campaign. A few days after their sad parting there was a joyful reunion – with Conrad. They met in the clearing above the fortress, both aware that this was where they had had their first meeting almost a year before. For a few moments they regarded one another shyly. Tilly noted that her friend had grown. He seemed taller than she remembered and broader about the shoulders. His hair seemed a darker shade of brown but the clear blue eyes and the strongly boned face were the same. His sturdy muscular limbs hinted at the kind of man he would become.

Conrad found the child's innocent gaze disconcerting; to hide his embarrassment he said abruptly, 'I have made this for you, Tilly.' He pressed a wooden disc into the girl's hand. She found that it was a pendant with a goat's face carved upon it in intricate detail. The boy had threaded a narrow strip of leather through the top of the wood so that she might wear his gift around her neck.

'Conrad! It is beautiful,' Tilly exclaimed with genuine delight. 'I have never seen such wonderful carving. Thank you! Thank you! I shall keep it all my life. It will always remind me of the beast which caused us to meet. Please, help me to put it on.'

Conrad blushed with pleasure that his present had been so well received. Nervously, he tied the pendant and in so doing he had to lift Tilly's long tresses away from her slender neck. He had never before touched anything so soft and silky. 'Your hair is the colour of ripe corn,' he muttered, speaking his thoughts aloud. Conrad was as startled as Tilly by his impetuous remark. Both children were perplexed, unable to cope with the strange new sensations aroused within them. Tilly ended their confusion by thrusting a gift of her own into Conrad's hand.

'I have made something for you also.' She watched anxiously as he un-wrapped the material. She had used the remainder of the pale yellow silk which the skald had given her to fashion a sash for him. She had embroidered it generously with the gold thread, depicting the story of their friendship. The goat was there under the trees; Tilly was fishing by the stream under Conrad's instruction; the boy was shown pouring over his books.

'Tilly!' he gasped, quite overwhelmed. 'It is splendid. I shall wear it always and when I ride into battle it will protect me against my enemies.' So saying, the boy pulled open his coarse shirt and wrapped the sash around his bare waist. Then a horrifying thought struck him. 'Tilly!' he cried. 'Did you steal the material?'

'Have no fear,' Tilly reassured him. 'Both the cloth and the gold thread were given to me as a present.'

Conrad smiled with relief. 'Nevertheless, I had better keep your gift safely hidden. No one would expect a poor peasant like me to have come upon such a rich treasure honestly.'

Tilly nodded. 'And I must let no eyes but mine enjoy your pendant. Now we share another secret!'

The pair enjoyed many happy hours together in the next few weeks, Conrad conversing in Burgundian French almost as easily as in his own German dialect. So things might have continued had habit not made Tilly careless. She ran towards the main gates one afternoon, her head full of the things she wanted to tell her friend. She had not even bothered to cover her beautiful golden hair. Oblivious of her surroundings, she did not notice the man standing beside his horse, talking to the blacksmith. She did not see his startled expression nor hear the hasty excuse he made to his companion before hurrying after her. She did not look back once as she rushed up the hillside, neither did she guess that her meeting with Conrad was being observed, nor did she sense that she was being followed as she returned to the fortress.

In the Great Hall, the Lord Bardolph sat at his table with Lady Adela and Lady Gertrude at his side. For the moment, all was harmony between them as they watched and applauded the dancers and jugglers who were performing before them. Then Bardolph called for the musicians to cease playing. All kinds of entertainers were welcome at Bardolph's stronghold, but none more so than a gleeman. Bardolph loved a good story and provided the man had a ready supply of tales to tell he could stay as long as he liked and be well rewarded for his trouble. Now Bardolph called out, 'Enough! Enough! Bring on the gleeman. I want to hear more tales about our idiot Frankish overlord.' The man had only just begun his work when Gareth the Bailiff appeared. 'Ah! Gareth! Come listen to the tales this fellow tells. He has news also – very welcome news. He has just come from the court of our Frankish monarch. It is as we have heard: the man is mad – an idiot! Come, sit here and listen to the news.'

'I would, my lord, but I must speak with you on most urgent business.'

'Not now, bailiff, not when I am enjoying myself,' Bardolph protested. 'See, the ladies are with me; they will tell you that this man deserves a hearing.' Lady Adela and Lady Gertrude nodded their heads in vigorous agreement.

'I beg you, my lord,' Gareth insisted. 'This matter is most grave; it is for your ears only.'

Bardolph was surprised to see his imperturbable bailiff so agitated. 'Oh, very well,' he agreed. 'But first I must reward Lady Adela and Lady Gertrude for entertaining my guests in their usual elegant manner. See my men, ladies? I will give any one you desire to you as a husband. Take your pick.'

'Thank you, my lord,' replied Lady Adela in icy tones, 'but we must decline your offer and take our leave.'

Both ladies got to their feet together, bowed to Bardolph and walked with as much dignity as they could muster up the staircase. As soon as the door to Lady Isolda's room closed behind them, Bardolph collapsed in laughter. Two of his henchmen mimicked the ladies' walk and manner. Bardolph looked at Gareth. 'You do not approve, bailiff. Come, before your face sours the wine.'

Bardolph's own sleeping quarters were situated at the back of the Great Hall behind a partition and directly under the Lady Isolda's room. Gareth closed the door carefully behind them as Bardolph slumped down on a chair beside his bed. 'Well, what is so urgent that it could not wait?' he demanded.

'My lord,' Gareth began, 'I have seen the Lady Matilda leave the fortress unaccompanied.'

'What!' Bardolph thundered. 'You must have been mistaken.'

'No, my lord,' the bailiff insisted. 'I know the Lady Matilda well. She is always present when I visit the Lady Isolda.'

'And you did not stop her?' Bardolph interrupted. 'What folly was that? Where is she now?'

'She is safe in her room upstairs,' answered Gareth. 'I did

not detain her, my lord, because I felt it more important to find out where she was going. It was obvious from her carefree manner that she had left the fortress on previous occasions. I followed her up the hillside and saw her meet a young goatherd. It was apparent that they were old friends. They spent about an hour together and then the Lady Matilda returned home. I did not cease from watching her until I saw her enter the chapel.'

Bardolph had listened to the bailiff's story in silence, his knuckles turning white as he gripped the arms of his chair. Now he leapt to his feet, purple in the face. Words exploded from his mouth as he paced up and down the floor, one hand rubbing his throbbing thigh. 'Do I deserve this: to be cursed with such a child?' he demanded, shaking his fist at the rafters above him. 'Nine sons I have sired and every one dead within the year. One daughter is born to me and she alone survives to deceive me. Where is the justice in that? What evil is in her mind? Does she plot a peasants' revolt or is that boy in the pay of my half-brother, Ulric the Bold? Perhaps they plan my murder.'

'My lord, be calm,' Gareth entreated. 'I am certain there is no plot against you. I assure you there is no evil in the Lady Matilda. I repeat I know her well whereas you, my lord, have scarcely set eyes on her since the day she was born.' Bardolph glowered at the bailiff but he stood his ground. 'I am convinced the explanation is a simple one, my lord. The Lady Matilda has always lacked companions of her own age and in her desperation she has found a remedy. I know the boy also and I am sure there is no evil in him either. My only reason for reporting this matter to you is my concern for the Lady Matilda's safety. I am disturbed to find that she has been able to come and go as she pleases. Think of the dangers that might have befallen her and could befall her in the future if this was allowed to continue.'

'Continue?' yelled Bardolph. 'Of course it will not be allowed to continue. But I am much more concerned with the reason for her deception. I am not convinced that it is a simple matter. You say you know the boy? Tell me about him.'

'Very well, my lord,' said Gareth quietly. 'The boy came here about four years ago with a sick old woman. As far as I know they belong to no one. They built a hovel in the forest above this fortress.'

'In *my* forest?' snapped Bardolph. 'Who gave them that right? What do they pay in rent?'

'I will explain, my lord,' Gareth continued calmly, 'if you will allow me. I did not challenge the couple because I did not expect them to settle here. The old woman is ugly and afflicted and possesses powers of healing. It has been my experience that such women are usually suspected of being witches and are soon driven out by the other inhabitants. I made inquiries and found that the pair had indeed been hounded from their previous home. Perhaps our people are more tolerant – or more cowardly. They did not interfere with them and the boy quickly proved himself to be hardworking and honest, so much so, that many of your tenants have entrusted him with the care of their goats. All he has taken from your forest is a little firewood and the occasional bird or rabbit. These I felt you could spare, my lord.'

Again Bardolph glared at Gareth. 'One day you will presume too much,' he snarled menacingly.

The bailiff continued his defence unperturbed. 'The boy proved himself such an able guard last summer whenever robbers attacked the herds on the high alp that I felt the time had come to regulate his position and bring him into your service. It has been my plan to mention this matter when a suitable opportunity presented itself. I intended to recommend that the boy replace your own goatherd who is getting too old to defend your beasts when the necessity arises. The boy is young and strong and would be a useful acquisition. The old woman too could earn her living. Many of the peasants here about take their sick animals to her. I myself have taken a lame horse to her and she cured him most speedily.'

Bardolph's painful leg had forced him to sit down while he listened to Gareth's explanation but once more he sprang from his chair. 'Have you gone mad? You would have me bring this boy, my daughter's conspirator, into my fortress – into my very home? And a witch – you would have me harbour a witch? No! Never will I allow such a thing! There is only one answer: the rascal must be removed from her sight immediately. Have him sent to my brother, the Lord Gustavus. While you have been away his messenger reported that the Burgundians have all the good fortune. Already our casualties are heavy, though the fighting has scarcely begun. Send the boy to the battlefield and let Raoulbrun solve my problem. Let him bare that boy's flesh to the bone as he did mine.'

Gareth, accustomed to his master's rages, tried reasoned argument. 'My lord, there is no evidence of any plot against you. I am certain you are seeing danger where there is none. I know of no crime, save a little poaching to stave off hunger, which has ever been committed by either the boy or the old woman.'

'Enough! Silence, bailiff,' shouted Bardolph. 'You will do my bidding or I shall pull down that fine house I built for you and return you to the humble dwelling from which you came. Remember, Gareth, you know my strengths and weaknesses but I also know yours. Your strength lies in your integrity and ability but your weakness lies in your love of soft living. Cross me and you will rue the day. My brother's men will be in the district tomorrow to collect our reinforcements. See to it that you include the boy on your list. And get rid of the old woman also. She may well be the cause of this trouble. Yes, perhaps she has bewitched my daughter. Well, you shall break the spell. No witch shall come between me and mine again.'

'And the Lady Matilda?' Gareth inquired, seeing it was useless to argue further.

'She shall know nothing of this. I must match cunning with cunning. If I am to discover what she schemes I must win her confidence and trick her into making a mistake.'

'My lord,' protested Gareth, 'you are speaking of a little girl.'

'A clever, devious, wicked little girl,' asserted Bardolph. 'You will advise the boy of his fate today so that he has time to tell the Lady Matilda. I want her to know that it is useless to search for him. After they have enjoyed a last meeting I shall so fill her time that never again shall she have a chance to deceive me.'

'Very well, my lord,' Gareth said resignedly.

'And mark my words well, bailiff,' added Bardolph threateningly. 'Carry out my exact instructions with none of your usual impudence.'

'Whenever I have taken independent action, sire, it has always been because I felt it was best for you.'

'And when you buy goods for those women upstairs, how is that best for me?'

'My lord, I know that the Lady Isolda fears your wrath and dares to request only bare essentials. I am certain that in time you will come to regret the barrier you have placed between yourself and your family. I seek only to maintain a link between you and them in anticipation of the day when you may need their goodwill.'

'And so you spend a fortune on them.'

'My lord, in one year you spend on the Lady Isolda's entire household only one fifth of what you spend on adornments for the female servants of this hall.'

'Who are you to judge me?' Bardolph snarled. 'Why should I suffer your insolence any longer?'

'Perhaps, sire, because no man's affairs are run more efficiently than your affairs and those of the Lord Gustavus.'

'And no man's servant was ever less modest.'

'Modesty is a sign of weakness in a man,' replied Gareth politely.

Bardolph could not disagree with that statement so he tried another line of argument. 'And how do you justify the time you spend with those women upstairs when you are supposed to be running my affairs so efficiently?'

'I linger only to pass on any interesting news. You forget, my lord, I too have an invalid wife so I am very aware of the isolation which the Lady Isolda feels.'

'Enough of this!' snapped Bardolph, seeing that he could not win. 'You are trying to divert me from my purpose. See to the boy and the old woman. Cross me in this and you will regret it.'

'Master,' said Gareth, bowing, 'I am ever mindful that your interests and mine walk hand in hand.'

'Never forget it!' warned Bardolph.

The next afternoon, Tilly was surprised to find that she was free again although there were no special guests in the Great Hall. Her father had summoned the ladies and Father Almeric to a meeting. Tilly joyfully made the most of her good fortune and was soon speeding towards the forest clearing. Conrad was bursting with news. He scarcely greeted her before he began to explain what had happened, the excitement evident in his voice.

'I have wonderful news, Tilly, wonderful news! I am to be a soldier with the Lord Gustavus.' Tilly's heart missed a beat; her smile faded. The boy did not appear to notice her dismay. 'The bailiff himself came to tell me I had been chosen,' he continued. 'He came himself, Tilly – he did not send one of his men. I am to leave this evening. Of course, my happiness was mingled with sorrow ...' Tilly looked up hopefully, only to be disappointed. 'I feared for the survival of Hulda with no one to fend for her but the good bailiff assured me that he would see that she was taken care of and that I could leave without concern. I am so happy, Tilly. Say that you are happy for me too. My greatest ambition is to be realized: I am to ride with the Lord Gustavus.'

At last the boy let Tilly speak. 'But Conrad, are you not sad to leave me?' she asked with tears in her eyes.

'Tilly,' said Conrad placing his hands on her shoulders and facing her intently. 'Of course I am sad to leave you but it is all part of my plan for our future. Ever since we met I have been tormented by the worry of how to provide for you. You have lived in the fortress and have known a way of life which is far above mine. How could I ask *you* to live in a hovel? But if I become a great soldier and win many battles, I shall be well rewarded. Then I shall be able to buy your freedom from the Lord Bardolph and build you a home that is fitting for one so beautiful and learned.'

The shock of Conrad's words made Tilly stop crying. 'Do you mean that you will return and claim me when you are a man?'

'Of course, Tilly,' replied Conrad earnestly, astonished that she should have needed to ask the question. 'You must know that that has always been my intention. Why, only a few weeks ago, did we not exchange gifts as is the custom between two people who are betrothed? Did I not tell you then that I would never be parted from your gift? I shall carry it everywhere, Tilly, and dream that you are with me.' Then for the first time, Conrad kissed Tilly gently and brushed away the tears that had trickled down her cheeks. 'Come, little one,' he said, 'I must return you to the fortress. It would be a tragedy if you should incur the Lord Bardolph's displeasure now. If he should send you away I might never find you again.'

They walked in silence down the hillside, hand in hand. Tilly's mind was in turmoil. She felt stunned by the news of Conrad's departure but she was also disturbed by the fact that he considered her his betrothed. Tilly had never given a thought to their future relationship: somehow, she had pictured them as perpetual children playing, working and laughing together on the hillside forever. All at once she was conscious of the futility of their friendship. Whether goatherd or soldier,

Conrad could never be her husband. For as long as she could remember, she had accepted that when the time came her father would arrange a suitable marriage for her and political expediency would be the only consideration. What could she say to her friend? How could she reveal in their last moments together that she had deceived him: that she was the Lord Bardolph's heir, not his servant; that she would one day inherit the chieftainship of their tribe; that all thought of a union between them was absurd? How selfish she had been, thinking only of herself. She glanced at Conrad cautiously as he strode along and saw that his face displayed only contentment. She realized that he had taken it for granted that she acquiesced to his proposals for their future and expected no declaration on her part. Perhaps it would be kinder to keep silent and certainly it would be easier. She could not bear to hurt her friend and now she knew how much he cared for her. The thought that she would never see him again was almost too much to bear. They approached the gates and Conrad stopped, took both of her small hands in his and turned her so that they stood face to face.

'Promise me that you will never again leave the fortress without permission, or deliberately do anything to displease the Lord Bardolph.' Tilly could not speak. Tears welled up inside her. Tight-lipped she nodded her agreement. Conrad embraced her promising as he did so, 'I give you my word, little Tilly: I will return and claim my betrothed as my wife.' Then he pushed her gently towards the entrance to the fortress. Reluctantly she went, pausing for a last sight of him before she waved goodbye.

Conrad trudged back up the hillside with a heavy heart. He had not reckoned that parting from Tilly would be so painful. His eyes too were misty with tears so he did not see the bailiff walking along the ramparts and entering the stronghold soon after Tilly. Conrad bade farewell to the boy who had come to replace him as goatherd and then went back to the shack for a last meal with Hulda. He packed his only belongings, the books which Tilly had made for him, in a cloth. He sat on a tree stump to wait for the soldiers to collect him. When they arrived, he hugged Hulda. She was weeping bitterly. He climbed into the cart beside the other recruits and waved to her until she disappeared from view. Then Conrad sat back on his haunches on the hard boards and felt black despair overwhelm him. He was leaving behind all he loved and all who loved him. What did the future hold? Would his hopes be fulfilled? He suddenly felt sick with the fear of the unknown.

No sooner had the cart driven by the soldiers left the forest and begun its descent towards the plain than a second wagon drew up outside the shack. Men climbed down and went inside the hovel. When they emerged they had Hulda with them. They placed the old woman in the back of their vehicle and drove away.

VI

A new beginning

When Tilly reached the safety of her dormitory she threw herself upon her bed and gave vent to her misery. For a long time she sobbed uncontrollably but when she could weep no more she lay still, feeling completely exhausted. It was then that sounds penetrated her thoughts – sounds of an argument. She raised her head. She could identify several voices. They were coming from the Great Hall. Then she heard her own name mentioned. At once she was gripped with fear. Perhaps someone had come to look for her, searched the fortress and found her missing. She leapt from her bed and rushed to the door. Opening it slightly, she peered warily down the staircase. She saw her father sitting in his huge chair his back to her and, in front of him, anguish on their faces, stood Father Almeric, Lady Adela and Lady Gertrude. There was no doubt that she, Tilly, was the subject under discussion. She leaned a little farther out of the doorway so that she might hear more clearly what was being said. A floorboard creaked and the bailiff, who had been standing at his master's side, looked up at Tilly. He whispered something to the Lord Bardolph who turned, glanced up the staircase and beckoned to the child.

'Come down here, Matilda,' Bardolph commanded. Tilly obeyed, filled with trepidation.

The old priest and the ladies gasped at the sight of her red and swollen eyes and tear-stained face. They rushed to put their arms around her. 'The child has overheard what was being said,' cried Lady Adela. 'She is distraught.'

'Leave her!' ordered Bardolph. 'Come, Matilda, stand here where I can see you clearly.' Tilly meekly did as she was told, betraying none of the fear she felt. Bardolph stared at her, long and hard. As he surveyed the slim figure, the small tight-lipped face, he was reminded of another girl so very like this one who had stood before him in this same hall such a long time ago. His bride, the Lady Isolda, could not have been so many years older than this child when she had come to be married. He recalled that first meeting so vividly. Book-learning had never come easily to him but he had laboriously rehearsed a few phrases of welcome in her native French. He had scarcely begun to stumble out the words when she had interrupted, informing him in German that she and all her company spoke his language perfectly. He had never been able to forgive that first rebuff. Bardolph forced himself to concentrate on the present. 'How old are you, Matilda?' he asked. 'Seven? Eight?'

Tilly's eyes widened with surprise at the question. 'I am ten years old, my lord,' she replied.

Bardolph continued to sit motionless studying his daughter, trying to assess what evil lay beneath that innocent countenance. He stared into the huge eyes searching for the answer. The child returned his gaze and again he was reminded of his wife. One scathing look from her and no words were necessary. How often during their stormy marriage had she slain him with one glance and reduced him to a stammering idiot. He knew that arrogant stare so well. Truly she was the image of her mother; he must tread very warily.

'So you are ten years old,' said Bardolph at last. 'Then it is time we got to know one another. You are my heir, Matilda, and one day you will lead our tribes. My father – your grandfather – was also King of *all* the Alemannian tribes. That title is rightfully mine but Ulric the Bold, my half-brother, also claims it and some tribes, curses upon them, support him. It is a matter which I and your uncle, the Lord Gustavus, intend to resolve in the near future. By the time you succeed me, Matilda, you will be the undisputed leader of all the Alemannian peoples. If you are to survive you must be carefully schooled. It is my duty to see that this is done. I have decided that I shall teach you myself all that is necessary for you to know of the ways of leadership. Do you ride, child?'

Tilly was as surprised by this question as by the first. Perhaps she had been wrong after all; perhaps her fears of discovery had been unfounded. She began to relax a little and smiled as she answered, 'Yes, I do. My uncle, the Lord Gustavus, gave me a pony when I was eight and you gave me a most beautiful cloth and side seat. If you remember, Father, I wrote you a very long letter of thanks.'

'Yes, Matilda, I remember,' Bardolph replied, glaring at Gareth. The bailiff had insisted upon reading him every word of the letter in spite of the fact that he had omitted to advise his master beforehand of his intention to purchase the equipment. Looking at his daughter now, Bardolph was forced to admit that there may have been some merit in Gareth's reasoning. Certainly, he had the child's goodwill over the matter of the gift. As soon as the subject of riding had been raised her face had become transformed. No longer sullen and haughty, she was beaming at him now and her eyes shone.

'But I have only ever been allowed to ride him inside the palisade. Oh! Father, my pony looks so fine in its rig,' Tilly continued eagerly, her reticence pushed aside, 'might I not ride with you some time so that you may see for yourself your wonderful gift?'

Bardolph was astonished – and cheered – by his daughter's sudden enthusiasm. He responded at once. 'Of course you may ride with me, Matilda. Tomorrow morning you will join me in the hunt.'

The ladies and Father Almeric gasped in dismay. The latter rushed forward, arms outstretched. 'My lord, I beseech you – I beg you to reconsider. The Lady Matilda is but a child, delicate like her dear mother. She has been nurtured like a flower –

protected – sheltered. The rigours of the hunt would distress her; the horrors of the kill would sicken her.'

Bardolph would hear no more; he crashed his fist upon the table. 'Silence! Enough! A flower, you say? You have nurtured a flower! What use is a flower to me? What use is a flower to my people? A flower cannot rule them. A flower cannot defend them against their enemies. My eyes have been opened just in time. There will be no more discussion. The matter is settled. You will tutor the Lady Matilda for four hours a day only; the rest of her time shall be spent under my personal supervision.'

The old priest hid his head in his hands, whilst Tilly could scarcely conceal her joy at this unexpected turn of events. She was, however, very fond of Father Almeric and sought to comfort him. 'Please do not be upset, Father Almeric,' she entreated. 'The hunt will not unduly tire or distress me.' Then, addressing her father she inquired, 'Will the beasts we kill be used to feed us, my lord?'

'Of course,' confirmed Bardolph in amused tones.

Tilly turned again to the priest. 'Have you not taught me that God in his wisdom put other creatures upon this earth for the help and comfort of us, his people? To kill wantonly for the thrill of killing would be wicked, but to kill in order to feed ourselves ... Surely, there can be no harm in that, dear Father Almeric?'

'Well spoken,' said Bardolph. 'You will ride with me tomorrow.'

At that moment Lady Adela, more courageous than her cousin, stepped forward. 'Have you forgotten, my lord, that many years ago you promised my mistress that she should have sole charge of the Lady Matilda?'

'Times have changed,' muttered Bardolph, rising from his chair and motioning with a wave of his hand that the meeting was at an end.

Lady Adela would not be dismissed. 'I trust, my lord, that you will inform the Lady Isolda of this change.'

Bardolph paled at the suggestion. 'No! You can inform her,' he declared.

'That would be wrong,' Lady Adela maintained bravely. 'It is your duty, sire, to advise the Lady Isolda yourself that you intend to break your word.'

Bardolph scowled. 'Who are you to tell me my duty?' he thundered.

The bailiff decided he had better intervene. He whispered in his master's ear, reminding him of the close bond between mother and daughter. 'My lord, perhaps the Lady Matilda has confided in her mother.'

Bardolph nodded in agreement. 'Very well, I shall speak to the Lady Isolda now – this very moment,' he declared. The ladies moved towards the staircase; Bardolph called out to them. 'You will remain here. I shall go alone or not at all!' he roared. At least he would retain the element of surprise. As he ascended to the upper storey, the years of tempestuous quarrelling came back to him. Just as she had used her flashing eyes like a sword, to hurt and wound, so she had used her tongue. His language may have been foreign to her but so well did she master it that it became another weapon in their battles. Worst of all, he had never succeeded in learning Burgundian French. She had been able to insult him to his face by conversing with her ladies knowing he was ignorant of what they were saying. He had never doubted that their intermittent laughter had been directed against him. He would be spared that indignity today. He would have no witnesses; the conflict would be equal between husband and wife.

Bardolph entered the room hesitantly and paused just inside the door. Bertha, who had been dozing in the chair beside her mistress's bed, woke with a start. Bardolph ordered her to leave the room. She did so eventually with great reluctance and stood outside on the small landing, feet firmly planted and arms resolutely crossed, making it clear that she intended to remain there on guard.

Bardolph crossed to the bed and looked at the sleeping Lady Isolda. Years of chronic ill-health had taken their toll. She was even smaller and thinner than he remembered. The once beautiful face was gaunt; hollow cheeked. The long fair hair which he had secretly admired so much was still lovely. Bardolph sighed. How could any man hope to raise healthy sons from such sickly stock? The marriage had been arranged by his father: a union of his elder son and Raoulbrun's only daughter. Some insult caused the fighting to recommence the following year. Bardolph had considered sending his bride back to her father – nothing had changed his first instinctive feelings towards her – but she had been with child. He had had great hopes of a son so he had kept her. The child had been born dead, the first of so many bitter disappointments. Years of sorrow and recrimination had followed and finally, rejection and mutual hatred. Bardolph recollected the last time he had stood in this room. He had come to see his ninth son. The baby was but a few hours old – a tiny puny thing. He had ceased to breathe even as Bardolph looked at him. His wife too had given every appearance of being dead and had not been expected to live through the night. The Lady Isolda had survived but never since that day had she left her bed and never since that day had he set eyes upon her.

Bardolph pulled the chair which the nurse had been sitting on further away from the bed and sat down. The noise woke the Lady Isolda. She opened her eyes and for a fleeting second, Bardolph saw cold fear in them as she recognized him. Quickly, she regained control of her emotions and demanded icily, 'Where are my ladies?'

'They are below, ma'am,' replied her husband striving to keep his voice steady. 'I wished to speak to you alone.'

'It is a long time since you wished that,' retorted Lady Isolda.

Bardolph was determined not to quarrel so he continued quietly. 'What I have come to say concerns Matilda. I have decided that the time has come to take her in hand myself.'

Lady Isolda struggled to raise herself on her pillows, her hooded dark-rimmed eyes registering alarm. 'No! No! You cannot do that!' she protested vehemently. 'You gave me your solemn promise when she was born that I should have sole charge of her upbringing.'

'That was many years ago, my lady,' Bardolph argued, trying not to raise his voice. 'I did not think then that she would be my heir. Till now I have pushed the thought from my mind but I must resign myself to it and accept that one day she will succeed me.'

'Why now, my lord,' Lady Isolda demanded sarcastically, 'why now must you resign yourself to this awful truth?'

Bardolph moistened his lips nervously, searching for the right words. 'It was not my intention to alarm you, ma'am, but if you insist upon knowing I will tell you the reason. The bailiff has uncovered a plot involving Matilda's safety.'

Lady Isolda recoiled as from a blow. Horrified, she cried, 'Someone plans to kill my child?'

'Do not distress yourself, ma'am,' Bardolph said with genuine concern. 'Gareth has already carried out my instructions regarding all parties to this plot and Matilda is no longer in any danger.'

'Thank God! Thank God!' whispered Lady Isolda, wringing her hands in anguish.

Bardolph saw that this shock had weakened his wife. He made the most of his advantage but he proceeded gently, knowing he could afford to be generous now that he was in command of the situation. 'So you see, my lady, our daughter has been much in my thoughts of late. Apart from ensuring that no further harm comes to her, I feel it is my duty to prepare her for her future. To lead our tribes is an arduous enough task for a man, but for a woman ... Unless she is strong and powerful other nobles will contest her for the leadership when I am gone. Ulric the Bold will be among the first to try to overthrow her and many others will follow.'

At these words, Lady Isolda's eyes blazed with some of her old fire. 'That must never happen; you must not allow it to happen. Matilda must keep what is rightfully hers.'

Bardolph was gratified by this unexpected support. 'You, of course, will continue to supervise her in book-learning, religious education and the feminine arts,' he conceded. 'But I wish her to be with me when I sit in council or in judgment, and to ride with me when I journey through our lands. In this way she will become so well-known to my people, from the richest vassal to the lowliest serf, that when I die they will follow her without question and her position will be unassailable.' Bardolph was amazed at his own eloquence and even more amazed when his wife agreed with his argument.

'You are right, my lord. I have been misguided in wanting to keep Matilda to myself. But I beg you to take great care of her – she is all I have.'

Bardolph saw tears in his wife's eyes and for the first time in his life he felt compassion for her. 'She is all I have, my lady,' he murmured.

'I fear she may have inherited my weak constitution,' Lady Isolda confided. 'Many times of late she has entered my room breathless and flushed.' Bardolph looked down at the floor and smiled to himself. He could think of a very different explanation for those symptoms but he kept his thoughts to himself. 'We have always been so close but recently, I have felt her growing away from me,' continued his wife sadly. 'A bedridden mother is no companion for a healthy child. She will be more content with you, living life to the full.'

Bardolph was convinced there was no guile behind these remarks. He was certain now that his wife knew nothing of her daughter's exploits. All feelings of hostility left him and he responded with a kindness that surprised Lady Isolda. 'I have no wish to take Matilda from you or to alienate her affection for you. Your ladies may accompany her at all times and I swear that she will never be left in the charge of anyone except me or possibly, Gareth the Bailiff. There is much that she can learn from him but I give you my word that she will never come under the influence of any other of my nobles.'

'I thank you for your understanding, my lord,' replied Lady Isolda. 'I have no fears regarding your bailiff: I know him to be a man of sound judgment. I am sure he is universally respected.' Then, showing that she had accepted the situation, she changed the subject. 'Your mention of the bailiff has reminded me that I can at last thank you in person, my lord, for the many gifts he has brought us on your behalf.' Bardolph began to feel uncomfortable. His wife continued. 'I assure you your kindness has always been appreciated, and never once have you denied us any request.'

Now Bardolph felt ashamed. He glanced briefly at his wife and saw that her gratitude was sincere. To hide his discomfort he answered gruffly, 'There is no need to thank me, ma'am. You have asked only your due.' Then he heard himself say, 'It is I who should thank you. Your demands have always been minimal. If there is anything further you would like you have only to ask.'

Lady Isolda looked at her husband in astonishment and wondered what had become of the man she once knew. Could this be the same uncouth, uneducated monster whose sheer brute strength had terrified and repelled her? She considered for a moment and then suggested, 'There is one thing I should like, my lord. I should like a little of your time – to discuss our daughter's progress.'

Bardolph passed the indignant Bertha in a confused state of mind. He had braced himself for conflict only to find himself the victor after scarcely a fight. What was more the gulf between him and his wife had been bridged. He descended the staircase with a bemused smile on his face. He almost bumped into Lady Adela, Lady Gertrude and Father Almeric who were waiting anxiously at the bottom of the steps. He bowed to them and ushered them upstairs with a sweep of his hand. As they hurried past him he caught sight of the bailiff smiling knowingly. 'How insufferable is the man who is always right,' he muttered to Gareth good humouredly.

Next morning Bardolph found Tilly eagerly awaiting him. She greeted him warmly. He could scarcely believe that she wanted his company. He stood and looked at her in the fresh clear light of early morning. She was already mounted, dressed in a blue woollen gown with a close-fitting hood which completely hid her hair and framed her tiny heart-shaped face. What a fool he had been, Bardolph thought. Once more Gareth had been right. If only he had given this child more of his attention that regrettable incident with the goatherd would never have occurred. But he would make up for his negligence a hundred-fold, he vowed. He climbed onto his horse with his servant's help and called jovially to Tilly, 'Come my pretty little lady! Let us away!'

The child glowed with pleasure at the compliment. The company left the inner courtyard, Bardolph and Tilly leading the way. They were followed by the usual party of hunters, surprised and bewildered by the presence of a little girl. A covered wagon made up the rear and seated uncomfortably in it were Lady Adela and Lady Gertrude. It had been decided that Tilly should join them as soon as she became tired; she had determined that she would never succumb to such weakness.

As the procession advanced across the outer bailey, many stopped to stare at the spectacle. Some people came forward and lined the route to the main gates, many bowing their heads in salute to the beautiful child who sat straight and imperious on her white pony. As they approached the drawbridge and the sweep of land down towards the plain became visible, Tilly's excitement grew. She turned and gave her father a smile of such radiance that it brought a lump to his throat. He sat taller upon his horse and felt the first flush of paternal pride. Father and child rode forth – to a new beginning.

PART TWO

I

A dream shattered

The wagon which carried Conrad towards his new beginning was soon joined by several others. They stopped at a number of villages to pick up the recruits whose names were on the long list prepared by the bailiff. The convoy sheltered for the night at a riverside settlement and set off again at first light. Conrad felt a little more cheerful by morning and he tried to strike up a conversation with his companions. Hardly a word had been exchanged the previous night: everyone had been lost in his own thoughts. The younger occupants of the wagon replied to Conrad's questions but the older ones still sat morose, worried at leaving their families and fields at a time when there was so much work to be done.

All went well for Conrad until he made the mistake of confiding to his new acquaintances that he had always wanted to be a soldier and serve in the Lord Gustavus's bodyguard. The men driving the vehicle and those inside who had taken a turn at military service before laughed uproariously at this revelation. Conrad found himself the subject of taunts and jeers for the remainder of the journey; no one was more relieved than he when the encampment came within sight on the third day. The carts passed through the gates of the wooden palisade and began to move through the camp unloading men and supplies at intervals. Conrad was the last one left in his wagon.

The driver called out to a white-haired man with huge muscular shoulders, standing with a group of soldiers. 'Hey! Otto! Can you do with a boy?'

'Yes, I will take him if he is strong,' the man replied, coming up to the vehicle and peering at Conrad.

The driver could not resist adding, 'Mind you take good care of him, Otto. This is no common foot soldier – this is a young nobleman who would ride with the Lord Gustavus himself!'

Conrad's heart sank. Would he now endure more misery at the hands of his new companions? He climbed down from the wagon with the driver's mocking laughter ringing in his ears. Otto looked at him not too unkindly and ignoring the soldier's jibes said, 'Well, boy, you look sturdy enough. Come and tell me what you can do.'

Conrad glanced at his new master's weather-beaten face and liked what he saw. 'I am good at hunting, trapping and fishing,' he replied, adding as an afterthought, 'and I have fought the Raetians.'

The big man laughed. 'That will do for a beginning. What is your name?'

'My name is Conrad,' answered the boy.

'And I am Otto the Axe-man and this is my company,' said the man, indicating the group of seasoned soldiers who had been watching the proceedings. 'A braver tougher band of warriors you will never meet – nor a hungrier one. It is as well that you are a good hunter for it will be your task to feed this ravenous company.'

In the weeks that followed, Conrad worked hard to supplement the rations of Otto's men with fresh meat and fish. He fashioned traps, mesh nets and a bow and arrows and he always left the encampment just before dawn. He would return soon after the men had woken up with birds or fish strung around his neck and would be clapped on the back for his trouble by his grateful new comrades. But in that time he also came to realize how foolish his aspirations had been. The camp was full of horses and Otto confirmed that his lord depended heavily upon his mounted soldiers in battle. Every member of the cavalry, however, was a wealthy man: he had to be since he was expected to provide and maintain his own horse and equip himself with armour and weapons at his own expense. Serfs and peasants, Conrad was now aware, could only be infantrymen. He found it very difficult to reconcile himself to these harsh facts. He had lived with his ambitions for so long, and had made such promises to Tilly, that he could not shake off his depression. He was homesick too: for Tilly and Hulda and for his pastures and forests where his dreams had never been threatened by reality.

Early one morning, Conrad had settled himself in the undergrowth to wait for some unsuspecting animal to pass by when he spied a group of riders through the trees. One man detached himself from the others and rode slowly towards the spot where the boy was hiding. The man sat tall and erect upon his horse and on his arm perched a falcon. As he approached Conrad recognised him – it was the Lord Gustavus. The boy held his breath and gazed in awe at his general. Although he was enjoying a rare moment of relaxation the Lord Gustavus's features were stern. His high forehead and cheekbones, deep set eyes and aquiline nose gave him an unmistakable air of authority. Conrad felt he was in the presence of greatness. So intent was he upon silently worshipping his hero that he did not hear Otto creep up behind him.

He jumped when the soldier placed his gigantic hand on his shoulder and whispered, 'Come, boy, leave our master to his sport.' Otto led Conrad firmly away and then decided that this was as good a time as any to give him a few words of advice. 'There is nothing wrong with dreams, boy. Even old Otto has his dreams: pleasant thoughts to dwell on before I go to sleep. But that is all they are, Conrad, and if you do not rouse yourself before the fighting starts again you are going to be in trouble. Either you will be amongst the first to die or one of the commanders will notice your negligence and you will suffer the punishment of all criminals in our master's infantry – you will be sent to join Carlo's Company.' Otto had used this threat before to shake Conrad from his lethargy but the boy had not bothered to ask the Axe-man to explain. This time, seeing a flicker of interest in Conrad's eyes, Otto continued. 'At one time, cowards, murderers and thieves were dealt with by execution or maiming but then our lord decided he could not afford to waste men in such a way. But it was still necessary for wrongdoers to be seen to be punished, so he formed Carlo's Company both as a deterrent to others and to fill a military need. Because they are worthless scum he deploys them where he does not wish to risk his other troops – where the danger is greatest. They are sent in to test the enemy's strength or to fight hopeless rearguard actions to cover a withdrawal. Men do not survive long in Carlo's Company: if the enemy does not get them they get each other! Cut throats all, they would kill for a mouthful of bread. Take care, Conrad, great care that you do nothing to warrant relegation to that company. To serve in those ranks is the worst dishonour that could befall you.'

Otto waited to see if his predictions of doom would arouse any response in Conrad. When the boy continued to stare at the ground in silence the Axe-man decided to change his tactics and try encouragement. 'Resign yourself to the fact that the likes of us can never join our general's own Companions in Arms but we can serve him just the same. What is wrong with being an ordinary foot soldier, eh? So long as you are the best! It is an honourable calling. I have been in the service of our lord and his father before him, since I was a boy. I have been proud to fight for them; I would not have had any other way of life. You listen to old Otto, boy, and I will make you the best infantryman in our lord's army. But you must help me in return by making up your mind to work hard and heed all I say.'

The old man talked for a long time, doing his best to fire

the boy's imagination; eventually he succeeded. 'Very well, Otto,' Conrad agreed, 'I will try to be a good infantryman.' He continued to leave the encampment early to hunt for food in the surrounding countryside – his skill with bow and arrow became renowned – and when others returned lightly laden Conrad's baskets were brimming. He soon earned a reputation as an excellent forager and with his responsibility for feeding his comrades fulfilled he could spend the rest of the day with his tutor, thus keeping his word to try to be a good infantryman.

Otto found his pupil strong, agile and eager to learn. Since he was already proficient with bow and arrow, they began with simple weapons. Otto demonstrated that a well-chosen rock accurately propelled from its sling with the correct amount of force, could stun or even kill a man. Next he fashioned a round, wooden, hidebound shield for the boy and taught him how to use it to the best advantage.

'In close hand to hand fighting, Conrad, your shield not only protects you but becomes another weapon. You can use the rim,' Otto lunged forward to illustrate his point, 'to crack your opponent's ribs or crush the bones of his face. And do not forget your feet – they are weapons too. Use them to trip your enemy and when he is down, strike him with your axe or knife. Later, Conrad, I shall train you to fight shoulder to shoulder with the other men behind a shield-wall. In open country our general uses a shield-ring or square but where our flanks are protected by a river or cliff, he favours a "swine-array" with our champions leading the way and forming the "snout". One man, famous for his skill and valour, leads the champions. Do as old Otto tells you and one day that honour may go to you, boy.'

Conrad was pleased with his shield and thanked Otto for it but as he pointed out, 'I have no weapons except my small woodcarving knife.'

'You have now,' his teacher replied. 'Last night one of my

men died. He had been wounded in the last fight with the Burgundians. I was too late to get his tunic – he had a stout leather one like mine – but it would have been too big for you anyway. I managed to save his weapons though. Here is his knife – a better one than yours – and his spear and axe. A man without weapons is not a man at all; he is worthless to his chieftain and to the Lord God. Now you can truly call yourself a man, Conrad.'

The boy proudly weighed the weapons in his hands but then he cried, 'Where is his sword?'

Otto laughed. 'Will you never learn, boy? The sword is the king of weapons. It is for chieftains, nobles and champions; not for the ordinary warrior like you and me.' The Axe-man saw the disappointment in the boy's face and knew he must divert him quickly before he sank back into his former melancholy. 'Look at this spear, Conrad,' he instructed, pointing to the weapon the boy was holding. 'I wager you do not realize that this once belonged to a Frank.'

'How do you know that, Otto?' asked Conrad, his interest captured at once.

'I will tell you,' replied the old soldier. 'It is a light throwing spear, much like the javelins we use, but the head is attached to the shaft in a different way. See, it is a small barbed head with a long thin neck. When a Frank throws his spear he aims at your shield – and he never misses, boy! The neck is made of soft iron so that it will bend and the heavy shaft will drag your shield down and you will be defenceless. The Franks call this kind of spear an Angon. You must learn to use it like a Frank. But learning to aim and throw accurately and forcefully is not all there is to spear-fighting. Spears are very useful weapons at close quarters; then you adopt thrusting movements like this!' Otto seized the spear and began leaping about, piercing the imaginary enemy to the right and to the left of him and finally charging the few remaining with blood-curdling yells. Breathing heavily, he returned to Conrad.

'Prepare to defend yourself, boy! You will not always be the attacker; you must be sharp-eyed and agile to stay alive. Learn to jump, boy, to jump aside as the spear darts at you and to jump high, right over the spear if necessary – like this!'

Conrad suddenly found himself jumping for his life as Otto prodded and thrust the spear in his direction. After a few minutes the old man threw the weapon down, laughing. 'You will not die that way – you are too quick, thank God! There is one more spear trick you must master, but not today. It takes a lot of strength and courage but you must learn to catch a spear in flight as it leaves your enemy's hand, turn it and hurl it back at him.'

'I have a lot to learn, Otto, have I not?' said Conrad with a sigh.

'Indeed you have but I am here to help you. Anything you need to know, ask old Otto.'

'Then tell me, Otto, about these Franks you speak of? I thought the Burgundians were our enemies.'

'They are, boy, they are. Burgundians, Franks, even Alemannians – the tribes that follow Ulric the Bold – they are all our enemies.' Otto squatted on the ground and dragged Conrad down beside him. 'I will tell you what I know of the Franks. They once had a great warrior king called Clovis – or so our Lord Gustavus tells – and he conquered us: all the Alemannian tribes and the Burgundians too. But that was a long long time ago. Although the present King of the Franks is supposed to be our overlord he is a weakling and a simpleton. Our lords have taken back their lands and pay him no homage. From time to time he sends an army to put us down and demand tribute. Hah! He gets no tribute from us. Every force he has sent against us we have destroyed. The Franks are no match for the Alemannians, Conrad. They fight like an unruly rabble. They rush upon you like madmen. But they are dangerous because they make no attempt to protect or defend themselves; they think only of attack and do not care how many of their number are killed or injured. In their frenzy they take many of our good soldiers with them, but we always beat them in the end. Discipline, boy, discipline is the best weapon we have. Our Lord Gustavus sets great store by discipline. A Frank could never hold a battle formation as we do – could never maintain a shield-wall. And as for their leaders, they are no match for our general. He can outwit and out-manoeuvre them every time! But one thing we have learned from the Franks is how to make the best use of this.' So saying, Otto took his axe from his belt. 'The Lord Gustavus says you should never under-estimate an enemy; watch him closely and see if he can teach you anything. About the only thing a Frank can do well, Conrad, is throw an axe. Many years ago, the Lord Gustavus had axes made for us after the style of the Frankish throwing-axe. It was a weapon I took to straight away. That is how I got my name – Otto the Axe-man! My "widow-maker",' the old man paused and stroked his axe lovingly, 'has given me good service and has saved my life many, many times. When I have done with you, boy, you will be as skillful an axe-man as I am.'

Once again Otto got to his feet, this time to demonstrate his favourite weapon. 'In close combat you must use your axe thus, changing the direction of your blow as it falls and as your foe tries to avoid it. Your aim must be accurate and your timing perfect. Then you must learn to do this!' With scarcely a pause, Otto sent the axe hurtling in the direction of a young tree, standing alone. In an instant, the sapling was split in two down the middle.

'I think I am going to need a lot of practice before I can do that,' said Conrad. 'You must be the best axe-man that ever lived.'

So the days passed for Conrad and very soon he found himself enjoying life once again. His fondness for Otto grew and it became important to him that he should please the old man. Otto found much pleasure in Conrad's company also and their evenings would be spent together around the camp fire. Conrad would listen in rapt admiration whilst his friend recounted tales of past glories and adventures. Otto had accompanied his master on many campaigns and his loyalty and love for the Lord Gustavus was unquestioning. He never tired of telling Conrad how revered their general was by all his men; how it was said that he never ate, drank or slept; how he recovered from terrible wounds that would have killed a lesser man; how he was respected not only as a great leader but as a saint for his sober and austere way of life.

Conrad was not the only one who enjoyed listening to these tales. Most nights the pair was joined by Thorkell the Skald, eager to hear in particular details of the Lord Gustavus's past battles, for these were the tools of Thorkell's trade. The first time that they met Conrad admitted that he had never heard of a "skald".

'Of course you have not,' replied Thorkell. 'It is not an Alemannian word. I am a Norseman. In my homeland all chieftains have their skalds just as they have their champions. We are very important people! Where is the glory in being a hero if no one knows you are a hero? Through me – through my sagas – men live forever. Their names and their deeds will be remembered for generations. My songs will be handed down like jewelled swords.'

Otto interrupted, laughing. 'Do not be fooled, Conrad, he is good for more than words. He is no mean fighter himself.'

Conrad was surprised to hear this. 'You take part in the fighting? Is it not dangerous to pause on the battlefield to look around at what others are doing? Would it not be better to stand apart on higher ground to observe the battle?'

'Indeed no! To know how a warrior feels I must be a warrior. How can I tell in my songs what it is like to perform remarkable feats if I have never performed any myself? How can I describe what it is like to be wounded if I have never been wounded myself?'

'I think you must be a very brave man,' concluded Conrad solemnly.

'I am sorry you said that – very sorry,' Thorkell replied shaking his head, 'for now I am forced to admit that I am a coward. To tell the truth, Conrad, I only became a skald so that I would not get killed. I had been a fighting man all my life – I knew no other skill – but being small in stature, unlike my friend here,' he prodded Otto in the ribs, 'I suffered greatly at the hands of taller stronger men. It became apparent to me that I should not live long. All my people – all Norsemen – are poets at heart, so I decided to become a skald. I get wounded from time to time but the wounds are never serious. No man with a morsel of wisdom deliberately tries to kill a skald for to do so would be to kill himself. I sing of the wonderful acts of both friend and foe. Our enemies know me too and they know I will record their heroic deeds also. I am every man's immortality, Conrad.'

The boy did not know what to make of this confession since the skald told his tale with a gleam in his eyes and with exaggerated expression in his voice and face. It was true that Thorkell was not of Otto's stature but Conrad judged that he was only a little below average height. He was strong and sturdy and appeared quite capable of returning blow for blow in combat. Conrad decided that not all of his new friend's words could be taken seriously.

On one matter the boy was in no doubt – the Norseman was the most popular man in the camp. The Lord Gustavus would permit no entertainers of any kind to follow his army. The skald knew that his master did not number him in such company but regarded him as a military historian, recounting facts in a manner that the average soldier could understand and appreciate. What is more, he inspired men to emulate the brave deeds of the heroes of his sagas. To the Lord Gustavus's men, however, Thorkell *was* first and foremost an entertainer who sang the kind of songs they loved to hear. Unbeknown to his master, the skald did not confine himself to accounts of battles past; he had a stirring selection of poems which the Lord Gustavus would have condemned as pagan. They described the adventures of famous weapons – usually swords – whose magical properties made their owners invincible. These tales extolled the mystical powers of the smiths who had made the weapons. They included praises to Weland, the smith of the gods once worshipped by Teutonic soldiers, or to Vulcan, the Roman soldiers' god of fire and metal-making. Otto took great exception to this liberal attitude to religion. He himself followed his master in all things and he had embraced Christianity with the same fervour as the Lord Gustavus.

One night as the crowd dispersed at the close of Thorkell's performance, Otto reprimanded the skald. 'You should not speak such heresy – especially in front of the boy. If the Lord Gustavus knew he would have you whipped. If you do not fear him you should fear the fires of hell.'

'Otto, I fear a religion that has no poetry in it,' replied Thorkell. 'What rousing songs can I sing about your one and only God? There are so many I can sing about my Norse gods – tales of Odin, god of war and for that matter tales of Mars, the Roman god of war – same god. They are tales to fill a man with excitement and passion!'

Otto ignored Thorkell's dramatic rhetoric. 'You know how our master feels on this subject. You have deceived him by pretending to embrace his religion while continuing to worship Odin. You should not have come here.'

Conrad found the conversation confusing and difficult to follow. Religion, so far, had not touched his short life but he did not like to hear his new comrades quarrelling so he tried to change the subject. 'How did you come here, Thorkell?' he asked. 'Your homeland must be far to the north.'

'It is so, Conrad,' answered the skald. 'The land of my birth is far to the north but I have always been an adventurer and over the years I have had many masters. As I have left the service of one chieftain to seek another – one where the pickings were better – I have always travelled south. Language has never been a problem to me: I have been blessed with a gift which enables me to assimilate any man's tongue quickly. When I reached this country I had no wish to travel further. The mountains and the snows remind me of my homeland; furthermore, the Lord Gustavus is the greatest warlord I have ever encountered. His exploits provide me with a never-ending tapestry of tales to tell. And best of all, Conrad, since he is almost always victorious, the plunder is never-ending too!'

'So for earthly reasons you pretend to our master that you are a Christian,' exclaimed Otto, returning to his argument.

'I do not pretend,' Thorkell protested. 'I do worship your God – and Odin, Weland, Mars and Vulcan – and any god who is a warrior's god. To me they are all one – different peoples give them different names.'

'Then tell me,' persisted Otto, 'why you call your spear, "Odin's Messenger"?'

The skald sighed. 'You know me, Otto. I have fanciful names for all my weapons – as you do for your axe – but if it disturbs you and, because I value your friendship so highly, from now on my spear shall be known as, "God's Messenger".'

'Pah!' snorted the Axe-man. 'I do not know why I suffer you. You stand by nothing. You value only the easy life.'

Conrad, bewildered by the passion roused in Otto, felt it was time to intervene again. 'Today I saw a flock of wild ducks flying in the direction of the lake. If you both like to eat duck I could try to get some for you.'

Both men were silent for a moment then simultaneously, they started to laugh. Otto clapped a heavy hand on the boy's shoulder. 'We understand, Conrad. It clearly pains you to hear us wrangling. I should know better than to be agitated by this fellow's words. He likes nothing better than to tease and play jokes. Pay him no heed.'

'Otto is right – I am nothing but a player,' confirmed

Thorkell, 'and tomorrow night we shall expect to find you roasting wild duck for us over this fire.'

Anxious to please his two friends, Conrad rose even earlier next morning before it was light and whilst Otto was still asleep. Only the sentries on duty at the gate and by the perimeter wall saw him set out on his hunting expedition. It took him some time to reach the lake and his first attempt to enmesh the ducks in the rush net he had made, failed. He trod on a dry root and immediately, the flock rose into the air as one bird and was gone. Conrad cursed himself for his carelessness but did not admit defeat. He followed the course the ducks had taken, making his way further down the lakeside. He was overjoyed when he caught sight of them through the bushes, settled once more on the surface of the water near the bank. He approached more cautiously this time, careful that the wind did not blow a warning of his presence. He crept to the edge of the lake, sparkling now in the early morning sunshine. With a swift deft movement of his arms he threw his net. To his delight, six ducks were instantly entwined in its mesh as they attempted to rise from the surface of the lake. Quickly he hauled the net ashore and as he untangled each struggling terrified bird, he swiftly wrung its neck with his strong hands.

Conrad surveyed the heap of game on the bank with much satisfaction. He was just considering whether to pursue the flock for another attempt when rough hands seized him from behind. So engrossed had he been in his work that he had not heard the two men creeping through the undergrowth towards him. They dragged and half-carried the protesting boy further down the lakeside. The larger of the two men had not forgotten first to wrap the dead ducks in Conrad's net and fling the bundle over his shoulder. Try as he would the boy was power-less to escape. At last, they reached a small boat moored at a point where the lake narrowed. His captors flung Conrad into the vessel and clambered in after him. They quickly rowed across to the opposite bank where their own camp lay on the further shore of the lake. Conrad's worst fears were realized when he saw all the soldiers and the unfamiliar standards fluttering in the breeze – he had been taken prisoner by the enemy! He looked about him in alarm as he was marched along between the two soldiers. But horrified though he was at the thought of the danger he was in, his anxiety was mitigated by another feeling – one of complete amazement: he could understand every word his captors uttered! They were speaking the secret language that Tilly had taught him; he knew instinctively that he must keep his knowledge to himself.

Suddenly, as they passed a tent much larger than the rest, a young boy came hurtling through the entrance and fell headlong at Conrad's feet. He was followed by a short, thick-set man, bald-headed but for a few curls at the nape of his neck. His most striking feature was his flaming-red beard. The man was cursing the boy when he caught sight of Conrad in the grip of his captors. He demanded to know what was going on and the two men informed him that they had seen the boy netting ducks on the far side of the lake. They explained that he was just a peasant boy but a skilful one so they had captured both him and his prize. The bearded man felt the heavy net and nodded his approval. To the soldiers' disgust he grabbed the boy and the ducks and threw both into his tent. As Conrad picked himself up off the ground the man addressed him. '*Mon domestique. Comprennez-vous?*' Conrad looked blank, pretending not to understand. The man then spoke again in poor German, 'You my servant. Him, thief. You not thief or die like him.' At the same time the man grabbed Conrad's shirt and pulled him towards him so that his face was close to his own. The man then pretended that his head was in a noose and he let his tongue loll out of the side of his mouth and rolled his eyes backwards. Conrad shivered as he accepted the awful truth that he had just been made the servant of Raoulbrun the Burgundian.

II

A prisoner in both camps

Raoulbrun proved to be a most demanding master. He allowed Conrad very little time for sleep and no opportunity whatsoever for escape. Although in late middle age, he was a man of indefatigable energy. He spent the daylight hours tirelessly supervising his followers; no aspect of their daily lives was too trivial for his attention. He would laugh and chat with any man; he would take surplus food off one group, thrust it into Conrad's arms and then give it to another group on the other side of the camp; he would stop to inspect weapons; he would watch training sessions, often intervening and demonstrating himself; he would visit and cheer men recovering from wounds. Everywhere he went Conrad was required to be one step behind. He fetched and carried, ran hither and thither all day at the Burgundian's bidding. By night Raoulbrun dined with his commanders, three of whom were his own sons. The evening would begin soberly enough with discussions on tactics and propositions for the next attack and end, hours later, with drunken reminiscences of past glories, real and imaginary. Conrad was instructed to remain close at hand throughout these nocturnal meetings. He would curl up against the wall of Raoulbrun's tent and snatch what sleep he could. Frequently, he was rudely awakened by kicks and blows to fetch more wine, more food or whatever the generals required.

It was at night when he was so tired that Conrad found it particularly difficult to conceal the fact that he understood what the Burgundians were saying. When someone struck him a cruel blow as he lay sleeping and ordered him to bring something, it took great self-control to recover quickly and pretend that he did not understand. He usually received more abuse together with the explanation, reiterated in his own Germanic tongue. There were a few occasions when he did not recover his senses soon enough and obeyed the instruction without waiting for the translation. Fortunately, these lapses occurred only very late at night when his tormentors were too weary or too drunk to notice. Soon Conrad became accepted as part of the surroundings and went unnoticed until his services were required. He was treated in the same manner as and, was regarded as being equal to, Raoulbrun's dog.

Night after night Conrad dozed off to sleep while the enemy discussed plans for the annihilation of his people. He had heard all the arguments so many times that he had ceased to listen for very long. Then one night he awoke to find that the Burgundians had at last agreed upon a plan and were working out the details of its implementation. Both armies had suffered heavy casualties in the last battle – the Burgundians more than the Alemannians had realized – and had withdrawn to their respective base camps to lick their wounds. Now Raoulbrun felt he had enough reinforcements and a sufficient number of warriors restored to health to successfully launch another attack. He was anxious to press home his advantage before his adversary was ready. It had been agreed amongst the commanders that sharp swift action was required. A surprise assault on the enemy camp itself was the most favoured solution.

Conrad listened with bated breath as he lay on the damp ground, his back to the assembled company. It took all the self-discipline he could muster to make his breathing even and steady, as though asleep. He heard Raoulbrun repeat the instructions once more to ensure that everyone had understood. The Burgundian forces were to make their way to the other side of the lake by night. They would encircle the Alemannian position under cover of darkness and just before first light appointed assassins would kill the guards on the gate, creep into the stockade and silently deal with the other sentries. The Burgundians would then swoop upon the encampment in an avenging horde, massacring most of the inhabitants before they were even awake. The plan was to be put into operation the very next night.

Conrad lay rigid with horror, convinced that someone must hear his heart pounding. He must escape. He must warn his people of the impending danger or they would be wiped out. Suddenly he felt a kick in his back. Someone was shouting in German, 'Water! Water!' Conrad got up, took the empty jug and hurried from the tent towards the lake, his thoughts racing. He must get away but how was he to do so without arousing suspicion and causing Raoulbrun to change his plan?

There were guards stationed at intervals along the water's edge. Their job was to patrol what was, in fact, the border between the two territories. Conrad came abreast of the nearest guard, raised his pitcher aloft and pointed to the lake, indicating that he was going to fill the utensil. The man nodded in assent: he recognised the boy from previous occasions. He turned and walked slowly along the path towards the next soldier on duty. Instantly, Conrad knew that he held the solution to his problem in his hand. He had only seconds to put his thoughts into action. He rushed down to the water and hurled the pitcher out to where it would be caught by the current. Next he jumped into the lake himself, thrashed about, shrieked for help and then dived into the nearby rushes. He squatted there, hidden by the overhang of the bank and listened to the sentries hurrying back to investigate the noise. One man caught sight of the pitcher in the moonlight as it floated by. He assumed at once, as Conrad had intended, that the boy had slipped and overbalanced into the water as he was filling the jug. He and his comrade spent a few minutes running up and down the lakeside looking for some sign of Conrad. Eventually, one of them went to Raoulbrun's tent to report the incident. The man returned shortly afterwards carrying another pitcher which he carefully filled only an arm's length away from where Conrad was hiding.

When the boy estimated that the guard was on his way back to the camp, he cautiously raised his head above the reeds. He could see the other soldier who had searched for him, some distance away telling his comrades further along the bank what had happened. This was Conrad's chance. Slipping quietly back into the water he made for the narrowest part of the lake where he had crossed with his captors. Fearing the moonlight might betray him he swam under water as much as possible. He was a strong swimmer but the under-currents were treacherous. He was swept well off course but at last he managed to battle his way to the other side of the lake. He waited until the moon had mercifully disappeared behind a cloud before daring to climb onto the shore. He dashed for shelter and collapsed exhausted in the undergrowth. He lay there panting for a long time, listening intently for any indication from the opposite bank that his ruse had been discovered. No such indication came and when he had rested he got up and crouching low, made his way from the water's edge towards the Alemannian encampment.

It was dawn when Conrad reached his own lines and surrendered to the startled sentries on the gate. The men recognised him as Otto's boy whom they had presumed had deserted. Conrad quickly explained that he had been taken prisoner by the Burgundians and had escaped, bringing urgent news to the Lord Gustavus. The soldiers let him go and he ran headlong towards the general's tent. Here he was challenged again, this time by the guards on duty outside the tent. The boy made such a commotion at being hindered that he roused the great man himself. At the sight of the Lord Gustavus, Conrad was momentarily at a loss for words. Then he blurted out that he had information about an imminent enemy attack. The general raised his hand in an imperious gesture to silence the boy and then ordered him into his tent. There he listened as words tumbled from Conrad's lips: the boy described how he had been captured and made Raoulbrun's servant; how he had overheard plans for the attack and how he had escaped to warn his people.

The Lord Gustavus never took his eyes from Conrad's face as he related his story and he said nothing for several moments after he had finished. Then he inquired in relentless tones, 'How is it, boy, you understood so well what the Burgundians were saying?'

'I understand the language of the Burgundians, my lord,' Conrad explained, 'but I was careful not to let them know that.'

'Where would a peasant like you find such learning?' the general scoffed. 'What were you before you were brought to serve in my army?'

'I was a goatherd, my lord,' confessed Conrad, 'but I had a friend who taught me a new language. I did not know until after I had been captured that it was the language of the Burgundians,'

'Your tale becomes more incredible by the moment,' snapped the Lord Gustavus. 'Who was this friend and what devious purpose did he have in teaching you a foreign language? Was he one of our enemies? Did he mean you to take our plans to the Burgundians? Is that so, boy? Are you a traitor? Has the enemy sent you back here with this tale to trick us into leaving the safety of our stockade that they might ambush our forces?'

Conrad, with mounting consternation, interrupted the general. 'No! No, my lord! I swear to you that I am no traitor and nor is my friend. I can tell you nothing of why or how I acquired my knowledge for to do so would be to betray my friend whom I love. I would rather be put to death than forsake that trust.' Conrad searched in desperation for a way out of his dilemma. He had supposed that escaping from the enemy would be the most difficult part of his mission. It had not occurred to him that convincing his own people of the truth of his story would be even more difficult. His position seemed hopeless until he remembered that Otto was well-known to the Lord Gustavus. 'I beg you, my lord, to send for Otto the Axe-man. I was in his company and he knows me well. He will tell you that I am to be trusted.'

For the first time the hard lines on the general's face softened a little. 'Guards!' he called out and when the men appeared he instructed them, 'Send for Otto the Axe-man.'

'There is no need, my lord,' replied one of the soldiers. 'He is here already with Thorkell the Skald. They came as soon as they heard of the boy's arrival.'

'Send them to me,' commanded the Lord Gustavus.

Otto and Thorkell entered the tent, their faces betraying their delight at seeing Conrad. Bowing briefly to his master, Otto said, 'My lord, we searched for days for Conrad, then we concluded, sadly, that he must have fallen into the lake and drowned as he netted ducks for us. Thank God he is safe.'

Otto and the skald made towards Conrad to embrace him but the general motioned to them to remain where they were, demanding in harsh tones, 'What was your assessment of this boy whilst he was under your command?'

'He was the best apprentice I have ever had, sire,' replied Otto without hesitation. He exchanged worried glances with Thorkell – it was obvious that their young friend was in trouble. 'No one was ever more anxious to learn the skills of a warrior than Conrad. And he was the best hunter and forager I have ever known. No one could have worked harder to feed your men, my lord.'

'You never suspected that he might be a traitor?'

Both men were taken aback by this question; they rushed to the boy's defence. 'Conrad, a traitor!' exclaimed Otto, aghast at the suggestion. 'Never, my lord! This boy is your most loyal follower. Many times he has told me how honoured he felt when he was called to your service. His ambition has always been to be a soldier under your command. You can trust this boy, sire. I would stake my life on that.'

'Otto speaks the truth, my lord,' asserted Thorkell. 'There is no guile, no deceit in this boy. You can believe every word he utters. I too would trust him with my life, master.'

Again the general raised his hand. 'Enough! It is clear that you both support the boy. Leave us now.'

Otto and Thorkell accepted their abrupt dismissal reluctantly. As soon as the tent flap had closed behind them the Lord Gustavus resumed his interrogation. He proceeded to ask detailed questions about the enemy camp. Conrad replied without any difficulty. He knew the layout of the encampment well since he had spent a large part of every day accompanying Raoulbrun on his rounds. His memory was excellent and he gave exact information as to men, horses, equipment, weapons and supplies.

At last the Lord Gustavus seemed satisfied. For a few moments he sat deep in thought then he said, 'Your statements correspond exactly with the information brought back by my scouts who have been observing the Burgundian position. In view of the fact that you have not lied in this respect and, bearing in mind the testimony in your favour of Otto the Axeman and Thorkell the Skald, I shall act upon the information you have given me. If it transpires that you have been telling the truth you shall have any reward that you desire.' The general got up from his chair and advanced upon the boy. He towered over Conrad who did his best not to show his discomfort. 'But if you have betrayed me or told me any falsehoods,' the general paused then continued speaking the words quietly and deliberately, 'I promise you that you shall suffer the slowest most painful death that I can devise.' Straightening himself, he recalled the guards. 'Take him away and secure him safely. On no account must he escape.'

Without further ceremony Conrad was marched to the area where the supplies were stored and flung, face down, into an empty wagon. He was gagged and ropes were tied around his wrists and ankles, and lashed to the outer ribs of the vehicle. Another rope was passed around his neck in such a way that if he tried to raise his head or move it, there was a very real danger that he would strangle himself. Thus poor Conrad spent a most uncomfortable day, unable to look up and see what was going on or to move his arms or legs, spread-eagled as they were on the hard wooden floor of the wagon. During the long lonely hours he had plenty of time to think: to contemplate all that had happened to him in the last few weeks and to speculate on the dire consequences should his information prove to be false. It was this last thought which tortured him the most. On the journey back from the enemy camp he had never for a moment stopped to consider that Raoulbrun might have guessed that he understood Burgundian French. Doubts gave way to conviction; very soon Conrad was certain that his secret had been discovered by the enemy. As he lay imprisoned in the bottom of the wagon he suffered agonies of mind. What if the Lord Gustavus had been right and Raoulbrun had used him to lure his comrades from the safety of their stockade to a certain death? The torment was almost too much to bear.

All around Conrad were the sounds of preparation for the coming battle. He listened to the shouting of orders, the tramping of feet, the trundling of wagons. As nightfall came he shivered more with fear than with cold. He heard the soft tread of the soldiers as they quietly left the stockade to take up their positions to await the arrival of the enemy. The night seemed interminable to Conrad. Then he found he could see the patterns in the wood of the wagon floor in front of him more clearly. He realized dawn must be approaching. Suddenly the silence was broken by the blast of a horn – the signal for the commencement of the battle. The noise was deafening: the air was filled with the cries of the combatants, the hiss of arrows and the clang of metal. Conrad's frustration reached fever pitch. He strained at the ropes confining his limbs but to no avail. Worst of all, he could not tell from the confusion of sounds which side was winning. When eventually the din abated he held his breath, straining to hear the voices of the soldiers entering the stockade. Would they be Alemannian or Burgundian? The wagon shook. Someone was cutting his ropes. Men he had not seen before pulled him roughly from his prison. He had been in a restricted position for so long that at first he had no use in his limbs and the men had to drag him along between them. By the time they stopped in front of a large tent, some feeling had returned to his legs. Who would he find inside? Would it be the Lord Gustavus and if so, would he praise or punish him? Would it be Raoulbrun the Burgundian, gloating over the success of his deception? The men removed the gag from his mouth. He managed to stagger forward as they pushed him towards the entrance to the tent. Tentatively, he raised the flap and stepped inside.

Conrad found the Lord Gustavus and several of his commanders, blood-stained and battle-weary, waiting for him. The general came forward and confronted him. 'We have won a great victory; the enemy is dead or in flight. You may claim your reward.'

Conrad was so relieved and overjoyed that at first he was speechless. Then he stammered out, 'My lord, I have but one wish – to ride with you as one of your Companions in Arms.'

The request had an instant effect on all present. Some faces expressed disbelief, others derision. 'Boy, you do not know what you ask!' exclaimed the Lord Gustavus in a tone which indicated that he too was appalled at the suggestion. 'Those who ride with me are noblemen – not peasants. Ask for land. It is every peasant's desire to own his land. I will give you any that you choose.'

'I thank you, my lord, but I do not want land,' Conrad insisted. 'You promised I could have any reward I wanted and I want only to be trained as a mounted warrior in your service.'

'A goatherd with ambitions to live like a nobleman,' muttered the Lord Gustavus. He paced up and down considering the proposition, glancing at Conrad from time to time with a piercing gaze which the boy felt must have cowed many a brave man. But Conrad refused to be cowed and he forced himself to stand resolute, head held high, beneath the inquiring stare. The general did not ask his commanders for advice and they did not offer any. When his silent deliberation was over he announced his decision. 'I am greatly impressed by your conduct. You have shown bravery, intelligence and initiative – qualities unusual in a peasant but essential for a Companion in Arms. It seems most unlikely even so that one of your low birth could be trained to the standards of excellence I demand of my Companions ... However, I enjoy an element of challenge even when the proposal is as preposterous as this one. Furthermore, I am a man of my word so I shall accede to your request.'

'Oh! Thank you, my lord. Thank you,' cried Conrad vehemently.

The Lord Gustavus continued. 'Let us understand what obligations are demanded of each of us by this agreement. My Companions are rich men who maintain themselves while in my service. You, I assume, have no possessions?'

'No, my lord,' Conrad admitted, 'and no family either.'

'Are you a freeman?' asked the general.

'As far as I know, my lord,' replied the boy, 'although I have hired my labour to many men, in return for food, since I was a small boy.'

'Then I must support you for life, not as a serf,' emphasised the Lord Gustavus, 'but as a nobleman. I must provide you with training, horses, armour, weapons and shelter. You ask much, boy!'

'You will not regret it, sire, I swear. I shall be a true and loyal follower,' vowed Conrad.

The general ignored the boy's emotional outburst and spelt out the rest of the agreement. 'You for your part must serve me faithfully to your dying day. Should you fail in that duty in any way our contract is invalid. During training, should you not reach the required standard, I would reduce you to the status of a foot soldier in time of war and a common serf on my estates in time of peace; as a Companion, should you show cowardice, disloyalty, negligence or incompetence I would have you put to death. Do you understand these conditions?'

'I do, my lord,' Conrad declared, 'and I accept all the conditions of our bargain. I swear that I shall never fail you or betray your trust.'

'I hope not, boy. I hope not,' replied the Lord Gustavus gravely. Then, as though shrugging off his doubts, he announced, 'It is customary for cadets to serve on campaign in a menial capacity. Normally, I assign them to my commanders but in your case I shall make an exception. You are fortunate – you will serve only me.'

III

Under siege

Once more Conrad became the servant of a warlord, spending the remainder of the summer and autumn at the Lord Gustavus's side. His military training was to begin in earnest when they returned to the general's estates for the winter. It had long been the Lord Gustavus's practice to put the most promising of his vassals' sons through rigorous schooling in the martial arts and Conrad would join the next intake of cadets. Meanwhile, he was employed upon tasks similar to those he had previously performed for Raoulbrun. His way of life changed little except that he was not beaten by his new master. He now followed the Lord Gustavus around just as he had followed the Burgundian general. Before long, Conrad found himself comparing the two leaders. Where Raoulbrun had been involved in every aspect of his men's routine, the Lord Gustavus took no interest. He had little regard for his soldiers' comfort or their problems. They were there for one purpose – to fight – and he was concerned only with their fitness to perform that function satisfactorily. In Raoulbrun's camp all major decisions had been made in council, in collaboration with the other commanders; in the Lord Gustavus's camp no decision was ever reached as a compromise, based on a consensus of opinion. The Lord Gustavus would listen to his generals' advice but he alone would determine the course of action to be taken. He alone was in command of his army.

Conrad also observed striking contrasts in the personalities of the two men. Raoulbrun had been gregarious, needing the company of his fellows at all times. The Lord Gustavus was a solitary figure, aloof and unapproachable, shunning even the company of his nobles. Otto's description of his master proved to be quite accurate. The Lord Gustavus was indeed a man of austere habits: he ate and drank very little; he could exist for long periods without nourishment or rest; he was refreshed after only a short sleep. It was easy to understand how legends had grown up around him. He expected absolute loyalty from his followers and the devotion he received was akin to that accorded to a deity.

On the matter of religion too, Otto had been correct. The grandfather of the Lord Gustavus and the Lord Bardolph had been converted to Christianity. Gustavus was a fanatical believer who never doubted that God was on his side and would ultimately ensure him total victory over all his foes. His chaplain always travelled with him and every day began with the celebration of Mass. A public service for the entire army was held, whenever possible, before battle. The general did not share his skald's belief in freedom of thought; he tolerated no other form of religion amongst his men but Christianity.

The Lord Gustavus made one concession to Conrad's arrival: he normally spent the concluding hours of each day reading alone in his tent, but now this became the time when he would summon the boy. He explained to Conrad that it was his belief that there was much to be learned from the experiences of the great warrior leaders of the past. For this reason, he insisted that all the boys he trained had a working knowledge of Greek and Latin that they might read for themselves the military histories of Greece and Rome. Knowing that Conrad had no such grounding, he had decided to undertake that part of his education personally and immediately.

Conrad brought the books that Tilly had made for him to his first lesson. He had retrieved them from Otto's safe-keeping when he had gone to tell his friend his wonderful news. He had departed with the old man's warm congratulations and Thorkell's cheerful conviction that he, Conrad, was destined to be the hero of his greatest saga, ringing in his ears. If the Lord Gustavus was surprised to find that Conrad possessed books and could read and write in his own language, he did not reveal his thoughts. He had never since their first confrontation referred to the origins of Conrad's learning. On reflection, the boy concluded that this must be because his master lived by high moral principles himself and sympathised with Conrad's refusal to betray a trust.

Conrad proved himself once more to be a quick and able pupil. He soon grasped the rudiments of both Greek and Latin and found much satisfaction in his lessons. He often thought of Tilly and how right she had been that his master would want only learned men for his Companions. He was under no illusion that, but for her teaching, he would never have had the opportunity to realize his ambitions. Many times Conrad thought of writing to her to express his gratitude and to tell her of his good fortune. He refrained from doing so because he was afraid that he might cause trouble for her. He had worn her gift concealed around his waist since the day she had given it to him. He was certain that it had protected him from harm during those perilous weeks in the enemy camp. Whenever he was alone he would look at the sash, see Tilly's pretty little face in his mind's eye and renew his vow to return to her one day, riding at his lord's side.

The Burgundian army had been routed, at least for the present, so the Lord Gustavus decided to turn his attention to a particular town which, for a long time, had been a thorn in his side. This Burgundian town had been built in a commanding position where the river, which formed a border between the two enemies, swung in a large deep curve into Alemannian territory. The Burgundians made frequent sallies from it attacking the Alemannian settlements across the river and making off with cattle, grain and even on some occasions, the young people. Several unsuccessful attempts had been made in the past to subdue the town but protected as it was on three sides by water it had proved to be in an unassailable position. The Lord Gustavus now turned the full weight of his forces against the town. He would accept nothing less then total victory. He was determined that his own Alemannian tribesmen should replace the Burgundian garrison before the onset of winter.

Conrad observed the proceedings with great interest. The Lord Gustavus was a master of the art of siege warfare: he had many times been both an attacker and a defender. He had told Conrad that as a young man he had journeyed to Byzantium and offered himself as a mercenary to the Emperor of the Eastern Roman Empire. He had served his time at many a frontier outpost, defending the Empire against the Persians and successive waves of nomadic barbarians sweeping down from the Danube. In the year 626 he had been one of the successful defenders of the capital, Constantinople, when that great city had been simultaneously attacked by Bulgars, Avars, Gepids, Slavs and Persians. He had never forgotten the lessons of his youth; there was no trick of besieger or besieged that he did not know.

Gustavus was convinced that, since he had the time and the men and, with Raoulbrun unable to come to his people's aid, he would soon solve the problem of how to crush the garrison town. Two hundred years before it had been an administrative centre during the Roman occupation. The Romans had fortified it and built a bridge across the river. The Burgundians had repaired the town walls and painstakingly removed the stone slabs which formed the centre of the bridge, thereby hindering any Alemannian advance. Gustavus travelled with an elaborate siege train but he knew that his giant catapults and mobile assault towers would be useless unless he could transport them across the river to the very walls of the town. Conrad was present when he called his engineers to his tent.

'The buttresses of the bridge are still intact; you must find a way of spanning them,' he instructed them curtly. 'I can send some of my men across the river by boat and raft but it is essential that I have the use of the bridge for my main force and, most important of all, for the wagons containing the dismantled siege machinery. The crossing of the river must be accomplished in one night so it is imperative that the bridge surface be strong enough to support the full weight of an army.'

The engineers went away to deliberate on the difficult problem their master had set them. For the next three weeks the stockade which had been erected on the Alemannian side of the river was the scene of much activity. Many trees were felled and the trunks dragged back to the base camp; good swimmers and climbers were dispatched under cover of darkness to take exact measurements of the bridge's remaining structure; experiments were carried out to determine what weight could be supported by a surface of logs lashed together. At first, the system was found to be too fragile to take the required load; when this fault had been rectified the Lord Gustavus decided the result was too noisy. To retain the element of surprise a silent operation was absolutely necessary so a massive thick cover was made, woven of rushes and mosses, and secured to the wooden base to muffle the sounds of the invaders. Rafts were also constructed to accommodate some of the horses and men. They would be used at the same time as the bridge to accomplish a speedy crossing of the river.

When the preparations were almost complete, men were dispatched at night with chisels and hammers padded with scraps of hide and fur, to remove small sections of the stonework from the sides of the buttresses. The exact positions of these recesses had been calculated by the engineers. They would be used as slots for the stout timbers supporting the new wooden roadway across the river. At last all was ready and every man knew exactly what to do. All that was required was a moonless night and when the general's prayers were answered, no one was more excited than Conrad.

The entire length of the opposite bank of the river was patrolled by Burgundian soldiers. They had been on the alert ever since the Alemannians had established their camp. Day after day they had listened to the sounds from inside the enemy stockade, brought to them on the wind. They had prepared and waited for an attack and had been bewildered when none had come. Many of the guards in the pitch blackness now wished that they had had the good fortune to be on duty inside the walls of the town instead of out in the open, by the river and in such close proximity to the enemy. When it was feared that the clouds obscuring the moon would not break, reinforcements were sent from the town to double the guard on the river bank. This precaution did not save the Burgundians.

The expertly trained Alemannians, at a given signal, swam silently across the river and equally silently throttled and slayed the Burgundian sentries. More Alemannians followed with oiled ropes tied around their waists. Their task was to select suitable trees on the enemy bank to act as improvised pulleys for the rafts. At the same time others swam to the far end of the bridge, also bearing well-greased ropes, which they passed around the stone pillars supporting what was left of the structures on either side. All the swimmers returned to their own side of the river, untied the ropes from around their bodies and handed them to their waiting comrades, already mounted on the sturdiest horses. The rafts were pushed into the water as quietly as possible and the first contingent boarded them. The draught horses hauled on the heavy ropes and the ferrying of men, animals and machinery across to Burgundian territory began.

Near the Alemannian side of the bridge more horses strained on the ropes attached to the framework of intersecting supports, the pillars on the far side acting as their pulleys. Many men, clinging precariously to the remains of the bridge, assisted in the difficult operation of lowering the contraption between the buttresses and lodging it in the prepared recesses in the stonework. Next, the horses pulled on the ropes attached to the portable wooden floor which was to span the gap over the river thus dragging it into place on top of the props, where willing hands waited to secure it into position. The engineers who had designed the new section of bridge crossed to test the success of their theories. The road held and the first wagons with wheels well lubricated made their way slowly to the other side. Once on enemy soil every man moved to his appointed position. There was more work for the engineers and their assistants. The siege machinery had to be unloaded from the carts, assembled and made ready for action. In spite of the blackness of the night this was accomplished relatively silently and without mishap because the men engaged upon the operation had practised the routine day after day wearing blindfolds.

When the first fingers of light appeared and the mist from the river began to clear, the sentries on the town battlements were stunned by what they saw. They were completely surrounded on all sides by the Alemannian army and its siege machinery: assault towers, mobile battering rams, mechanical slings, catapults and dart-firing machines. Before they could give the alarm a horn sounded and the onslaught commenced. The first the townspeople knew of the attack was when stones and boulders began to land in the streets and crash through the roof of the shacks built along the inside of the Roman wall.

Conrad had a privileged position from which to observe the hostilities. He stood with Thorkell the Skald beside his master's horse on the meadowland which stretched from the river to the fortified town. The Lord Gustavus sat upon his mount resplendent in full armour. Tall and lean, his height served to enhance his majestic bearing. There was no sign now of the austere man of simple tastes – in his place was an emperor. The early morning sun glistened on his elaborately embossed shield, on the jewels encrusted in the silver-plated hilt of his sword, on his gilded mail shirt and in particular, on his wonderful gleaming helmet.

As Conrad glanced at his lord he was reminded of a conversation he had had the previous night with the skald. The boy had been busily polishing the general's armour and weapons when his friend had arrived. At once Conrad had expressed his amazement at the richness of his master's possessions.

'When you know our lord better you will find that he is not one man but two,' Thorkell had informed him. 'But tell me, Conrad, which of these treasures do you admire the most?'

Without hesitation, the boy had picked up the helmet. 'I marvel at the beauty and craftsmanship of this. No one else in this camp or in Raoulbrun's has anything to compare with this. See how cleverly it has been made. It even has eyebrows, a nose and pieces to protect the cheeks. How it shines! I wonder why it has a boar's head on the crest.'

Thorkell had laughed and explained. 'The helmet shines so because the iron has been covered with small plates of tinned bronze. See – they have been embossed with pictures of gods and warriors. The eyebrows which conceal the visor, and the nose and the crest, have all been inlaid with gold and silver. As for the boar's head, my people believe the boar has great protective powers so they put him on the top of helmets to guard the wearer.'

'Your people? Do you mean that this is a Norse helmet?' Conrad had asked.

'Indeed it is,' the skald had replied. 'And I can tell you that its original owner was a Swedish king.'

'How do you know that?' the boy had demanded.

'Because *I* gave the helmet to the Lord Gustavus,' Thorkell had answered, 'when I requested that he take me into his service.'

'But how did you come by it?'

'A long story, my friend, but suffice to say that it had been in the possession of my previous master, a mean man who never rewarded my efforts on his behalf in a manner proportionate to my skill. When I decided that I was not properly appreciated and should move on, the helmet seemed an appropriate parting gift.'

'You mean you stole it!' Conrad had accused.

'Not I!' Thorkell had professed to be greatly pained at the suggestion. '*He* stole it – from the grave of the Swedish king. He was not a Norseman himself; I am a Norseman! I had every right to remove it from his possession and to present it to one more worthy of its ownership. Through me justice has been done. When you see our lord wearing it tomorrow, you will agree that I was right.'

Looking at his general now, the boy was forced to admit that the skald's reasoning had been correct in one respect: the splendid helmet had found a most fitting recipient in the Lord Gustavus.

Conrad's reverie was brought to an abrupt end by his master. 'Observe closely, boy. Time spent in careful preparation is never wasted. The Burgundians will be hard-pressed to recover from the suddenness of our attack. Panic will spread through their midst. I doubt their garrison commanders will be able to marshal their forces and organize an effective defence quickly enough to deny us our prize' There was a hint of jubilation in the general's voice. 'We must press home our advantage. Send in the battering rams,' he called out to his horn-blower who stood a little distance in front of him.

At the horn's signal, men and horses trundled the battering rams forward. Soon, huge ones were pounding against all four gates. Smaller ones whose bases had been constructed to span the ditch that surrounded the fortified town, bored into any part of the wall which was seen to be in need of repair. Again and again, the Lord Gustavus shouted instructions to the horn-blower and men rushed to obey the various commands. Mechanical slings sent a constant shower of rocks and stones onto the battlements and into the town. Larger engines fired darts and the bigger catapults, designed originally for hurling boulders, flung small barrels stuffed with inflammable material. These were ignited just before the missiles were released and as a result, fires broke out all over the town.

'Can you imagine the pandemonium on those streets?' Thorkell whispered to Conrad.

'I can and I am very glad I am not there,' said Conrad with feeling.

Gustavus looked down at his cadet. 'It is not sufficient in circumstances such as these to rely entirely upon war-engines – even a collection as formidable as mine.' The general almost smiled as he continued. 'Now you will see a sight similar to the one which astounded me many years ago when I served on the frontier of the Eastern Roman Empire. These men have been modelled on the Hunnish horsemen I saw then.' Once more he raised his arm in the direction of the horn-blower. 'Send in the mounted archers!' he commanded. Conrad stood amazed as teams of horsemen charged round the fortifications letting fly a deadly hail of arrows with unbelievable speed, accuracy and ferocity. It was an onslaught to strike fear into the hearts of all the defenders. 'While the archers divert the enemy's attention we have the opportunity to put into force the next stage of our attack,' the general continued, addressing Conrad. 'Send in the tortoises!' he shouted to the horn-blower. As soon as the signal was given, groups of men ran to the waiting carts and unloaded strangely shaped shields quite unlike the round ones normally used by the Alemannians. They were rectangular and curved.

Conrad whispered to Thorkell, 'What is happening now?'

'This is an old Roman tactic,' replied the skald. 'It is called sapping.'

As they watched, the soldiers arranged themselves in teams of six and at a given word each group leant forward, placing the shields over their heads and backs in such a way that they interlocked. At a second command, they began to run forward towards the beleaguered town.

'I understand!' cried Conrad. 'They do indeed look like tortoises.' He watched fascinated as the teams managed to climb into the ditch and up the other side without breaking formation. They reached the base of the town walls despite the concerted efforts of the Burgundians to hinder them with rocks hurled from the battlements. Once in position, either where the stonework was already weakened or at a corner, the "tortoises" were joined by other men.

'Those are the tunnellers,' Thorkell explained. 'Their task is to undermine the wall while their comrades hold the protective shell of shields over them.'

As the boy watched, the valiant defenders on the battlements, faced by attack on all sides, ran this way and that in their efforts to stave off their enemy. At the height of the chaos the Lord Gustavus gave another order to the horn-blower. 'Send in the assault towers!' Men rushed to obey their master. Protected by shield walls and assisted by horses they dragged the heavy ramps across the ditch. Next they trundled the huge mobile towers into place over the ramps and archers climbed into their upper storeys.

'Look, Conrad,' said Thorkell. 'The lower storeys of the towers house battering rams. The ones with pointed heads are for boring into the fortifications and the others, with rounded heads, are for pummelling the walls.'

'Surely the Burgundians cannot hold out long against us?' reasoned Conrad.

The Lord Gustavus heard his remark and commented, 'I do not have your confidence. From my observations there are now more defenders on the walls. It would appear our enemy has recovered to some extent from the initial surprise of our attack and a degree of order has been restored. I suspect many of the townspeople have rallied to the support of their garrison.'

Conrad saw that his general was right. Everywhere assault parties were met by a hail of missiles as they attempted to storm the battlements. The Alemannians in the assault towers met the same fierce resistance whenever they tried to lower the drawbridges at the top of their machines. As they rushed forward onto the parapet of the Roman wall, they were beaten back and forced to retreat over their drawbridges to the safety of their towers once more. Then the Burgundians began to retaliate with flaming arrows in an effort to set fire to the engines. Seeing this, the Lord Gustavus decided to withdraw his assault towers rather than risk having them destroyed at such an early stage of the fighting.

'I had hoped for instant success but it seems this is not to be,' he declared. 'I must resign myself to a longer siege.' As Conrad listened, he dispatched men to search the river bank for signs of sewers or ducts carrying water. 'It may be that the Romans piped water into the town and if they did, it will be a simple matter to cut off the supply,' he announced.

When the searchers returned, they reported finding an old Roman sewer large enough for a man to crawl through but it appeared to have stout metal grilles at intervals along its length to foil any invaders' plot to enter the town undetected. When it was confirmed that the gratings were still in good condition, the general decided it would take too long to remove them. His other plan also failed when no evidence was found of the existence of aqueducts.

'The town must get its water from wells sunk in the ground inside the walls,' concluded the skald; then making sure his master did not overhear, he continued, 'and at this time of year there should be adequate supplies of grain and livestock too. The siege could go on indefinitely. A speedy victory is essential for us: we must not be pinned down outside these walls until a larger force comes to the rescue. Whilst we were encamped on the other side of the river a messenger would have gone to Raoulbrun. Though powerless to help himself, as a loyal vassal of the Frankish monarch – like most of the Burgundian chieftains – he has the right to demand his overlord's protection. Since neither our master nor his brother, the Lord Bardolph, has paid any dues to the King of the Franks for years, we could find ourselves facing a Frankish army if the siege is prolonged.'

'Are you saying that we might be defeated?' asked an incredulous Conrad.

'No' replied Thorkell. 'The Franks have never beaten us but I should think that our master would not consider this the best time or place for such an encounter.'

Thorkell appeared correct in his assumption. The Lord Gustavus called his commanders to him and told them, 'You must concentrate your efforts on undermining the old fortifications. See that the men work in relays so that no time is lost. I prefer the tortoise formation for its flexibility but as I do not have the vast numbers of men at my disposal that the Romans had, you may use carts covered with wet skins for protecting the sappers wherever you think fit. But remember, every effort must be made to draw attention away from the mining parties.'

The general's orders were put into operation immediately. The horse-archers harassed the defenders on the battlements with repeated charges while catapults and slings delivered a continuous barrage of missiles. Battering rams maintained a constant pounding on the barricaded gates. The assault towers packed with archers were pushed close enough to the wall to give cover during the changing over of work parties. But the task proved to be a formidable one: the Romans had built the wall to last and to withstand just such a determined attack as this. It was thick and the foundations went deep but the miners laboured on tearing out earth, rubble and rocks. The highly disciplined shield-bearers who protected them bore bravely the brunt of the enemy's wrath. In spite of the concerted efforts to divert them the defenders rained stones, boulders and flaming arrows down upon the Alemannians and even molten lead, boiling oil and pitch. For the most part the warriors courageously stood their ground but where the tortoise-shell of shields broke under the onslaught carts, covered with curtains of skins soaked with water so that they would not catch fire, were hauled across the ditch to reinforce the position.

By the third day the objective had been achieved: there were gaping holes under many sections of the wall. As they had worked the miners had propped up the tunnels with wooden supports. When the order was given by Gustavus, 'Sound the withdrawal!' the teams left the Roman wall under cover of the "tortoise shells" or the carts, and the last man out of each tunnel set fire to the supports. The miners and the shield-bearers then ran to join their comrades lining up in battle formations on the meadowland.

The Lord Gustavus, surveying the sight from his horse, turned to Thorkell and Conrad and addressed them both. 'Skald, go about your business! Boy, you will remain here with me and learn from what you see.'

'Take care, Thorkell,' whispered Conrad as his friend hurried to his appointed place among the warriors.

A hush fell upon the Alemannian army. The war-engines ceased their relentless barrage. Every man waited in silence to see if his efforts had succeeded. The only movement was the flapping of the standards in the light breeze. First, clouds of dense smoke began to drift upwards from the base of the wall, filling the Burgundians on the battlements with a sickening fear. In places, flames began to lick the outer stonework. Now the crackle of burning timber could be heard clearly as the fires caught a firm hold. Some members of the assembled army began to show their excitement; they gripped their axes and spears more tightly in eager anticipation. At last they heard the sound they were all waiting for: the sound of the wooden supports crashing down inside the tunnels as the flames ate through the timber.

When the first cracks appeared in the wall itself, a great cheer went up from the Alemannians. In some places the wall held in spite of the gaping void beneath it, but in most instances the undermining was a complete success. The masonry above began to crack, then to crumble and finally to collapse sufficiently for the invaders to gain access. The Lord Gustavus raised his hand to the horn-blower and the charge began. The Alemannians scrambled over the rubble in terrifying hordes, screaming their war-cries and hurling their axes. Once inside, the archers made for the gates and some gave covering fire whilst others hauled away the barricades and let the remainder of their forces into the town. The cavalry could now play its part, racing through the streets tracking down the remaining Burgundian soldiers like avenging angels. Soon it was all over; the town capitulated.

IV

Revelations

Throughout the final stages of the battle the Lord Gustavus sat upon his horse watching the proceedings in silence, betraying no emotion whatsoever. When his generals, in exultant mood, returned to inform him that what remained of the garrison had surrendered, he appeared unmoved by this final confirmation of his victory. Conrad heard him give his orders with his usual air of authority. 'The gates will be left open until dusk, then closed and guarded. The walls will be patrolled, particular attention being given to the places where they have been breached. All men will be permitted to celebrate our triumph but in rotation, each one taking a fair share of sentry duty. When I make my entry into the town in the morning I shall expect to see my men sober and proper in their bearing. You will have any remaining members of the garrison, and civic leaders, ready for my inspection. Deal with all valuables in the usual manner.'

So saying, the general dismissed his commanders and was about to depart when Conrad asked, 'My lord, what can I do to help?' This was a question the boy had asked repeatedly over the last few days only to be given always the same answer, 'Look, listen and remember. The lessons you learn here will live with you all your life.' But now his master gave a different reply. 'Do what you can to help the wounded.' Then the general turned his horse and rode back over the bridge to his base camp.

Conrad looked around him and was appalled by what he

saw. In the excitement of the final thrust, amid the noise and confusion he had somehow, incredibly, failed to see men fall. In the tumult he had seen only the continuous stream of warriors surging over the crumbling wall; he had been oblivious to everything else. Now he became aware that the ground between himself and the town was littered with the bodies of his comrades, some stirring and moaning, others deathly still. He stood in a daze. There were so many. Where should he begin? Then he saw some of his fellow Alemannians on the wall itself, searching amongst the rubble. At once he thought they must be looking for men trapped in the debris. He rushed forward to help, covering the distance across the meadowland with all speed but stopped, frozen in his tracks, when he realized how wrong his assumption had been. These men were not rescuers – they were thieves. They were systematically searching the bodies of the Burgundian defenders and worse still, not content with robbing the dead and dying, they were mutilating the corpses and disembowelling them in an orgy of wanton violence.

Conrad felt sick with horror. Waves of nausea enveloped him. He turned and dashed headlong for the river. The cold water revived him but failed to blot out the hideous scene he had just witnessed. He forced himself to stumble back up the riverbank and here he was confronted by neat rows of wounded, laid out for the physician's inspection. As he approached, more carts arrived from the town bearing the men who had fallen in the last moments of the battle inside the walls. The boy helped to unload the injured. He went from man to man doing what he could to aid and comfort until he came to a youth, not so many years older than himself. As he attempted to bathe a wound on the young man's head he was startled to hear him murmur something in his delirium. He spoke, unmistakably, in Burgundian French. Conrad stared hard at him. This was not an Alemannian yet he did not look any different from an Alemannian. There was nothing about his appearance to distinguish him as a Burgundian. He could not have been a regular soldier because he wore no protective clothing of any kind. He must have been one of the towns-people who had helped in the defence of his home. The youth stirred again and resumed his mumbling. Conrad placed the cloth with which he had been staunching the blood from the wound, over the young man's mouth to muffle the sounds. What should he do? Should he call out that here was one of their enemies? If he kept quiet would he be a traitor to his own side? He looked again at the youth's face. He felt no animosity towards him – only compassion. He knew that had he been in the same position he would have fought to defend his home and family with the ferocity of an animal defending its young. Yet he had sworn never to betray his lord's trust. Would sparing the young man's life be a betrayal of that trust?

At that moment Conrad chanced to look up and see once more the men on the wall going about their dastardly business. He hesitated no more. He examined the youth quickly. He appeared to have no other injury save the one on his head. Conrad called to an old man kneeling on the ground nearby, tearing up rags for bandages. He threw him a few strips of material and Conrad bound the Burgundian's head tightly. He saw two soldiers lifting men whose wounds had already been tended, into a wagon. He went over to them and asked them to help him lift another injured man into the vehicle. He added that he would then be willing to take over their duty and drive the wounded back to the stockade across the river. As he had hoped, the men welcomed the offer. They dumped the youth unceremoniously into the back of the cart and made off with all speed in the direction of the town before all that was worth looting had been taken.

Conrad glanced furtively around. No one was paying him any attention. He drove the wagon slowly towards the approach road to the bridge but when he reached it he veered towards the town instead of the river. As he drew near to the town gates he found the highway which joined the one he was on, packed with refugees fleeing from the conquerors. Most were on foot; a few were in carts. All were clutching what few meagre belongings they had been able to salvage. Mostly they were old people or young children. Conrad supposed that the young men and the middle-aged must have died in the carnage. He was just wondering what had happened to the women when high-pitched screaming provided him with the answer. He looked towards the gates and saw that the soldiers were searching everyone who was leaving the town. Anything of the slightest value was quickly found and requisitioned. The women and the young girls were being hauled out of the line and herded together at the side of the road by armed guards. Conrad was mystified by this procedure until he saw the leering expressions on the faces of the Alemannian soldiers who surrounded the prisoners. He saw too the fear in the eyes of the women; he remembered seeing that same look once before in the eyes of his mother as she held him, trembling, to her breast whilst they hid from the men ransacking their village. For the first time his mother's simple statement, 'Your father was a soldier,' assumed a sinister significance. Conrad shook himself and pushed aside the ugly thought. He could do nothing to help the unfortunate captives but he could help the Burgundian youth.

At that moment a cart driven by an old couple passed Conrad. He jumped off the seat of his wagon, grabbed the mule's reins and stopped the vehicle. With his finger to his lips, he beckoned to the terrified driver to follow him. The man obeyed and as he stepped down the boy explained quickly, in a low voice, in the man's own tongue. 'I have a youth from your town in my wagon. He is wounded. My people do not know he is a Burgundian. Take him quickly. He has suffered enough.' At these words the old woman, who had been weeping, climbed down from the cart also to help her husband. Both were bewildered by Conrad's action but when they had placed the youth in their vehicle they thanked him for his charity.

Conrad returned to the bridge, praying that his action had not been witnessed. He spent the remainder of the day ministering to the suffering and ferrying survivors back to the Alemannian encampment. By nightfall he was weary and depressed. It was a very subdued boy who answered his master's summons to his tent that night.

'Tomorrow you may ride in my procession when I make my triumphant entry into the town,' Gustavus announced. 'I have already given my thanks to Almighty God for our victory but we shall hold another service in the town so that our entire army may give thanks.'

Conrad felt too dejected to give any thought to ceremonies of rejoicing and he said sadly, 'There are many dead and wounded, my lord.'

The general did not reply immediately but then he said, 'War has many faces – not all of them glorious – but if you wish to be a great warrior you must learn to live with them all. Today you have seen death and destruction on a scale which you had never imagined; I can tell you – and your own future experiences will confirm this – that our casualties have been light. Had the siege continued, and I have known few sieges to be as short in duration as this one, many many more would have died. Take comfort from that, boy.'

But Conrad was not comforted and as the evening progressed his discomfort grew. The wind was carrying the sounds from the town to the Alemannian camp: sounds of cheering, shouting and awful screaming. They combined to give a graphic picture of what was going on inside the battered walls. Conrad kept trying to tell himself that the townspeople had brought their punishment upon themselves; that this was just retribution for the many raids that they had made upon the Alemannian settlements. But he kept thinking of the families trapped in the town who had not managed to escape before the gates were closed; most of all he kept seeing the faces of the frightened women who had not been allowed to escape. It seemed also that the screams were getting louder and more desperate. It became increasingly difficult to concentrate on Latin grammar and eventually it became impossible. Conrad could contain himself no longer. 'Why do you permit this, my lord?' he demanded.

It seemed the Lord Gustavus had been expecting an outburst of this nature for he answered calmly, 'To the victor, the spoils! So it has been, Conrad, since time began and so it will always be. It is a soldier's right to rape and pillage. It is his just reward for a battle well fought. If I deny my men what is lawfully theirs, how can I ask them to fight so bravely again?'

Conrad was not content with this argument. 'But, sire,' he persisted, 'it is your victory more than anyone's yet you do not celebrate in this way.'

'Indulge in drunken debauchery?' The general was aghast, his composure for once shaken. 'It would not be fitting for me to descend to such depths. To be worthy of the loyalty of other men – men who would follow me unto death – I must show myself to be above their weaknesses.' He struggled to regain control of his emotions and as his anger subsided Conrad saw a look of great sadness enter his master's eyes. He seemed lost in painful recollections; then he said slowly, 'But it was not always so and the Lord God in His wisdom deemed me unworthy and took away all that I held dear ... Leave me, boy. I am weary.'

Conrad gathered up his books and glanced anxiously at his master who sat staring ahead of him lost, it seemed, in tormented thoughts. 'Good night, my lord,' said Conrad as he left the tent but the Lord Gustavus did not appear to hear him.

When Conrad lay down to sleep that night he looked back upon the day and knew it was a day he would never forget. As his master had predicted, he had indeed learned many lessons and it seemed to him that the aftermath of the battle had been as much a revelation as the battle itself. He fell asleep pledging that if ever he should become a great general he would show generosity and mercy towards his vanquished foe.

V

The villa on the plain

Conrad sat uncomfortably in the wagon, cradling his friend's head in his lap. As the vehicle lurched into yet another rut in the road, Otto groaned and shut his eyes. 'Have a care!' yelled Conrad to the driver.

'I am doing my best,' the man replied, 'but it is a bad road.'

'Never mind,' Otto murmured wearily. 'We do not have much further to go.' Then, seeing the distress in the boy's face, Otto attempted in his customary way to cheer him. 'I am a lucky man, Conrad, a very lucky man. Even if I never fight or work again, my lord will take care of me.'

'It is your due – your right, Otto,' replied Conrad. 'You have served our master well all your life. You have done your duty by him; now he must do his duty by you.'

'And he will, Conrad, he will,' declared the Axe-man vehemently. 'There is no finer master than the Lord Gustavus. Did he not give orders that I was to be brought home just as soon as I was strong enough to travel? And did he not give you leave to accompany me?'

Conrad nodded and his thoughts went back to that first morning after the siege was over when he awoke suddenly to find Thorkell bending over him and shaking him. 'Wake up, Conrad!' the skald had urged. 'Otto has been badly wounded and he wants to see you before they take off his arm.' The two of them had hurried through the darkness to where the badly wounded men had been assembled. Otto had been so weak and in so much pain that he had only been able to grasp Conrad's hand. They had held him down whilst the physician and his assistant had removed what was left of Otto's mangled arm – amputation being the only alternative to certain death. The old man had, mercifully, passed out and Thorkell had watched Conrad bandage Otto after the physician had moved on to another wounded man.

'I was brought up by someone who had the power of healing,' Conrad had told Thorkell. 'I can recall her treatment of wounds and fevers. Once it is light I will search in the woods for what I need. After that I swear, Thorkell, that I will not leave Otto.' Conrad had kept his word and when a messenger had come to take him to join the general's victory parade he had refused to go with the man. Those around who had witnessed his disobedience had predicted dire consequences but no punishment had followed and he had not seen the Lord Gustavus since. In the days that followed, Conrad had left his friend only briefly to search for fresh supplies of the herbs and plants in which Hulda had put so much faith. Slowly, Otto had begun to regain his strength and now they were on their way to the Lord Gustavus's estate – the only home Otto had ever known.

'Just think, lad,' the old man went on, 'if I had not been wounded, you would have made this journey alone while I remained behind to garrison our newly-won town. Instead of lying here in comfort, I would have been rebuilding that wall which took so long to fall down. As it is, we shall be together all winter. Does that thought make you happy?' Otto tried to laugh but his face once more contorted with pain and he instinctively put his remaining hand to his broken ribs.

'Do not try to talk too much,' pleaded Conrad, his voice full of concern. 'Of course I am happy that we shall be together, Otto, but I am sad that we have your suffering to thank for our good fortune. I do pray that you will soon be well again.'

'I shall soon be well again. You have saved my life with

your stinking poultices and your foul tasting potions and now I am going home. I shall feel better as soon as we are inside the gates. I love that place as much as my master does. Have I ever told you about it, Conrad?'

'Many times,' the boy replied, smiling indulgently.

Otto continued, undeterred by the reply. 'The house was once the home of the Roman general who governed this region. They called it a villa in those days. When our lord's ancestors drove the Romans from this land, the house fell into their hands. Sadly, successive chieftains of our tribe, in the years that followed, neglected the villa and its estates. Well I remember the first time I saw the place.' Otto was happy in his reminiscences and Conrad was pleased that for a little while his friend could forget his pain. He listened in silence to the tale his tutor had recounted many times before as they had sat around the camp fire.

'Well do I remember,' Otto mused. 'I was a young man then and the Lord Gustavus was only a boy – younger than you. I was his personal bodyguard; I went everywhere with him. This day, Conrad, we were pursuing a wild boar. The Lord Gustavus, even at that early age, was already a fine horseman; soon he had left the rest of the company behind and I alone was with him. He was riding so fast that somehow he lost track of the boar. Child-like, to hide his disappointment, he looked for some new diversion. Finding he was in a part of the forest he had not seen before, he insisted upon exploring. Through the trees he could see meadowland. At once he galloped out into the sunlight and down onto the plain below. There we came upon the ruins of some vast building. I had no knowledge of what it had once been but my young master, who had had much book-learning, had no doubts that that heap of rubble had once been the home of a very powerful man – a Roman general no less!

My young lord dashed from one side to the other shouting, "Here would have been the guardhouse for the soldiers! Here would have been the stables!" When at last he returned to my side, he was breathless with excitement; his eyes were shining. "One day, Otto," he said, "when I am a great general like the Roman who once lived here, this shall be my home – and your home too." He was as good as his word, Conrad. He rode straight back to his father and demanded that those ruins and the surrounding land should be included in his share of his father's estates. And so it was that when King Theodoric met his death – and that is another tale, Conrad – and his possessions were divided between his sons, the Lord Bardolph was happy to take the mountain fortress and let his brother have this estate on the plain. Since that day my Lord Gustavus has used his share of the war-plunder to rebuild the villa and restore it to its original state. It is there that he trains the young men who will lead his army. Ah, Conrad, I am so proud that you are to be one of them and, that the villa is to be your home as well as mine.'

Since Conrad's classical education had only just begun he had no conception of how a Roman villa must have looked. When he first caught sight of his master's home he assumed he was looking at a small town, built in a neat rectangle. As they got nearer, he realized that it was not a town but one group of buildings, heavily fortified. Sentries were much in evidence and as they passed through the gateway, Conrad decided the villa was as much a fortress as the Lord Bardolph's stronghold. In the vast inner courtyard, boys and youths of varying ages were energetically engaged in practising the martial arts. Around the perimeter of the courtyard stood their instructors, veteran soldiers all, shouting commands at the top of their voices. The wagon made its way slowly between the pairs of combatants and passed through a second smaller gateway, set in a dividing wall at the far end of the training ground. Now they were in a much smaller courtyard where the paving stones were broken by gardens. The cart finally came to a halt at the bottom of a flight of steps leading up to a most imposing building – its ornate portico supported by marble columns. Conrad had never seen anything like it before. Roman Emperors, he felt sure, must have lived in such a place.

Otto, perceiving the boy's open-mouthed wonder, whispered, 'This is where the Lord Gustavus lives.' There was no time for further discussion. Men came hurrying to lift Otto from the wagon and bear him on a litter into the house. Conrad made to follow his friend but found his way barred by the servants.

'No one is permitted to enter these apartments except on the instructions of the Lord Gustavus,' he was told. Conrad protested in vain and relinquished his grip reluctantly on Otto's hand.

'You will be Master Conrad,' said a voice behind him. The boy turned and faced a middle-aged man whom he recognised as being one of the instructors he had seen in the outer court-yard. 'Follow me,' ordered the soldier curtly. Conrad obeyed, but not without a few backward glances at the door which had closed behind his friend. He was upset at being parted from Otto so abruptly, especially when he had assumed he would be allowed to go on caring for him. As he re-crossed the outer courtyard, Conrad's discomfort was increased by the curious, even hostile, stares of the youths who were now drawn up in orderly formations awaiting the command to commence their drill. The walk seemed unending but finally the soldier flung open a door at the far end of the east wing and said, 'You sleep here.' The room was long and narrow; it was completely bare except for some small chests arranged along one wall. The man pointed to a heap of straw and animal skins behind the door. 'You can help yourself to some bedding,' he said. He then left the room without any further explanation.

Conrad chose a corner where he hoped he would be incon-spicuous to his companions, deposited his share of the bedding on the floor and sat down. Since nothing further appeared to be expected of him he decided, after a few minutes, that he might feel less depressed if he were outside in the fresh air. He found a quiet sunny spot against the wheel of a cart standing near the main gate. On the journey he, Otto and the driver had stopped for the night by a stream, close to a huddle of peasants' huts. One of the inhabitants had invited them to rest under his roof and in the morning had given them some coarse bread and goat's cheese. Conrad had had little opportunity to eat goat's cheese since he had left his own herd so he had saved some of the delicacy to enjoy later. Now he took the cheese, wrapped in some of the bread, from inside his tunic and ate it slowly, savouring the flavour and with it the memories which it brought back – memories of the mountains, the high alp, of Hulda and most of all, of little Tilly.

Conrad's happy thoughts were interrupted by a commotion at the gate. He looked up and saw that several more newcomers were arriving. His worst fears were confirmed when he saw that all the youths were quite obviously from wealthy families. He looked down at his own filthy smelly rags and compared them to the rich clothing of his future companions. Each boy rode a fine horse and was accompanied by his own servants. Instinctively Conrad drew back, seeking cover from the cart. He was nevertheless close enough to hear the conversations. The soldier who had met him greeted the latest arrivals in the same abrupt manner. He carried a basket into which he ordered each boy to place the gifts he had brought to pay for his keep and training. The servants of those who had brought foodstuffs were allowed to carry them to the storehouses. Then the soldier told each boy to take his horse to the stable and attend to its needs. Immediately arguments broke out. None of the boys had ever stabled his horse before: that was the duty of their servants.

'You will have no servants here,' the soldier stated. 'You will dismiss your followers and instruct them to return to your fathers. We have no room for them here. Furthermore, the first lesson you must learn is how to care for yourself. That is the Lord Gustavus's order.'

So it was throughout the day. Some thirty boys arrived in all and each was received by the soldier-in-charge with the same lack of ceremony. When nightfall came Conrad knew he must face his fellow pupils. Hesitantly, he opened the door of the room they would all share and was met by a barrage of noise. The soldier-in-charge was there supported by several other guards. He was facing a hail of protests from the boys who had never before been expected to live in such cramped conditions. It was clear that they would have to sleep side by side, crushed together. All of them had brought a wealth of belongings and the wooden chests were overflowing. The one small space left in the centre of the room was occupied by pots containing a steaming broth. To Conrad's nostrils the smell was appetising but the other boys did not share his opinion. As the bowls were passed round they were cast aside by the disgusted recipients. Conrad managed to retrieve one and consume its contents unobserved.

'You will regret this action,' the soldier shouted sternly. 'You were given hot food tonight as a concession, to help you to recover from your journey. There will be no more hot food for several days. It is our Lord Gustavus's wish that I use the time until his return to determine which of you is strong enough to withstand the rigours of training. From tomorrow, you will eat as an ordinary soldier eats on campaign. Our general eats the same rations as his men. If they starve, he starves – only then can he tell what reserves of strength they have left to continue the fight. You will learn to live by the same rules. As for your crowded quarters – time will solve your problem. The Lord Gustavus has based this establishment upon the military schools he saw in Byzantium; those were copied from the Spartans. He tells us the Spartans were a fine warrior race. They did not tolerate weaklings – they put them out in the cold to die! Our lord does not tolerate weaklings either – he sends them home to their mothers! As each one of you fails to meet the test more room will be left for the remainder.' The soldier looked around him and added disparagingly, 'This room will probably be quite empty by the spring.'

The boy standing in front of Conrad whose protests had been among the loudest, turned round to elicit the support of his fellows. His eyes fell upon Conrad. He wrinkled up his nose in disgust. 'Who is this stinking peasant?' he yelled. 'What is he doing here?'

The soldier-in-charge pushed aside the onlookers. 'This boy is here on the Lord Gustavus's instructions,' he replied sharply.

'Do you mean he is to be trained alongside us?' demanded the youth incredulously.

'Yes!' snapped the soldier.

'I will not have it!' screamed the boy. 'My father is one of the Lord Gustavus's generals; he will not permit this.'

Others joined in the dispute. 'Ingram is right. He is a common serf. Put him with the livestock.' The clamour increased: all were glad to find a scapegoat on whom to vent their anger after the day's frustrations.

'Silence!' commanded the soldier. 'Our lord has already decided what is fitting. The boy remains until the Lord Gustavus decides otherwise.' The soldier stared hard at Conrad, noting for the first time his torn clothing, stained with the blood of the wounded he had tended after the siege. 'Come with me,' he ordered.

Conrad was glad to follow the man and leave the uproar behind. He heard the other guards still shouting for order as they passed through the inner gates into the garden area. The soldier turned sharply to the left, away from the Lord Gustavus's palatial apartments, to a building screened by trees. Once inside, Conrad found himself in a large hall with a fire blazing in the hearth in the centre. The place was crowded: it was obviously the living quarters of all the soldiers and servants who worked at the villa. Conrad looked quickly around, hoping to catch a glimpse of his comrade. He even ventured to inquire, 'Is Otto here? Is he alright?'

The soldier's voice had a little warmth in it as he replied, 'You can stop worrying about Otto. He is among friends. You will see him again when he is better.' The man rummaged about in a large trunk then threw some garments at Conrad. 'Put these on and throw your old clothes on the fire.'

The boy was about to comply when he remembered Tilly's sash around his waist. He hesitated then said, 'My body is as dirty as my clothes.'

To his immense relief the man nodded and said, 'There is a well just outside the door.'

Conrad hurried out into the welcome darkness, undressed, quickly washed himself and put on the clean garments. He returned to the hall, tossed his bundle of old clothes into the hearth and followed the soldier back to the east wing. Thankfully the room was in darkness, the silence broken only by the breathing of the sleeping boys. Conrad picked his way carefully over the bodies and reached the safety of his own corner. As he settled for sleep, he remembered the first dreadful journey from his home to the encampment when he had endured the taunts and jeers of his fellow recruits. It seemed little had changed.

Next morning there was no opportunity to continue the wrangling of the night before. At dawn the door of the barrack room was flung open and the first day of training began. After a hasty meal of bread and water, which no one this time felt obliged to refuse, the newcomers were ushered outside to watch the senior cadets put through their paces. The soldier-in-charge, whose name they learned was Sigurd, barked the orders as the young men firstly drilled with enviable precision, then gave an agile display of gymnastics and finished by wrestling in pairs like champions. The new cadets spent the remainder of the day, with only a few short breaks, on the parade ground learning the rudiments of what they had seen. By evening, the majority of the boys were quite exhausted and when food was brought to their barracks, the first since the early morning bread, most of them were too tired to complain. The meal, as promised, was a cold one consisting of unleavened bread and slices of tough salted meat. Conrad had eaten many such repasts before and attacked his share hungrily. His obvious enjoyment of the meagre rations was not lost on Ingram, the general's son. After Sigurd had departed, informing Conrad quietly on his way out that he was to report to the stables where a horse had been allotted to him, Ingram could contain himself no longer.

'Why are you here, peasant?' he demanded. 'Why should our lord single you out for this privileged training?' Everyone in the room stopped talking and gave their attention to the two boys confronting one another. Conrad felt their eyes upon him and his face began to colour and his cheeks to burn. He was at a loss for words; he shifted his feet uncomfortably. 'Well, boy, answer me!' shouted Ingram. 'You have no family rich enough to support you, I am certain, so our lord must be maintaining you himself. Why peasant? Why is he doing that?'

'Yes, the Lord Gustavus is supporting me,' Conrad stammered at last. 'He wished to reward me for good service.'

'Good service! You?' jeered his interrogator. 'There is some mystery here. Perhaps you have knowledge of some dark secret or perhaps our lord is not the saint he would have us believe.'

Conrad was no longer tongue-tied. He hurled himself at

Ingram. 'You insult my master! Take back your words!' The pair was at once locked in combat. Most of the boys present had been brought up to revere the Lord Gustavus and they too resented Ingram's remarks. Other fights broke out between them and Ingram's supporters. Soon the entire dormitory was in uproar. It took the guards, lead by Sigurd, to separate the participants and to restore order. Sigurd was in no doubt as to who had started the fight – Conrad and Ingram were by far the bloodiest combatants.

'You two will rise an hour before daybreak for extra drill,' he ordered. Then turning to Conrad he added, 'I told you to go to the stables. Off with you!'

As he hurried across the parade ground to the west wing Conrad was grateful to Sigurd. With luck the other boys would once more be asleep by the time he returned. A groom directed him to the end stable. Conrad walked around the horse several times, patting and stroking him, unable to believe his good fortune. Though the animal was not his, since he alone would ride it he could pretend that it was his. It was a game he had played with the goats. The boy was about to tell the horse his thoughts when a cheerful voice said, 'No one would pay a ransom for him but he will serve you well enough.'

Conrad looked up, startled and embarrassed that his performance had been witnessed. He saw a boy, two or three years his senior, leaning over a wooden partition. He was a big red-faced lad with broad shoulders and muscular arms. 'You are Conrad,' the stranger said. 'Otto sent a message that I was to keep a look-out for you.'

At these words Conrad forgot all about his new acquisition and rushed over to the boy. 'How is he? Have you seen him?' he asked eagerly.

The boy shook his head. 'No, I have not seen him but my master, the blacksmith, has been permitted to visit him. They are old comrades. But Otto is getting stronger and says he will soon be able to visit you.'

'Oh! I hope so, I hope so!' cried Conrad with feeling.

'I am Roderic,' announced the boy. 'I live at the workshop next door. When I was a child I lived with the blacksmith but now that I am a man – or almost – I prefer to live where I work. Come!' The boy pushed himself away from the wooden partition and struggled towards the doorway. Conrad watched his efforts in astonishment. He had not guessed that the youth was a cripple. When he saw the heavy torso on the spindly misshapen legs he marvelled that one so afflicted could have such a happy disposition. His own troubles seemed minor by comparison with this boy's handicaps.

When they reached the adjacent building, Conrad was greeted by a sight to stir his imagination. The walls were hung with implements of war. There were shirts of chain-mail, helmets, swords, spears and lances. Embers were still burning in the forge and their red glow was reflected in the metalwork. Conrad gazed around him in wonder. Roderic was delighted by his reaction.

'I have been apprenticed to my master for many years. There is no aspect of the blacksmith's trade with which I am not familiar but it is as a sword-smith that I excel.' The boy spoke proudly. 'I shall never have the honour of bearing arms for our lord as you will, Conrad, but I am content in the knowledge that all those who do take the fruits of my labours with them to the battlefield. When I fashion a sword or a piece of armour, I feel that I too am fighting for the Lord Gustavus.'

'You are justifiably proud of your craft, Roderic,' agreed Conrad. 'You fight for our lord every bit as much as any warrior.'

Roderic was somewhat abashed by the earnestness of the boy's response and was glad to change the subject. Pointing to a stool, he said, 'Sit down over there while I bathe the cuts on your face.' Conrad had forgotten about his fight with Ingram; he was wondering how he could explain his battered appearance when Roderic made it clear that he understood exactly how it had come about. 'You must not be surprised that the other boys resent you and are suspicious of you. They are afraid of you because you are not like them. I know – I suffered the same when I first came here. Have courage, Conrad. Look upon this as your first battle.'

Conrad saw the boy's smiling face. 'I do not know if I have as much courage as you, Roderic,' he replied.

The youth stumbled awkwardly across the room to throw the bloodstained water out of the door. With his back to Conrad, he suggested nervously, 'Perhaps you would like to visit me again. The blacksmith, his craftsmen and the other apprentices leave an hour before sundown. I am alone then.'

'I should like that very much,' Conrad answered warmly.

VI

The new warrior horseman

'Now young gentlemen, we are going to see if you can march. You will march and march until you drop.' There was a fiendish glint in Sigurd's eyes as he made his announcement.

'We are not foot soldiers,' Ingram protested. 'We are here to train for our lord's own mounted Companions.'

'You are quite right, Master Ingram,' agreed Sigurd. 'You are here to train to be a very special type of soldier – a mounted soldier – but first you must prove to our lord that you have the strength and stamina to be a soldier at all. So we march! Open the gates!'

The little column moved out lead by Sigurd and flanked by two guards. At first the going was easy, being across flat meadowland, but as the company neared the foothills the ground became stony and uneven. Many boys began to visibly flag under the weight of the equipment each one carried. Before they had left the villa each cadet had been given a spear, an axe, a sword, a sax, a shield, a spade and two wooden stakes.

Suddenly, Sigurd called a halt. 'You may take a rest from marching; instead you may dig!' There were howls of protest from the exhausted boys. Sigurd raised his hand for silence. 'This is the time an enemy strikes, when he sees his prey is weary. Imagine you are a small force caught out in the open and hopelessly outnumbered by hordes of Franks or Burgundians. What do you do? I will tell you – you dig!' Sigurd warmed to his subject. 'Our Lord Gustavus tells us that the Roman legions were the most disciplined fighting force the world had seen. Each man carried with his weapons wooden stakes, as you do. If the army was attacked as I have described, half the men would engage the enemy while the remainder dug a trench, threw up ramparts and erected a temporary stockade on top. Then the entire force would take refuge inside and defend itself from a superior position. This was a practice adopted by the Byzantines with whom our Lord Gustavus served as a mercenary – even he did this as a young man. Everyone in his service is trained to do the same today. Our enemies may call us cowards but victory is all that matters. Start digging!'

Only Conrad set about the task with a will. Although he had never had to build a stockade with the enemy on his heels, he had helped with the entrenchment of the camp every night when the army had been on the march. Otto had told him that this too was a practice of the Romans which the Lord Gustavus had adopted. In this way men slept easy, the Axe-man had explained, knowing that they were safe – protected from their enemies inside their palisade.

Sigurd and the other two old soldiers found a comfortable spot to rest while they watched the antics of their young novices. It was an amusing spectacle for only Conrad was adept with a spade. His area of trench rapidly assumed the correct shape and he effortlessly gave a hand to the boys on either side of him. He pummelled the loose earth which he had thrown up into a firm mound and then drove his stakes and those of his companions hard into the top of their rampart. Their small section of timber fencing stood out against the skyline like a monument. The remainder of the trench – the area being constructed by the rest of the class – either collapsed upon the labourers as they worked or subsided as soon as an attempt was made to hammer in the stakes. When most of the ditch appeared to be a seething mass of loose soil, bodies, tools and timbers, Sigurd reluctantly put an end to his entertainment.

'That is enough, gentlemen! Your entire force was wiped

out long ago.' He shook his head solemnly. 'Let us pray our brave warriors never have to depend upon you for their salvation.' As the boys dragged themselves wearily out of the dirt, Sigurd put his hand briefly on Conrad's shoulder and said quietly, 'Well done.'

Sigurd did not speak the words softly enough and Ingram immediately retorted, 'Peasants were made for work such as this.'

'And you will learn to do it just as well before our lord's return, Master Ingram,' Sigurd assured him.

It was a sorry company which staggered through the gates that evening. They were greeted by the knowing grins of the older cadets. They stood about the courtyard in groups recalling their own first march. Conrad alone had the energy to leave the dormitory that evening – to visit his friend Roderic. His fellow pupils were all too tired to move another aching limb and many were happy to forego their unappetising meal and collapse, overcome with fatigue, upon their bedding until morning.

So the first four memorable weeks passed and at the end of that time most of the new contingent could drill reasonably well, could march a full day without dropping and could erect an almost-square stockade on top of quite stable earthworks without serious injuries being incurred. One morning, Sigurd lined them all up in the big courtyard and announced that the Lord Gustavus had returned and was ready to inspect them. Conrad held his breath as the great man appeared. He seemed even taller and more imperious in his bearing than the boy remembered. He paused before each new entrant and studied his face for a few seconds in silence. When it was Conrad's turn he gave no sign that he recognised him and passed on to the next boy without a word. Having completed his inspection the

Lord Gustavus mounted his horse and proceeded to deliver his opening address.

'I regret that I was not here to welcome you personally when you arrived but matters of great importance kept me away.' Conrad knew from Thorkell that his master always followed each campaign with a visit to his brother, the Lord Bardolph, for a division of the spoils, but the Lord Gustavus did not see fit to mention this additional duty. He continued, 'I was confident that Master Sigurd would, in my absence, put you properly to the test. On his recommendation all but three of you will continue with the initial training.' Everyone present knew who the three were who would be sent home: they had collapsed repeatedly from exhaustion and were demonstrably unfit for such exacting service. 'As for the rest of you,' said the general, 'I must stress that you too will be sent home if at any time you fail to reach the standards required of you. I shall not tolerate any boy who shows he lacks strength of body or strength of will. Those who are privileged to serve as my Companions in Arms must be honourable men whose courage, skill and powers of endurance I need never doubt. From their ranks I choose my commanders. Promotion is won by ability alone. It is therefore within the capacity of any one of you to rise to great heights and to reap a just reward. But I must warn you that if, as an officer, you neglect your duty to the point of endangering the lives of others, or you show cowardice in the face of the enemy or commit an act of treason, you will be publicly flogged to death.'

After an appropriate silence, the Lord Gustavus declared in a lighter tone of voice, 'And now to give you an ideal to aim for, I have arranged a little spectacle.' He urged his mount forward and positioned it alongside the line of cadets. The instructors standing at the far end of the parade ground near the main gates pushed a wooden contraption resembling a gallows into position. From its top beam hung a stuffed sack crudely shaped like a man. At the opposite end of the parade ground, just inside the gateway to the smaller courtyard, a horseman was waiting. When the Lord Gustavus gave him a signal he galloped out, stringing his bow as he did so and in the time it took him to cover the length of the outer courtyard he shot not one but three arrows at the swinging dummy. Every missile found its target. The man completed his charge with a lance thrust and somehow managed to rein in his mount before animal and rider crashed through the main gates.

At a more leisurely pace the horseman came over to the admiring spectators and the general resumed his lecture. 'Many of you will not understand the significance of what you have just seen. Though this officer is one of my Companions and most proficient in all the martial arts, he could not have achieved such a feat without the aid of this marvellous invention.' So saying, the Lord Gustavus leant forward and with his sword tapped the piece of iron in which the horseman's foot rested. 'This, gentlemen, is called a stirrup. You will see that it is a simple device but I tell you that this simple device is the greatest single advance since man began to fashion weapons of war. It will change the entire course of history!' The general paused to allow the full force of his words to penetrate then he continued. 'Now for the second stage of the demonstration ...'

Again he raised his hand and two more horsemen charged at one another from opposite ends of the parade ground. Both were fully armed but their mounts had only backcloths. The men gripped with their knees as their horses gathered speed but they had no iron stirrups in which to rest their feet. As they came within striking distance, each soldier slashed at the other with his sword. Both men were instantly unseated and fell heavily to the ground. Scarcely waiting for the bruised riders to make their escape, the Lord Gustavus raised his hand again. Two more combatants charged into the big courtyard, mailed and armed as before but this time stirrups hung from their horses' backs. Although they met with a resounding crash as blades landed on shields, neither man lost his balance. For several minutes they displayed their prowess, each contestant matching blow for blow, but neither unseated the other.

When the general felt he had made his point he called a halt and dismissed the demonstrators. He resumed his former position in front of the boys and proceeded to explain. 'You have just seen quite clearly that a man on horseback is very unstable. Any attempt to attack his opponent with force will more than likely result in the man himself being unseated by the shock of the impact. He must hold tight to his horse at all times, even when hurling a spear or loosing an arrow. He is therefore no more useful than one foot soldier. But the man who uses stirrups is worth ten foot soldiers! He can turn, he can rise and reach out; he can use sword, spear, axe or bow, all at speed and all without falling off his mount. I tell you, gentlemen, the implications of this invention cannot be overestimated. All through the ages, kings and generals have ridden into battle and then dismounted to fight. During your lifetime you will meet few men who will fight on horseback. They will all fight on foot except those who, like me, have seen with their own eyes the mounted warriors from the East – the Huns and Avars of Central Asia. It is they we must thank for this great innovation. The stirrup has been known to them for centuries. They have used it as their supreme weapon and have become the scourge of emperors. They have been halted at the borders of Byzantium only by the grace of God and the foresight of the great general, Belisarius, who in the last century ordered the stirrup to be adopted throughout the army of the Eastern Roman Empire.

There is no doubt in my mind that in centuries to come the stirrup will be adopted throughout the world and the face of warfare as we know it will be fundamentally changed. The foot soldier will be of little consequence. Battles will be fought and won, empires held and lost, on the strength of mounted warriors alone. Great skill will be required both in horsemanship and in the use of weapons, but every man will be a hero.

He will be a new breed of warrior, the like of which has never been seen before. He will be fiercely loyal to his chieftain; he will honour and respect both him and his comrades in arms. I cannot tell you, gentlemen, what this new warrior horseman will be called – perhaps he will be known simply as a "rider", a "knight" – but I can tell you that his deeds will be written down for posterity and his praises sung for generations. You, gentlemen, are privileged to be among the first of this new warrior breed. See that you are worthy of the great honour the Lord God has bestowed upon you.'

After such rhetoric no impressionable youth could fail to be fired with enthusiasm. Every novice vowed to himself that he would be numbered among these new heroes. Inspiration drove each and every one to greater efforts and even Sigurd became almost lavish in his praise. Outdoor activities still filled most of the day: there would be more than enough time for book learning once the winter snows began to fall. Furthermore, the general was anxious to establish once and for all which of the new boys had the stamina and self-discipline to make further training worthwhile. He ordered that the few remaining weeks of good weather be used to the full. The long route-marches, interrupted by entrenching and stockade building, continued at intervals but posed little problem for any of the novices. All could drill properly and could run in close formation maintaining a shield-wall. Sigurd remained in overall control of the boys but they now went to other veteran soldiers for instruction in the particular skills they must acquire and perfect.

It was imperative that every cadet should be an expert horseman. All the boys, with the exception of Conrad, had been riding almost from the time they could walk. Conrad had on occasion jumped upon a goat's back just for fun, but this was poor preparation for the task ahead. When he first mounted his horse he was surprised at how far he seemed from the ground and how easy it was to slip about on its back. The other boys were delighted when they noticed his discomfort. At last they had found something at which he did not excel and when he fell off at the first gallop, in spite of his stirrups, they laughed long and heartily in derision. As he stumbled to his feet and ran after his mount, Conrad swore he would suffer no further humiliation. From that time on, whenever he could escape for a little while, he would make his way to the stables and with the help and encouragement of Roderic, would practise the equestrian art in secret. Within a matter of days he had mastered the basic technique and could confidently join the rest of his company in learning the finer points of military horsemanship.

There was nothing further Conrad's instructors could teach him about archery and he had remembered all that Otto had taught him about spear-fighting. He was soon acknowledged to be one of the most proficient exponents of the spear in the group. When it came to sword-play Conrad was once more at a disadvantage. He, of course, had never owned a sword whereas the other boys had been given small swords as their first toys. All their lives they had been accustomed to playing fencing games. Ingram made little attempt to conceal his pleasure when he observed how clumsy Conrad was with the weapon. Again, it was Roderic who saved Conrad from further mortification and the possibility of serious injury. Not only did he know how to fashion a sword but how to use it as well. He knew every movement, every parry, every cut, every thrust and he enjoyed himself immensely imparting his knowledge to his friend. Being so unsteady on his feet, the workbench upon which he sat astride was an indispensable piece of equipment to Roderic. It was from this perch that he gave his lessons, wielding the sword effortlessly with either muscular arm and contenting himself with shouting orders as to the necessary footwork which must accompany each stroke. Once Conrad gained confidence he realized that many of the actions needed in sword-fighting were similar to those he had already mastered in spear-fighting and axe-fighting. The combination of expert tuition with the eye of a natural marksman and the agility of a mountain dweller soon produced a first class swordsman – much to Ingram's disgust. The sax, another weapon used only by noblemen, was strange to Conrad at first but being in effect a very large knife, he soon became accustomed to it.

Only one weapon remained for which the novices had received no instruction – the battle axe. When it was announced that they were to attend such a class Conrad was thrown into despondency: his repeated efforts to see his old friend had been thwarted. He presented himself on the parade ground at the appointed time with no enthusiasm whatsoever for the lesson ahead. When the unmistakable figure of Otto strode through the inner gates and made in the boys' direction, Conrad's joy at seeing him, apparently fully recovered, knew no bounds. The old soldier stood in front of the group and announced, 'I am Otto the Axe-man. I am here to teach you everything there is to know about the art of throwing the axe. You may think that a one-armed man would make a poor teacher and you would be right – although I am no mean marksman with my remaining arm – but no matter, for you have among you the best pupil I ever had. As I talk he will demonstrate.' Otto beamed at Conrad and offered him his favourite "Widow-maker". The boy came forward and proudly took the axe and for the remainder of the morning he wielded and threw it like one possessed.

VII

A fight to the death

Conrad looked back on his early days at the villa with mixed feelings. The military training he enjoyed thoroughly; he knew he was making good progress. In his relationships with his peers he could make no progress at all; he was shunned by everybody. There was a little more room in the dormitory following the departure of the three boys, but his bedding had been flung into the draftiest spot behind the door. Here he slept apart from everyone else and here he hastily swallowed his meals whilst the rest of the class sat together in the middle of the room, laughing and joking. Even during training sessions, Ingram and his friends never lost an opportunity to make some cruel remark or hiss some obscenity, when the instructor was out of hearing.

Hardly a day passed without someone picking a fight with Conrad. Ingram was invariably in the vicinity when this happened although he himself had never been a challenger since that second day after they had arrived at the villa. Conrad began to suspect that Ingram had organised a rota and was sending the other boys to wear him down. He became convinced that his enemy was only waiting for him to become sufficiently cowed before stepping in himself for the kill. This thought sustained Conrad through every dual and made him so angry that he found renewed strength for every contest. By the end of the second month he had fought and beaten almost every member of the class, some several times over. This constant state of hostility might have had its desired effect had

Conrad not been able to find comfort from his tormentors in the welcome that awaited him at the forge. Every night, as soon as he had devoured his ration – and Sigurd always remained in the barrack-room until he had done so – he would make his escape to the west wing. Roderic would have a bowl of water and cloths ready and his first concern would be to treat his friend's wounds.

'Be cheered by the thought that there are not many left to challenge you, Conrad,' he said one night. 'You give them such a beating that few come back for more.'

'I just wish they would leave me in peace,' sighed Conrad. 'I know they will never accept me as one of them.'

'That they will not,' laughed Roderic ruefully, 'but they might one day accept you as their better.'

'How can that ever be?' asked Conrad in disbelief.

'If you prove that you are their better!' replied his friend. 'Listen – I will tell you how it was with me.' Roderic's normally cheerful face looked sad as he began his story. 'My family, whoever they were, threw me out when I was a baby. They left me in a ditch to die. If the good blacksmith had not heard my cries as he made his way home, I would have died – been eaten by wolves most like. He has been a good father to me; his wife has been my devoted mother and his daughters my loving sisters. When he thought I was old enough to under-stand, he told me how I had been abandoned because I was crippled and how happy he had been to find me, just as if the Lord God had at last answered his prayers for a son. When he first brought me here to teach me his trade I was so proud, Conrad, until I saw the expressions on the faces of the other apprentices and the craftsmen. I had not realized until then how hideous and deformed I looked. I had been so happy at home with the blacksmith's family – so protected, so spoiled by the girls – that I had not given any thought to my appearance. I shudder even now when I think of it, Conrad. One man said outright that I must come from an evil line. "The sins of the fathers are being visited upon the child," he said and everyone seemed to agree with him. They decided that I had been cursed and would have nothing to do with me. I was so miserable and wretched that if the blacksmith had not continued to take me home with him each night, I do not know how I would have survived.'

'How did you survive, Roderic?' asked Conrad sympathetically.

'The blacksmith convinced me that there was only one way: since they would never accept me as an equal, they must accept me as a better. He made me promise that I would work harder than anyone else, learn faster and make myself the best craftsman in the entire workshop. And I have done just that, Conrad, and one day I hope to succeed my father as the master blacksmith. My companions are still wary of me and afraid of my deformity but they respect me and look up to me because of my superior skills. So it must be with you, Conrad. You must be the best cadet this place has ever seen. I doubt then whether anyone will call you "friend", but respect and admire you they certainly will.'

Roderic's words, the echo of the advice Otto had once given him when he had despaired of ever attaining his ambition, lifted Conrad's despondency. The other boys, however, continued their campaign against him and there is no telling what the outcome might have been had there not occurred an unexpected change of plan. One morning at sunrise, Sigurd burst into the dormitory and ordered everyone outside onto the parade ground. 'Hurry up, gentlemen, you have no time to lose,' he barked as the boys rubbed the sleep from their eyes. 'You are going on a three day unaccompanied march. Line up in your group as I call your name.'

'But you told us we would not be going on any overnight marches until the spring,' protested Ingram.

'I did, Master Ingram,' answered Sigurd, unperturbed, 'but the Lord Gustavus has decided that as the weather is holding we should make the most of the opportunity. There is no finer test of stamina, discipline and initiative than a three day unaccompanied march.'

The class was divided into three groups and to his horror, Conrad found that he was in Ingram's group and that his enemy had been appointed group leader. Mass and a hurried meal followed then each boy was issued with weapons and three days' supplies. The leaders were told their routes and given the names of the men, all vassals of the Lord Gustavus, to whom they were to report on the way. Everyone was to be back at the villa no later than sundown of the third day, each boy bearing the same weapons and equipment with which he had been issued and each leader bearing, in addition, sealed documents as evidence from the vassals they had visited.

Sigurd stopped Ingram as the group was about to depart and said to him, 'A leader has many duties; one is to ensure the safety of his followers. Should any boy show signs of unwarrantable injury, our lord would regard his condition as a reflection on the ability of his leader.'

Sigurd's timely words saved Conrad a lot of suffering and Ingram proved to be a most able commander. He was determined that his group should be first back at the villa and to this end he drove his companions hard. Rest periods were short and infrequent; the last vestiges of daylight had almost disappeared from the sky before he would allow his group to make camp; they were marching again by first light. He made an even greater sacrifice in refusing all offers of hospitality at the homes of the Lord Gustavus's vassals. Ingram had been used to a life of feasting and comfort and he was sorely tempted, but his desire to win overcame all temptations. He obtained the necessary seals of confirmation and then hurried his little company on their way. He was even too busy to waste time persecuting Conrad and instead made use of him to scout ahead to ascertain the easiest and quickest routes.

By dawn of the third day, the party was only hours away from its final objective. Then there was dissent. As the morning wore on Conrad spent more and more time anxiously watching the sky. Eventually, he called out, 'Ingram, we must find shelter. There is going to be a terrible storm.'

For a moment Ingram was too shocked to reply then he yelled, 'Nonsense! The weather is fine. You are mad, peasant!' The truce which had existed between the pair for the duration of the expedition was instantly broken. They stood glaring at each other with blazing eyes.

'You are right, Ingram, I am a peasant and any peasant would tell you that that sky means a blizzard is coming!' retorted Conrad. 'A peasant would seek shelter for his livestock and for himself and that is what you must do.'

'You ignorant impudent upstart, I am the leader here and no one tells me what to do – least of all, you!' Ingram snorted contemptuously. 'We shall be back at the villa by midday; no one else will have made the fast time that we have. I am not going to lose the chance of victory because of your stupid whims!'

'Then you will lose your life,' Conrad persisted, 'and the life of every one who follows you. When the blizzard comes we shall not be able to see a hand in front of us. We shall get separated in the blinding snow and out here in the open we shall freeze to death. That is where we should be heading.' Conrad pointed far to the left. 'There will be cover in those hills – a cave maybe or a cleft in the rock where we can find protection.'

'Idiot!' screamed Ingram. 'Those hills are almost in the opposite direction to where we are going. Such a diversion

would add hours to our time and lose us the race, and for what
– a storm that will never come?'

'It will come,' Conrad maintained with conviction, 'and I
do not intend to sacrifice my life in a battle against the
elements. I am going to seek shelter in those hills. I urge the rest
of you to come with me.'

Ingram would have no such insurrection. He had seen the
fear creeping into the other boys' eyes as the argument had
progressed and he knew that if Conrad left, many of the others
would be panicked into following him. 'I am in command,'
Ingram asserted once more. 'I say we head for the villa – all of
us! You either come voluntarily or I drag you there.' He began
to disentangle himself from his heavy pack and to circle Conrad
menacingly, his fists raised at the ready. There was no alternative but for Conrad to do likewise. This was the contest both
boys had known all along that they would have. This was to be
the day of reckoning.

A tremor of excitement spread through the rest of the
group as they gathered round. They cheered as the first blows
were struck. The pair was evenly matched, being about the
same height and build. At first there was nothing to choose
between them but then Ingram's hatred of Conrad seemed to
rise to the surface and make his attack all the more vicious. He
began to get the upper hand. As Conrad lay on the ground
dazed from yet another heavy blow, one of the boys whispered
in his ear, 'Run, peasant! He means to kill you. Run!'

This was all the encouragement Conrad needed. He got to
his feet like a charging bull and hurled himself at his adversary.
Within seconds he had Ingram pinned to the ground with the
weight of his body, his forearm across his throat. With his free
hand he grasped a stone and raised it above his head. Then he
paused and looked into Ingram's eyes. He saw no fear there –
only defiance – even in the face of imminent death. Without
further hesitation Conrad let the stone fall harmlessly from his
hand, released his hold on his opponent, stood up, gathered his

belongings and walked away in the direction of the hills. After only a few minutes he became aware of footsteps behind him. He turned and saw Ingram, bruised and bloodied like him, following with the rest of the group. Conrad waited and when Ingram came alongside, each put a hand on the shoulder of the other in a gesture of peace.

They did not find a cave in the foothills but they did find a hollow in the rocks just large enough to accommodate them all. They built a wall in front of stones and small boulders and fashioned a roof from twigs and bracken. They completed their work as the first flakes of snow began to fall. The blizzard raged all through the remainder of that day, the night, and the early hours of the following morning. When it had at last abated, the little company crawled out of its shelter – cold, hungry but unscathed. All around them lay a white wilderness. They were dazzled by its brilliance and put up their hands to shield their eyes after the darkness of their hiding place. It was as though they had stepped out into another world: a strange world where sky and land merged and there were no visible landmarks.

'We are lost!' cried one boy, voicing the fear of his companions. 'How shall we know which way to go in all this snow?'

'I know the way,' stated Conrad calmly. 'The villa is in that direction.' He pointed without hesitation. 'We shall reach it before nightfall.'

'The snow is too deep. We shall never make it in time.' It was Ingram now who had misgivings.

'We must plait twigs together and tie them beneath our feet; then we shall not sink so far into the snow,' Conrad assured Ingram. 'I have done it many times before. We can use the branches we cut to make the roof of our shelter.'

'We shall be weighed down by the rest of our equipment.

Let us leave it here,' proposed another boy. His suggestion was favourably received – but not by Ingram.

'We leave nothing behind. We shall return to the villa as ordered, carrying every item with which we were issued. We can lash everything to our backs, leaving our hands free. Our spears will serve as staves to support us and aid our progress.' Ingram's authority prevailed and eventually the group set out in single file with Conrad leading the way across the bleak wasteland.

After a while they sighted horsemen, obviously searching for them. One of the riders broke away from the rest and rode over to them. It was Sigurd. He assured himself that no one was missing before addressing Ingram. 'If you are exhausted we can take you back to the villa on our horses.'

'Thank you, but we have come this far unaided; we shall complete the course unaided,' Ingram replied with dignity. Sigurd raised his hand in salute and rode back to join his men without further argument. The horses soon disappeared from sight as the soldiers continued their search for the other two parties of cadets.

It was late afternoon when the group reached the villa. They returned to a hero's welcome. As they passed through the main gates they were cheered, clapped and embraced by guards and senior boys – those who were not engaged in the hunt for survivors – servants and grooms alike. Otto and Roderic were there to give Conrad an emotional greeting. Even the Lord Gustavus came down from his apartments when told of their safe return. 'You have done well,' he told Ingram.

'No, my lord,' replied Ingram, hanging his head in shame. 'It was Conrad who made us seek shelter. But for him, we might all have perished in the snow storm.'

'My lord,' said Conrad, coming forward, 'until the blizzard struck we had made excellent time. Without doubt, we would have been the first group home and our success would have been due to Ingram alone – because he led us so well.'

'It seems you have both conducted yourselves with credit,' concluded the Lord Gustavus.

None of the boys in the two remaining groups returned on foot. Those brought back by the soldiers that day and the next were all suffering from exhaustion, exposure and frostbite in varying degrees. Two died the same night and two more a few days later from a raging fever. Six boys were sent home because frostbite had deprived them of the fingers essential for their military careers. The bodies of four more cadets, frozen to death, were returned to the villa by peasants and one boy was never found at all. By the onset of winter the dormitory which had housed more than thirty boys became home for only half that number.

VIII

New worlds to explore

The boys who had survived the tragic exercise found their way of life considerably altered and improved. They were permitted to eat with their elders in the Long Hall at the other end of the east wing; they were treated as equals by the senior cadets; their instructors and the villa servants showed them a deference which had been lacking before. It was generally acknowledged that they had passed the crucial test and were destined for a privileged existence. They studied and attended lectures in the Long Hall too and were encouraged to spend the closing hours of each day around its huge fireplace. The chapel also, which adjoined the Lord Gustavus's house, was open to them. Previously, the newcomers had celebrated Mass with their general's chaplain in the courtyard or their dormitory, but now they attended morning service with the other cadets in the chapel.

Conrad's first visit to the chapel made a great impression on him. A tablet set in the stonework caught his attention as he stepped through the doorway. Engraved on it were the words: *This chapel is dedicated to the Glory of God and to the memory of the virtuous Lady Eloise.* Conrad recalled at once the night the Burgundian town had fallen when the Lord Gustavus had spoken of the lady he had loved – the lady who had been taken from him. Even the knowledge that his master had built the chapel as a tribute to his lost love did not prepare Conrad for the splendour he found within. The room was square and dominated by its central dome. Every wall was entirely covered in glittering mosaics – tiny cubes of stone and brilliantly coloured glass – depicting martyrs, saints and apostles. Above Conrad's head a huge and awesome figure of Christ, also fashioned in glowing mosaics, looked down at him from the centre of the dome. Religious images – called icons, as he learned afterwards – were everywhere. On one side of the chapel was a second altar, much smaller than the main one. In front of it stood a stone coffin in which lay the bones of the Lady Eloise; a stone sculpture of a young girl rested on the lid. Above the altar was a painting of the lady. She was portrayed with a tranquil smile on her face, seated beside the Virgin Mary and surrounded by saints. Conrad, though stunned at first by the display of wealth, decided that Thorkell's assessment of their master – that he was two men in one body – must be correct. The Lord Gustavus was indeed an enigma.

Less surprising after the events of the long march was the fact that Ingram became Conrad's protector instead of his tormentor. In spite of his defeat at Conrad's hands, Ingram was still the undisputed leader of the class but he had learned his lesson and never again tried to abuse his power. He seemed to forget overnight how much he had despised Conrad and put aside all feelings of disdain and would permit none in others. No one was allowed to make fun of Conrad, either to his face or behind his back. Furthermore, he made it clear to Conrad that if he wished to spend his evenings in the Long Hall he, Ingram, would see that he was not molested. Conrad, although grateful, did not choose to alter his habits. He still felt uneasy in the company of the other cadets. They were not his friends; Roderic was his friend and he was happy to go on spending his leisure time with him.

If ever he found himself free during the day, Conrad liked nothing better than to watch Roderic at his work. He was fascinated by his dexterity and delighted in helping him whether he was fashioning a weapon, armour or siege machinery. At first, Roderic would only allow Conrad to work the bellows for him but later he relented and permitted him to assist with some of the semi-skilled procedures. Much of the apprentices's time was occupied in making the mail-shirts which the cavalry wore. Roderic called the small interlocking rings of metal which formed the shirts, "war-netting". 'Thorkell the Skald calls the shirts, "byrnies" and the material, "Odin's Web",' said Conrad.

'I know Thorkell well. He has a poet's name for everything,' replied Roderic, laughing. 'The mesh is so close it takes many, many links to form one garment. If you want to help me, bind those thin strips of metal tightly and evenly around this wooden rod.' Conrad did as instructed and when Roderic was satisfied with the result he cut through the coil of wire with one firm stroke along the entire length of the stick, thus separating the loops into open rings. 'The next stage is a skilled job,' announced Roderic. He then proceeded to take each small ring in turn, flatten out the two ends and pierce a hole in each of them. Conrad admired the speed with which is friend worked; soon he had a small pile of links prepared. 'Now you may pass me the rivets,' Roderic directed and as Conrad obeyed, he used the tiny pieces of soft wedge-shaped iron to connect each ring to four others. He held up his work for inspection. 'See, Conrad, what a strong net we have made – no spear will cut through that!'

Some days Conrad watched while Roderic made other items of armour: splinted metal leg-greaves and gloves with splinted cuffs. He made helmets too of iron, with comfortable padded linings, usually simple nut-shaped ones but some with cheek-guards for the use of the Lord Gustavus's noble followers. None matched the magnificence of the Swedish helmet stolen by Thorkell.

The process which intrigued Conrad the most was, without doubt, that of sword-making, and in particular he loved to watch the fashioning of the blade. Roderic's boast at their first meeting that he excelled at sword-making, had not been an idle one. 'In the past,' he told Conrad, 'sword blades, in spite of being fire-hardened, were often soft in places and would bend. Thorkell knows many songs about warriors who had to stop on the battlefield and stamp on their swords to straighten them! The old smiths tried many ways to strengthen the metal; some even quenched it while it was still red-hot in special oils or honey. Today, we have found the answer to hardening the iron. I will show you. Look at this sword,' ordered Roderic, passing Conrad a shining new weapon.

'I am almost afraid to touch it,' said Conrad in awe-struck tones. 'It is so beautiful; it seems to glow in many colours. And how did you get this pattern to run through the middle of the blade?'

'That is the answer I was telling you about,' announced Roderic, pleased that Conrad sounded so impressed. 'We forge separate rods of iron, twist them, plait them, arrange them alongside one another in any design we choose, and then we weld them together to form a metal bar. This we grind down to the required thickness, we burnish it and etch it with vinegar. The result, as you see, is a fine two-edged blade that is both strong and flexible. Where we have filed away the core to form the fuller – that is the name we give to this wide shallow groove that runs the full length of the blade to lighten and stiffen it – the pattern we made at the beginning of the process, by twisting the rods together, has been exposed. It is this welded pattern that makes the blade so hard.'

'You possess a wonderful gift, Roderic. You have the power to create priceless treasures. I envy you,' said Conrad sincerely.

On certain days, when the weather permitted, the cadets were allowed to exercise their mounts outside the confines of the villa. They were encouraged particularly to hunt and to hawk – both pastimes of the nobility which Conrad had never thought he would share. Ingram took it upon himself to teach Conrad the rituals of these sports and did so with unexpected tactfulness. They explored the surrounding countryside together and soon came upon the village settlement built to house the families of the men who worked at the villa. It was the Lord Gustavus's custom to allow his soldiers, servants and serfs over the age of twenty five to marry, but no one was permitted to bring his wife or children to live inside the villa. This total absence of women – there was not even a female servant to be found – had astonished Ingram and the other boys when they had first arrived. It had been no surprise to Conrad.

The women of the village would come out of their huts to greet the young gentlemen from their master's villa and offer them food and drink. The settlement was surrounded by the strips of land allotted by the Lord Gustavus to his retainers for their support. The women and children worked the land and as the young horsemen rode by they would look up from their labours, curtsey, wave and cheer. Conrad found such courtesies strange at first but Ingram would wave flirtatiously to the prettiest girls and tease Conrad for looking embarrassed. In time, however, Conrad came to enjoy the attention as much as Ingram.

A similar warm, but respectful, welcome awaited the boys whenever they stopped for refreshment at the monastery which was situated not far from the village. Their favourite amongst the monks was the ever-cheerful Brother Thomas who was always happy to leave whatever he was doing and come to greet them as they led their horses through the gateway of the monastery.

'Welcome, young gentlemen, welcome!' he would say in his booming voice. 'Brother John has just baked some fresh bread – delicious with the honey from our hives and washed down with our own brew of mead.'

'Travellers must be glad they are turned away from the villa and directed to your gates instead,' Ingram would reply, referring to the fact that the Lord Gustavus, unlike his brother, the Lord Bardolph, did not welcome visitors. Any weary traveller seeking shelter at the villa was always turned away; even if night had fallen no exception was made although an armed escort to the monastery might be provided to ward off would-be robbers. The general would take no chances of harbouring a spy who would tell of what he had seen to any of Gustavus's many enemies.

'We are glad to assume our lord's duty of giving shelter and hospitality,' Brother Thomas had explained on the boys' first visit. 'The Lord Gustavus is a most generous benefactor. He built this monastery for us on his land and he supports our order most generously.'

'I am certain our lord reaps many benefits in return,' Ingram had replied with a natural charm which Conrad had not realized he possessed.

'Yes, that is true,' Brother Thomas had replied. 'The Lord Gustavus's estates are vast and require many serfs to maintain them. There are a number of villages for the labourers besides the one which houses the families of the villa workers. We are responsible for the health and welfare of our lord's many retainers: we minister to the sick, care for the poor and provide some degree of education for certain of the children. Come, let me show you around.'

Ingram and Conrad had both been impressed as the monk had conducted them through the buildings and they had seen the range of work being carried out on their master's behalf. When they had entered a particularly light room with monks huddled in silence over tables positioned against the windows, Brother Thomas had announced, pride in his voice, 'The Lord Gustavus has established not just a monastery but a centre of scholarship. These monks are all learned men content to spend their time compiling in beautiful illuminated script the works of the great Christian teachers. In addition, they provide you – the pupils at the villa – with a constant supply of books. They copy scrupulously from the originals which the Lord Gustavus brought back from Byzantium: texts handed down from the time of the ancient Greek and Roman civilisations, as well as modern histories and military accounts of the Byzantine Empire.'

Conrad, on that first visit, had noticed monks working in small plots of land around the walls of the monastery and he had commented, 'I think not all of your brothers are scholars. Some seem happy to till the soil.'

Brother Thomas had replied, 'Our abbot, a personal friend of the Lord Gustavus, is particularly interested in agriculture. He invents new methods of farming and if his experiments are successful in the monastic fields they are implemented on the lands of our overlord.'

'The Lord Gustavus may be a generous benefactor, as you say, but I think he has the better part of the bargain,' Ingram had concluded. Brother Thomas had not replied but had beamed broadly at the two boys.

The monastery was also a source of tutors for the Lord Gustavus; it was the monks who taught the cadets theology, languages and mathematics. As for the other subjects included in their curriculum, military engineers visited the pupils to demonstrate the practical application of the mathematics they had learned, and military history and tactics was considered of such major importance that the Lord Gustavus gave the lectures himself whenever he was in residence. On these occasions, he never came to the Long Hall but would summon the boys to his apartments and would conduct the lesson in his study. Even Ingram was overawed at first by the marble columns, the frescoes and the mosaics which they passed on their way to their master's inner sanctum. It was impossible also not to be impressed by the resemblance of their lord to the Roman generals whose busts sat majestically on marble pedestals around the room.

The Lord Gustavus delivered his lectures from a rostrum and it soon became clear that he was as much an orator as any Roman senator. A recurring theme in his lessons was his ambition to inflict a resounding defeat upon the Franks. 'Till now they have sent only comparatively small forces against us under the command of officers of inferior ability. But one day, gentlemen, they may find a general who will be a worthy opponent. We must prepare for that day; be ready for the great battle when we shall overthrow the Franks once and for all and establish ourselves for all time as a free and independent people. To you shall fall this supreme honour! To this glorious end you must work and train relentlessly! We are few in number and the Franks are many but history is full of examples of smaller forces winning against overwhelming odds – at Marathon 60,000 Persians were defeated by 10,000 Greeks; at Cannae 86,000 Romans were annihilated by 50,000 Carthaginians; in North Africa the entire Vandal Kingdom was conquered by a mere 15,000 Byzantines. All that is required is superior training and discipline from the ranks and inspired skilful leadership from above. It is to ensure that we have these advantages in abundance that you are here.'

The Lord Gustavus's other obsession was with the example of the Eastern Roman Empire where he had spent the impressionable days of his youth. He never lost an opportunity to sing its praises. 'All that was best of Greek and Roman culture has been preserved in Byzantium and all that was evil has been cast out. The Eastern Roman Empire puts no trust in pagan gods! When the Emperor Constantine, in the fourth century, moved his capital from Rome to the East – to Byzantium – he founded the first truly Christian empire. He built there a great city which bears his name – Constantinople! When I first set eyes upon it as a young man I was overwhelmed. I saw a city built to the Glory of God. Its beauty and splendour are beyond compare. Not a picture, not a fresco, not a mosaic is to be seen which does not pay homage to the Almighty. Ordinary people seek His blessing in everything they do: every house that is built is dedicated to Him; every fishing fleet seeks His blessing before leaving harbour. So it is throughout Byzantium. It is an empire dedicated to God and Christianity. Its emperors rule as God's representatives on earth with the title, "equal to the apostles". Their lands abound with magnificent domed churches. I built my own chapel here after their fashion but it is a small tribute by comparison with the splendid places of worship in Byzantium.

The Lord God has looked with pleasure upon this Christian empire. He has allowed it to prosper; to grow rich and strong. He has helped it to stand firm against all invaders. He has blessed it with great rulers and permitted them to re-conquer much of the former Roman Empire in the West. So it will be with us, gentlemen: the Lord God will look with favour upon our cause because it is a Christian cause.'

Long hours of study followed for Conrad, Ingram and their fellows. They explored early Greek history: the wars with Persia; the Peloponnesian wars between Sparta and Athens; the rise of Macedonia and the career of Alexander the Great. They considered the Punic wars between Rome and Carthage; they marvelled at the rise of the Roman Empire and argued over the reasons for its fall in the West. They came to share their master's admiration for the Roman Empire's survival in the East under the Christian Byzantine emperors. They discussed at great length the relative merits of Greek, Carthaginian and Roman methods of military training and tactics. They delighted in comparing the skills of the great generals of the past. Was Alexander or Hannibal the master of strategical cunning? Which leader inspired more confidence – Alexander, who persuaded his men to march deep into India, the edge of the world, or Hannibal, who drove his entire army, complete with elephants, over the Alps? Was Julius Caesar the supreme opportunist and the best example of Roman efficiency? Were all the qualities of leadership embodied in the Byzantine general, Belisarius? Did he surpass all others at military deception? Were his victories against Persians, Vandals and Ostrogoths, where in every instance his forces were greatly outnumbered by that of his adversaries, the most brilliant military achievements of all time?

Conrad committed to memory all that was read and discussed and he enjoyed as much as any boy the war games that they played. They re-enacted with the aid of wooden models the major battles of history: the battles of Marathon, of Cannae, of Daras and many, many more. But in his moments of quiet reflection Conrad came to the conclusion that there was one leader above all others with whom he felt an affinity – Alexander the Great. He admired him not just for his spectacular military successes but for his humanity: for his interest in his men's welfare; for the way he cared when they were sick or wounded; for the importance he attached to praising and rewarding them. Even more Conrad approved of his compassion towards those he conquered and above all, he felt inspired by Alexander's vision of "one world" – a brotherhood of man which would include all men.

As time went by Conrad was able to see more of his old friend, Otto. It had been decided that when Otto was not instructing cadets in the use of the battle-axe he should spend his time in the stables. There was much work to do there for the Lord Gustavus bred many of his own horses – sturdy fast horses specially suited to the requirements of his cavalry. Otto had a natural way with animals and loved his work so much that he eventually moved out of the hall where the soldiers and servants lived and took up residence in a corner of the stables near to the forge. Being so close to the smithy it was warm and he was comfortable there on his bed of straw. Everyone respected the corner as Otto's territory.

When spring came Thorkell the Skald was summoned from the Lord Bardolph's fortress to re-join his master, the Lord Gustavus. This meant that on many an evening he joined Roderic, Conrad and Otto around the furnace. On one occasion he was praising Roderic for his skills in his own special way by telling him all the tales he knew about sword-smiths with magical powers. This led him to boast about how much the Lord Bardolph loved such tales. 'He truly appreciates my art – and he is generous in his appreciation! All his court loves to hear my sagas. The young Lady Matilda, the Lord Bardolph's heir, also loves them. This last winter, for the first time, she was permitted to sit in the Great Hall and listen to them alongside her father. Previously, I have had to tell them to her in secret. A beautiful child – and spirited too. She has the stamina and energy of a boy. She was thrilled by my tales of the Valkyries, Odin's maidens who ride invisible over the battle-field leading the slain warriors to their heaven – Valhalla.' Thorkell paused and glanced anxiously at Otto. The old man smiled but did not protest: he remembered all too well what had happened the last time he had objected to the skald's casual attitude towards religion. Thorkell grinned back and continued his account. 'And my stories of Norse heroines, the shield-maidens who fight as bravely as any man, have always been her favourite. This time they excited her so much that the Lord Bardolph forbade me to recount them in her presence – but she persuaded me whenever he was away! I hope our master settles this matter of the succession with Ulric the Bold. That child will make a fine Queen of all Alemannians. I can picture her now, leading her tribes into battle. I could compose many a great saga about her!'

Conrad could contain himself no longer. Since the first

mention of the Lady Matilda his excitement had grown. 'Thorkell, did you see any other young girl with the Lady Matilda?' he demanded.

'No, I do not remember any,' replied the skald. 'There are many children in the fortress but whenever I saw the Lady Matilda she was in the company of the older ladies who care for her.'

Conrad could not hide his disappointment. Otto, Thorkell and Roderic looked at one another in astonishment. 'But what is this interest in young girls?' inquired the skald, adding teasingly, 'Do you have a lady-love in the Lord Bardolph's court?'

Conrad was at once appalled at what he had done. How could he have made such a mistake and put his little Tilly in danger? And all to no purpose: he should have known she would never be allowed to sit in public in the company of the Lord Bardolph and the Lady Matilda. 'Please Thorkell – and you too, Otto and Roderic – pretend that I did not ask any questions. I do have a friend in the Lord Bardolph's household. She is very dear to me – I owe her so much – but if her master knew I dread to think what punishment might befall her. If she should come to any harm because of me ...'

Thorkell, seeing Conrad's distress, and realizing the significance of what the boy was saying, interrupted him to ask, 'Conrad, were you once a goatherd?'

'Yes,' replied the boy, surprised. 'I was a goatherd outside the Lord Bardolph's fortress.'

The skald smiled to himself and quickly adopted his usual comic manner. 'So tonight we have solved the mystery of how you acquired your learning and the books that Otto showed me. Have no fear,' he announced dramatically, 'for I am the last person to betray a fellow thief – especially one who steals in such a good cause. I shall not speak of your little lady-love to anyone.'

Otto and Roderic nodded their heads in agreement and

hastened to add their assurances. 'Your secret is safe with us,' they both said.

Warmed by the dying embers from the furnace, the four friends spent many a happy time together. Otto would reminisce on the past, Thorkell would sing his sagas and Roderic would entertain them with amusing tales of the people who visited the blacksmith's shop. Conrad alone had little to say; he was content to sit and listen. Yet try as he would he could not entirely ignore the fact that though he shared his evenings with his chosen comrades, his days were spent in preparation for a future which would be very different from theirs.

PART THREE

I

A dream realized

The cadets, now grown into sturdy youths, knelt at the altar rail as the Lord Gustavus's chaplain moved along the line blessing each one in turn. Behind the chaplain stood a smiling Brother Thomas and the tutor monks who had devoted so much of their time to their pupils. When the doors at the rear of the chapel opened, the cadets rose from their knees and, pausing for the chaplain and the monks to lead the way, filed outside to where Sigurd and their other tutors stood in the small courtyard waiting to join the procession. They made their way through the gates to the outer courtyard where a vast crowd of tribesmen was waiting for them. At Sigurd's command, the young men marched proudly forward into the centre of the parade ground and stood in line facing the assembled chieftains of the Alemannian tribes. The Lord Bardolph was not amongst them but the Lord Gustavus stood at their head.

Conrad suddenly felt uncomfortably warm, clad as he was in full armour: round iron helmet, metal ringed byrnie over hide tunic and trousers, and splinted metal greaves on his legs. His cheeks flushed as he became aware of the hundreds of eyes upon him. But these were not hostile eyes like those which had greeted him in that same square two and a half years before. These were the welcoming, approving eyes of the people who had gathered to witness this great occasion. Conrad knew he had no family amongst their number who had travelled many days to see him honoured, but somewhere in the throng his own special friends were present to give him their support – Otto, Roderic and Thorkell. This was the day he had longed for and worked for: the day he would be admitted into his master's tribe as a true warrior.

The Lord Gustavus raised his hand for silence and Sigurd announced the name of the first candidate. Ingram stepped forward. The Lord Gustavus confronted him and inquired, according to custom, whether he was qualified to become a warrior. Sigurd read out in a loud voice the details of Ingram's training and the high standards he had attained in all sections of his military education. When the list was completed, the Lord Gustavus proclaimed, 'I deem you worthy to be numbered among my tribal warriors.'

At his words, the youth fell to his knees and kissed the ring attached to the hilt of the sword the Lord Gustavus held out to him. Then he made his oath. 'I swear by Almighty God to honour, serve and obey you to my dying day and acknowledge that I owe total allegiance to you, my lord and my chieftain.' As Ingram got to his feet his father, who had been waiting a little distance behind the Lord Gustavus, approached and smiling proudly, presented his son with a shield, a spear and a sword.

Each cadet was called in turn to be formally questioned as to his abilities and to be accepted into his tribe. He then re-affirmed his loyalty to his chieftain, who was not in every case the Lord Gustavus. Boys from other Alemannian tribes who recognised the Lord Bardolph as King of all Alemannians were also trained at the villa. The cadet's father or near kinsman completed the ceremony with the customary gift of new weapons. Conrad was the last to be called. The Lord Gustavus conducted the interrogation and admittance rites and after Conrad had sworn his allegiance on the sword ring, it was the Lord Gustavus who also presented him with his arms. Conrad did not need to be told that Roderic alone would have made them: a magnificent embossed shield with metal rim, very different from his first shield which Otto had given him, a stout spear with shining head and a sword, its blade pattern-welded with a design like the backbone of a fish, which flashed in a myriad of colours in the sunlight. It was a moment to savour and remember forever.

As Conrad resumed his place beside his fellows, Sigurd, signifying the end of the ceremony, walked into the centre of the parade ground, raised his spear and turning a full circle, addressed the crowd. 'How say you?' he called out. 'Give your assent by voice of arms!' In reply, every tribesman present began to clash his spear or sword against his shield. Soon the air was filled with the noise as the Alemannians gave their assent to what had taken place before them, in the traditional manner.

The celebration feast which followed lasted the remainder of the day. Next morning, the Lord Gustavus lead his cavalcade – including his newest warriors – out through the villa gates to the cheers of a vast gathering of well-wishers. For Conrad, it was his dream realized; he felt he would burst with pride and joy. He had achieved his ambition: he was riding with the Lord Gustavus as one of his noble guard – a Companion in Arms. If he should die that day he knew he would die happy.

Ingram, who was riding beside Conrad, looked at him, grinned and shook his head. He had taken his elevation in his stride; as far as he was concerned his new status was his due. He was anxious only to get on with the profession for which he had been trained. 'I hope we fight our first battle soon,' he commented to Conrad as they left the villa behind them.

'Thorkell told me some good news last night,' said Conrad, jolted from his meditations. 'He has heard that the Franks are massing an army to attack us.'

'Who told him that?' Ingram demanded.

'He overheard some of the nobles talking,' Conrad replied. 'They were discussing a report by the Lord Gustavus's spies –

monks from our monastery who had been on a visit to a Frankish monastery. They saw the encampment not far from our borders. They said serfs and chieftains were arriving daily to swell the numbers.'

'Let us hope the reports are correct,' said Ingram earnestly. 'Perhaps this will be the great battle the Lord Gustavus has always anticipated, when we shall free ourselves from the Franks forever.'

'What an honour for us,' Conrad agreed.

The young men's prayers were to be only partly answered. Soon it was confirmed that they were on their way to join up with the rest of the Alemannian cavalry and infantry before advancing to meet the Franks. It was not, however, the battle to end all battles but merely another demand, under threat of arms, for payment of several years tribute owed by the Lords Bardolph and Gustavus to the Frankish monarch, their overlord. Ingram and Conrad were present, though out of earshot, when the Frankish envoys rode into the Alemannian stockade. The youths watched the proceedings with much interest.

'I wish I could hear what was being said,' Ingram complained.

'I can tell you what our master will say,' stated Thorkell as he joined the pair. 'He will assert that Alemannians recognise no overlord and warn them to be off before we annihilate them!'

The skald's prediction was confirmed when the Frank who had been doing most of the talking suddenly brandished his spear in the air and shouted something. War had obviously been declared! The Franks turned their mounts around and headed for their own camp with more speed and much less ceremony than when they had arrived.

'Now to action!' cried Ingram with undisguised pleasure.

Ingram's joy was short-lived. The Lord Gustavus summoned his former cadets to his tent and gave them orders which they least wanted to hear. 'It is not my intention to waste years of careful training on an unworthy enemy. The Franks have too many Berserks among their ranks: men who fight without armour, who make no effort to protect themselves but instead work themselves into a battle-frenzy and when the fever is upon them inflict many wounds upon our soldiers. We shall win, of course, but our casualties may be high at first. I did not spend time and effort on you to sacrifice you to madmen. You will take no part in this battle; instead you will observe the operation with me and add to your store of knowledge for the future.'

The reaction among the youths was unanimous and bitter disappointment. Ingram attempted to protest but one icy stare from his master rendered him speechless.

'It is useless to stake out the field against an unruly mob which has no discipline,' continued the general, 'so instead we must ensure that the fight takes place at a spot of our choosing. We shall prepare the ground beforehand to suit our purpose.'

Dawn of the next day saw the Alemannian army lined up on a plain facing the Frankish encampment and some distance away from it. Behind the Alemannians were low hills and it was here that the Lord Gustavus had chosen to position himself and his former cadets. There were signs that the Franks were preparing to come out and meet their foe. Ingram called to Conrad and pointed to a group in front of the Frankish tents who were bare-headed and stripped to the waist. It was just possible to make out their antics. They seemed to be gnawing at the rims of their shields and reeling about in a frenzied dance.

Conrad nodded to Ingram. 'Yes, I see them. They must be the Berserks working themselves into a fever.'

The Lord Gustavus heard his remark. 'You are correct. It is

a practice the Franks have copied from some of the Norse fighters; a few may even be Norsemen. They have had no difficulty in adopting the habit since it is in the nature of all Franks to fight as though possessed by the Devil. You will see that we, for our part, have drawn up our infantry on flat ground behind a shield-wall, with our cavalry protecting our flanks. This should fool the Frankish commanders into thinking that we intend to fight a conventional infantry battle like most of the tribes of Northern Europe.'

The Franks did not pause to consider before launching their attack. They descended upon the Alemannians in a rushing yelling mass, covering the large expanse of ground between their camp and their enemy at top speed. As they ran they hurled their Angon javelins before them at the shields of their adversaries and also their throwing-axes. It was just as Otto had described when he had given Conrad his first weapons. The young men feared for the stalwart Alemannian warriors, standing shoulder to shoulder behind their shield-wall. The screaming Franks must have been a terrifying spectacle. Now the Alemannians retaliated and flung their own axes and spears at the advancing horde. The surge was scarcely checked, so eager were the ferocious fighters to get to grips with their opponents. To the dismay of the young observers, the shield-wall began to pull back, especially at the centre where Carlo's Company of criminals had been positioned to take the brunt of the enemy's fury. The war-cries of the Franks grew louder as they gained the upper hand. Suddenly, the ranks broke altogether and about a hundred Alemannians turned and fled. The young watchers, appalled at the prospect of defeat, stood up in their stirrups for a better view.

Then Conrad noticed a smile on the Lord Gustavus's face. 'It is a feigned withdrawal,' he whispered to Ingram.

'Yes, I suspected as much,' agreed the youth, 'ever since I realized only a proportion of our forces was on the field. The remainder must be lying in wait somewhere.'

If any of the Franks had thought he was being lured into a trap he would have been powerless to stop the tide of his jubilant charging comrades. They chased the fleeing Alemannians straight into a gap between the low hills. It soon became apparent to the onlookers that their own tribesmen were following two clearly marked paths, one each side of the depression. Within minutes, almost all of them were safely under cover having dived into previously prepared dugouts. Their pursuers were in confusion, cries of victory changing to screams of pain. The whole area between the hills, except for the tracks which the Alemannians had taken, was littered with obstructions. The Franks disappeared into potholes; they ran into sharpened stakes carefully camouflaged behind greenery; they stepped onto metal spikes liberally strewn in the long grass. At the same time, they were assailed from above by a hail of arrows let loose by Alemannian archers, hidden until then at vantage points along the hillside. Those warriors who had been the bait to entice the Franks, once more joined in the fray, hurling axes and spears from the safety of their trenches. There was one more additional threat to come: horse-archers held in reserve at the far end of the shallow valley began their run in two columns, one along each of the unobstructed paths. Their deadly missiles brought absolute terror to the remaining Franks. As panic spread those who were still able, turned and attempted to escape the way they had come. They found their retreat blocked by the rest of the Alemannian infantry who had reformed their shield-wall across the full width of the narrow valley. The Alemannian cavalry, which at the commencement of the battle on the plain had stood on the flanks, was now deployed directly behind the infantry and fired its arrows over the heads of the shield-bearers. The Franks were completely surrounded.

As the massacre continued, the Lord Gustavus, who had watched the proceedings without comment until then, delivered his observations in the same tone of voice he had used in the classroom when discussing mock battles with wooden figures. 'As you will see, gentlemen, it is not difficult to induce a foe such as the Franks to leave the level ground which is most suited to his style of fighting, for an area which would give us the superior advantage. Our people worked well to prepare the ground in such little time, do you not think?'

The youths muttered their agreement but shocked by the magnitude of the bloodshed, they could scarcely drag their eyes or their thoughts from the carnage taking place below them. The general continued, apparently oblivious to the wanton butchery. 'You will note that we made full use of our archers, concealed in the hillsides. Many northern tribes despise the use of archers, claiming that it is cowardly and unmanly to fire shots from a distance instead of exchanging blows in hand to hand combat. Ignore such nonsense! Victory is all that counts and it should be achieved with as little danger to your own men as possible. Unnecessary casualties are wasteful and could result in defeat if you have to engage another enemy immediately after the first. Our horse-archers too are the supreme example of military prowess. The Franks, you will have observed, had no cavalry of any kind to challenge them. The Frankish leaders rode into battle but, as I explained to you at the commencement of your training, they dismounted to fight. Regretfully, victory against them is hollow. I must seek out a more worthy adversary for our next encounter. Let us hope that the Frankish camp yields just reward for our efforts. Come, gentlemen, there is no more to be learned.'

II

Ulric the Bold – and Raoulbrun!

'Ulric the Bold ... We are to challenge Ulric the Bold?'
Conrad's eyes shone with excitement.

'How do you know this, Thorkell?' demanded Ingram.

'I am a skald; I know everything!' Thorkell quipped as he
squatted down beside the other two and stretched his hands out
towards the campfire. 'Our master thinks that since we had few
losses against the Franks, we should attack Ulric while our men
are still flushed with victory. This could put the leadership of
the Alemannians beyond dispute.'

'I have never understood why there should be any dispute,'
said Conrad. 'Are the lords Bardolph, Gustavus and Ulric not
brothers? Surely their father must have decided which one of
them should inherit his title?'

'That is what they dispute!' answered Thorkell. 'The Lord
Bardolph claims his father, King Theodoric, wished him to be
the ruler on his death and the Lord Gustavus says he was a
witness to that decision. The Lord Ulric was the child of King
Theodoric's old age – and not by the mother of his two elder
sons either! Ulric maintains that the old king changed his mind
and decreed in public that he wanted him, Ulric, to succeed
him.'

'How is it that you know so much, Thorkell?' There was a
hint of exasperation in Ingram's tone. He was one of the few
people who often felt irritated by the skald's manner.

'I cannot resist a good story,' Thorkell answered, unruf-
fled. 'I have the nose to smell one out! It has taken me a long

time and I have had to question many people to get to the heart of this one but it has been worthwhile, I assure you.'

'Do not interrupt him, Ingram,' Conrad protested. 'Let him tell us what he knows.' Ingram shrugged his shoulders and pretended that he was not at all curious, but he listened just the same.

'It seems that when the Lord Gustavus was about your age,' said Thorkell, settling down to his tale in earnest, 'his father made peace with the Burgundians. He even married the Lord Bardolph off to Raoulbrun's daughter, though she was little more than a child at the time. The Lord Gustavus soon became bored – and there was some talk that he wished to be betrothed himself, to a lady in his mother's household but King Theodoric, of course, refused his request – and he went off to Byzantium where he knew there would be plenty of fighting. His father too looked around for a diversion since there was no war with the Burgundians to occupy him. He soon found one – at the stronghold of one of his tribal chiefs! When the chief's daughter was with child, it is said that King Theodoric persuaded the Church to annul his marriage to Queen Clothilda, the mother of the lords Bardolph and Gustavus, so that he could marry his young love, the Lady Almira.'

'How could he get an annulment?' asked Ingram in disbelief.

'By claiming that Queen Clothilda was already legally bound to another when he wed her!' announced Thorkell dramatically. He continued in confidential tones. 'She too had been the daughter of an Alemannian chieftain and it seems that since childhood she had been fond of one of her father's nobles – the commander of his forces. Many said they were lawfully betrothed. Even after her marriage to King Theodoric, she took every opportunity to make long visits to her family – and to her lover, it was claimed! If you have ever seen the Lord Bardolph and the Lord Gustavus standing side by side, or if you know them both well as I do, you will not be surprised that it was rumoured that they had only their mother in common.

Certainly, they are quite unlike one another in both looks and temperament.'

'Enough of your insinuations,' snapped Ingram. 'You slur the good name of our general.'

'I mean no disrespect; I only relate the facts as I have heard them.' The skald remained unperturbed and continued his story enthusiastically. 'King Theodoric told the Church – at the same time handing over a generous donation, so it is said – that he had proof that Queen Clothilda had been betrothed to her father's general as a child. Now whether his evidence was accepted and the annulment granted, and whether he went through a marriage ceremony with the Lady Almira, we do not know for certain – each side gives its own version of what happened – but what is indisputable is that King Theodoric was found dead with his neck broken!' Thorkell paused for effect, a gleam of delight in his eyes that his tale was captivating his listeners. 'The Lord Bardolph, supported by his mother, Queen Clothilda, immediately claimed the leadership of the Alemannians. The Lord Gustavus was still abroad and knew nothing of these events for several years. The Lady Almira, stating that a marriage had taken place and that she was the lawful queen of the murdered Theodoric, demanded that her young son, Ulric, be acknowledged as king. Her father and her tribe took up her cause, as did several other tribes, and there has been intermittent armed strife ever since.'

'Why did they not fight it out to the bitter end years ago?' asked Conrad.

Thorkell considered carefully before replying. 'You must remember that for many years Ulric was a child and depended upon others to fight for him. When he was your age, he too went abroad to learn his profession and for several years was a mercenary. The experience has stood him in good stead. Since he returned and took personal control of his army, the struggle against outside enemies has always taken priority. The Alemannians, Ulric's tribes as well as Bardolph's, have been at war almost continuously with the Burgundians for years. The border territories have changed hands many times. Then there have been the Franks; all Alemannians are united in their hatred of the Franks. What is more, the tribes have been almost equally divided between those who support the Lord Bardolph and those who support the Lord Ulric. Whenever there has been time for an internal confrontation, Alemannian against Alemannian, the two factions have been evenly matched.'

'But surely our general must be the better commander,' Ingram contended. 'He should be able to defeat Ulric the Bold easily.'

'He is the better commander,' agreed Thorkell, 'but not so much better. He has never been able to rout Ulric's forces as he has the Burgundians and the Franks. Ulric is too clever and cunning himself to suffer any decisive defeat. As I have told you, he too served his time as a mercenary and he knows almost as many tricks as our master. It is also my opinion that both men enjoy pitting their wits against one another. They look upon their encounters as moves in a personal game.'

The skald's conclusions seemed correct for the Lord Gustavus appeared to be in an almost jovial mood as he advanced in the direction of the Lord Ulric's estates. For once, the general's spy system failed him: Ulric the Bold was not at home but away, together with the greater part of his army, pursuing a territorial argument of his own with a cousin of Raoulbrun the Burgundian. As Thorkell told later, the Lord Gustavus refused to accept this disappointment. He set about ensuring that Ulric would return without delay, by ravaging his poorly defended lands in all directions.

This was a form of warfare for which Conrad had no liking. 'These peasants have just endured a long hard winter and now, just as their crops are beginning to show above the ground, we lay waste their fields.'

'No, Conrad,' Ingram corrected, 'we lay waste Ulric the Bold's fields. We pillage and burn his lands and for good reason. Remember also, that he would not hesitate to do the same to the Lord Gustavus's lands if it suited his purpose.' Conrad was not convinced and was unwise enough to voice his opinions where they could be overheard by those in a position of authority. Very soon he received orders, issued by the Lord Gustavus, to lead one of the forays the very next day. Ingram was not sympathetic. 'You should have realized this would happen, Conrad. You know our general will warrant no insurrection among his followers. Mind you bring back enough plunder – he is testing your loyalty.'

The men Conrad was to command were no more enthusiastic about his appointment than he was. It was a novel and an unwelcome experience for them to ride out with a member of the illustrious Companions – albeit a very young one – at their head. They suspected that their lord did not trust them. The day was spent riding from settlement to settlement, searching under threat of arms, the hovels of the serfs and the dwellings and the storehouses of wealthier men. When everything worthwhile had been found the soldiers departed, trailing burning bracken and branches behind them as they galloped through the fields. When the party returned to their own stockade that evening, they had carts loaded with spoils and a commander seething with bitter memories which he was sure would never be erased.

'That I, a peasant, should rob poor peasants ... They clung to my reins, begging me not to steal their food; to spare their fowls and their livestock for the sake of their children. But I ordered my men to take everything they had,' cried Conrad, putting his head in his hands.

'You had no choice,' said Ingram, placing a comforting hand on Conrad's shoulder. 'You had to obey your orders otherwise all you had strived for would have been for nothing. The Lord Gustavus would not have tolerated disobedience.'

Conrad could find no consolation in Ingram's argument. 'I have seen that same desperate look in my own mother's eyes when soldiers sacked our village. I know what it is to starve – my mother starved to death. I know what it is to plead for food. I know the despair those people felt today. Why, Ingram, why? I cannot understand our lord's reasoning. How can he expect these tribes to turn against Ulric and support the Lord Bardolph after the devastation we have caused? They must regard us as nothing more than marauders – bands of armed robbers!'

'I do not know what is in our master's mind,' said Ingram, sighing, 'but I do know that you brood too much; you suffer too much; you worry about others too much. I fear you will never make a great general, Conrad. To be like our Lord Gustavus, you must be as ruthless and as single-minded as he is – you must care only for victory.'

The effect of the forays upon Ulric the Bold was the desired one. News soon reached the Lord Gustavus that Ulric and his army was in pursuit. At once, he gave orders to break camp and as he headed in the direction of his own lands he was careful to leave a trail of havoc and scorched earth in his wake for the Lord Ulric to follow.

'It is sound military tactics,' Ingram assured a distressed Conrad. 'Our master must have decided where he wants to fight the battle and, as with the Franks, he is luring Ulric the Bold to the spot.'

At last the Lord Gustavus called a halt and turned his forces round to await the arrival of his half-brother. He had chosen to make his stand on a plain between two ranges of low hills. He drew up his infantry in the centre, forming a shield-square, with mounted units on either flank. Behind each group of low hills he concealed his reserve cavalry, Conrad, Ingram and the other un-blooded Companions among them. From their hiding place, the youths heard the horns sound for the commencement of the battle. They strained to make out what was going on, frustrated at being unable to see the action. They waited, impatient for their moment to come, until the signal was given and they galloped out onto the battlefield at the same time as their counterparts who had been lurking behind the hills on the opposite side of the plain.

The two cavalry units joined up and attacked Ulric's forces from the rear. It seemed to Conrad that the classic manoeuvre of double envelopment was going to be as successful in practice as it had always been in theory in the classroom. The enemy was wedged between the two firing lines of the Lord Gustavus. Ulric the Bold would have no alternative but to surrender or see his entire army wiped out – or so it appeared to the youths. At that moment, however, the air resounded to the notes of more horns and Conrad turned to see horse-archers thundering towards him from the direction of a forest where Ulric must have positioned them, screened from view, until needed.

The battle raged for some hours once each side had brought all its reserves into action. First Gustavus gained the upper hand and then Ulric. Both commanders, surrounded by their personal bodyguard, took part in the fray. As the day wore on, heavy casualties were sustained on either side. Horns sounded for combat to cease when the light began to fade. All was quiet, save for the moaning of the wounded, as a group of men bearing a flag of truce rode up to the Lord Gustavus. By chance, Ingram and Conrad, covered in scratches and bruises but otherwise unharmed, were close enough to hear the verbal exchanges.

The leader of the petitioners was obviously Ulric the Bold. Though dirty and bloodstained, he was an imposing figure. He was as tall as the Lord Gustavus and looked strong and virile. Although still in his twenties, he had the appearance of a seasoned warrior. His skin was dark and swarthy – Thorkell the ever-knowledgeable, had insisted during a previous story-telling that Ulric's maternal grandmother had been a black princess taken prisoner on some raiding expedition – and a scar ran the length of one cheek. He glowered tight-lipped at Gustavus as his henchman announced, 'Ulric, King of the Alemannians, would speak with the Lord Gustavus.'

Sigurd gave the response. 'The Lord Gustavus, commander-in-chief to Bardolph, King of all Alemannians, welcomes the Lord Ulric.'

The two generals ushered their mounts forward and confronted one another, undisguised hatred burning in their eyes. Ulric the Bold opened the negotiations. 'We have reached deadlock, brother, and have both suffered severe losses. News has reached me that the Burgundians have taken advantage of the situation to attack my territories to the west. Since you have already ravaged the remainder of my lands, I must stop these invaders or my people will starve. Regretfully, therefore, I must withdraw my forces. I would advise you to allow us to depart without further bloodshed since it is in your interest to return to defend your own lands as quickly as possible. No doubt, Raoulbrun will be as anxious as his cousin to reap the benefit of our conflict. He may at this very moment be launching an offensive in your absence.'

'Very well,' replied the Lord Gustavus. 'I agree that it would be prudent for both of us to cease hostilities until another more propitious occasion. But there will be another time I promise you, my lord. I shall not rest until you and all those tribes misguided enough to follow you, acknowledge my brother Bardolph as King of all Alemannians.'

Ulric the Bold reacted vehemently to these words. 'Never, never shall that day dawn ... Bardolph murdered my father; you and he brought about my mother's death also by your campaign of vilification. You branded her harlot; you branded me bastard, and now you rob my people. You have much to answer for. I will avenge my parents and my people; that I vow before God and my brave warriors. Take heed, Gustavus. I give you fair warning. Do not venture on my lands again.'

The Lord Gustavus's face, normally impassive, was flushed with rage. 'Go, Ulric, before I change my mind and fight you to the death!'

'I go, but remember,' Ulric the Bold shouted defiantly for all to hear, 'vengeance shall be mine!'

The next morning saw the battlefield almost clear of the dead and the wounded. Ulric had already departed with as many fit troops as he could muster to counter the Burgundian incursions. He left behind the walking wounded and his camp-followers to deal with those more seriously injured. As soon as his adversary was out of sight, the Lord Gustavus gave orders for all the wagons in the area to be commandeered. These were loaded with his own casualties while the dead were hastily buried. The convoy set out with as much speed as weary men and horses could manage. Carlo's men, as usual, marched some distance ahead of the main column followed closely by their guards, bows ready-strung to shoot the enemy or their charges if the latter were foolish enough to try to escape. Out-riders were positioned at intervals on either flank with instructions to keep a sharp watch for Raoulbrun the Burgundian whom the general now seemed convinced would attack once he learned how weakened they were after their encounter with Ulric the Bold.

All day the scouts searched diligently but found no signs of any hostile activity. By late afternoon, many of the exhausted warriors were on the point of collapse. The Lord Gustavus refused to make camp because he hoped to reach the border of his homeland by nightfall. The poor light, together with their fatigue, rendered the scouts less sharp-eyed and they failed to notice Raoulbrun's men waiting to ambush them. When the

Burgundian missiles, fired from the trees and the undergrowth on either side of the road, landed among the Alemannians – mainly upon Carlo's Company – chaos and confusion reigned, but only for a few moments. Panic did not spread among the well-disciplined troops. At once they utilised the wagons as temporary barricades and retaliated with their own barrage of arrows. In no time at all, the cavalry units which had been riding out of sight on either side of the main convoy to foil just such a plot as this, arrived on the scene and began to harass the Burgundians from behind. Suddenly, weariness had vanished and every man found renewed strength. While the cavalry and some of the infantry engaged the enemy, the remainder retreated to higher ground nearby and threw up ramparts and erected a stockade with lightning speed.

As the refuge was being constructed, Conrad fought as bravely as any man to beat off the attackers. He reeled his horse among them and delivered sword blows on all sides. Many attempts were made to unseat him and eventually, a hefty Burgundian succeeded. The youth was as confident in hand-to-hand combat as he had been mounted, and he managed to defeat all challengers until he found himself up against – Raoulbrun! The shock of being confronted by his former master caused him to momentarily lower his guard. It was all the opportunity the Burgundian general needed. He aimed a blow at Conrad's neck which would have beheaded him had he not in the split-second he saw the blade coming towards him, leapt back. He felt a sudden pain in his upper arm and almost simultaneously, another in the back of his head as he hit the rocky ground and blackness enveloped him.

III

The life-stone

When Conrad regained his senses, Thorkell and Ingram were bending over him. They both smiled with relief and the skald joked, 'I feared the hero of my greatest saga had deserted me before he had made me famous.'

As Conrad's vision cleared his one thought was of the enemy. 'Where are the Burgundians?' he muttered.

'Put to flight!' Ingram assured him. 'They underestimated us. They thought we were too weakened to put up a fight but we showed them how tough we are.'

'You are safe now inside the stockade,' said Thorkell. 'But lie still. You have a bad wound in your arm and it is yet to be cauterised.' Mercifully for Conrad, he lost consciousness again just as the skald took the red-hot iron from the fire.

Next morning the temporary stockade was dismantled and the homeward trek continued. The Lord Gustavus was anxious to reach a proper defensive position inside his own borders in case Raoulbrun should make another attempt to ambush him. Once they had reached a site which had a permanent stockade – it had been built years before to house a garrison at a border crossing – the physicians persuaded the general that the badly wounded, whose numbers had increased after the most recent encounter, would die if they did not rest. Having lost too many warriors already, the Lord Gustavus agreed that it would be politic to make camp there for a few weeks. He sent a messenger to the villa for more help with the wounded and Otto was one of the men who responded.

Otto was distressed to find that Conrad's wound, in spite of Thorkell's prompt treatment, was showing no signs of healing and that the youth had developed a fever.

'Did you find the plants Conrad told you about? Are you sure they were the right ones?' Ingram asked as he and Thorkell joined an anxious Otto.

'Yes, I think I found the plants Conrad had described,' replied the old man, 'but he seemed so confused and weak when he told me about them that they might not have been the correct ones.'

Thorkell knelt down beside Conrad who was barely conscious, and felt his burning forehead. 'As I see it, there is only one way to cure him,' he announced. 'Plants have been of no use and the physician can suggest only bleeding and purging; his ultimate answer is amputation and in his weakened state, that would kill our friend. Conrad is convinced that it was Raoulbrun who wounded him and that it was his sword which struck the blow. I know his sword well. He took it from a sacrificial mound of captured weapons that the ancients had made to their gods. It had rested for hundreds of years in consecrated ground ...'

'Thorkell,' Ingram protested, 'this is no time to boast of how much you know – and how could you possibly know such things unless Raoulbrun was one of the many masters you have served ...'

The skald hastily interrupted. 'I am not boasting. I only wanted to explain that I know that the sword has a life-stone.' This information produced an instant reaction in his listeners.

'I have heard of life-stones. They made the swords' owners victorious.' said Ingram.

'Pagan superstition,' muttered Otto, but without conviction.

'Superstition perhaps, but have your prayers been answered or those of the Lord Gustavus's chaplain?' Thorkell asked. Otto looked away, unable to contradict the skald. 'We have tried everything else; we have no alternative but to try this. You are right, Ingram, in that a life-stone was a talisman, to protect and bring luck to the sword's owner, but it also had the power to heal.'

'Then explain what we have to do,' said Ingram impatiently.

'We must rub the life-stone over the area of Conrad's arm, where it is red and swollen, then bind it to the arm and its magical powers will cause the wound to heal.'

'But how can we do that when Raoulbrun has the sword?' asked the youth. 'Surely any life-stone will do?'

'No!' replied Thorkell emphatically. 'Only the stone that belongs to the weapon which inflicted the injury can bring about a cure.'

'You speak nonsense, Skald,' retorted Ingram. 'It is pointless – and cruel – to mention such a means of helping Conrad when there is no way of getting the sword.'

'Of course there is a way.' Thorkell's eyes gleamed. 'I shall get the sword tonight.'

'How?' demanded Ingram.

'I shall steal it from Raoulbrun's tent!'

The sound of the Burgundian's name roused Conrad from his fitful sleep. 'Is Raoulbrun coming?' he asked weakly.

'No,' answered Ingram, 'but Thorkell has a plan to make you better. We shall return by morning.'

As Conrad drifted back to sleep, Thorkell said, 'Wrong, Master Ingram. *I* shall return by morning.' Then he added kindly, 'It will not be too difficult for one to gain access unnoticed to the Burgundian camp but it may be impossible for two. Stay here with Otto and see to it that our young friend does not give up the struggle before I have completed my heroic deed.'

Thorkell returned just as the sun was rising, bearing his prize wrapped in a woman's gown.

'How did you do it?' gasped Ingram.

'I shall enjoy recounting the tale in all its fine detail, later. First, the purpose of my escapade … Is he still with us?' Thorkell laid a hand on Conrad's fevered brow.

'Yes, thanks be to God,' replied Otto, 'but he has been racked with pain all night and bathed in sweat.'

'Take the covers from his arm while I prepare,' instructed Thorkell. Then he hesitated and looked at Otto. 'My friend,' he said quietly, 'this sword and scabbard was probably first owned by a Norseman and made in praise of Odin. I ought to offer a silent prayer to him to release the powers of the life-stone.'

Otto nodded his head in resignation. 'Do whatever you think you should. I, of all people, cannot bear to see one so young lose his arm, and if he should lose his life, it would be like losing my own son.'

'Trust me and trust in the sword,' said Thorkell. He carefully un-wrapped the precious weapon and reverently balancing it on the palms of both hands, he raised it on high, at the same time bowing his head and making his secret devotions. The sun glinted on the crystal life-stone as it swung from the scabbard beneath the hilt and made it sparkle. After a few moments Thorkell opened his eyes. He laid the sword on the ground and carefully prised the stone from its gold mount. It was shaped like a flattened disc, with a hole through the centre. Ingram had exposed Conrad's wound and the skald gently rubbed the crystal over the inflamed skin and then bound it against the arm. Conrad stirred, his agony plain to see. 'I do not wish to hurt you,' Thorkell assured him, his voice full of compassion, 'but this is the only way I know to make you well again. Your wound will heal now, Conrad, and your pain and fever will disappear. See, this is the sword which Raoulbrun used to injure you and its life-stone will take away the wound.'

Conrad struggled to speak. 'What are you saying, Thorkell? I do not understand.'

Ingram explained. 'Thorkell went to Raoulbrun's camp last night and stole his sword for you.'

'Brave deed, eh?' said Otto, smiling. 'For an avowed coward ...'

As realization dawned, Conrad was overwhelmed by Thorkell's generosity and the enormity of the risk he had taken. 'You could have been killed, yet you were prepared to sacrifice yourself for me.' He was so weak that tears glistened in his eyes.

To hide his own embarrassment, Thorkell resorted to banter. 'I would do anything to safeguard my livelihood. Have you forgotten? You are to be the hero of my greatest saga.'

'How can I ever repay you? How can I ever thank you?' whispered Conrad.

'You can thank me by getting well again. I shall regard it as an insult if you dare to die after the danger I have faced for you.'

Conrad managed a smile. 'I give you my word, Thorkell. I will get better.'

The wound began to mend, Conrad's fever left him and within a few days he was strong enough to get to his feet. Thorkell was triumphant at his recovery and celebrated by composing a song about his own adventure. The entire Alemannian army was cheered by the account of how he had tricked Raoulbrun. In the song, the skald told how he had lain in wait for the young female camp followers and had chanced upon a group on their way to entertain the Burgundian soldiers. In the darkness, he had stealthily and silently snatched one of the women, disrobed her, bound and gagged her, dressed himself in her attire and caught up with her companions as they entered the Burgundian camp. He sang of how he had found Raoulbrun's tent and hidden outside until the general was fuddled with wine and his noble followers were in a stupor on the floor. Then he had entered bearing another flagon of wine. He described how delighted Raoulbrun had been to see the "lady"; how he had told "her" how lonely he felt since he had out-drunk his companions; how he had pulled "her" onto his knee; how he had fondled "her" hair and complimented "her" on "her" fair curls, and how "she" had struck him on the head with the flagon of wine and had watched him join his henchmen under the table before relieving him of his sword and making a hasty retreat.

IV

'Vengeance is mine!'

Thorkell was so pleased with his composition and the acclaim which it brought him that he resolved to be content with the fame alone and presented Raoulbrun's sword – the life-stone restored to its mount – to his master, the Lord Gustavus. The latter, seeing the elated mood of his men following Thorkell's daring venture, decided to take the opportunity to punish Raoulbrun further for his effrontery in trying to ambush him. Three weeks after the skald's escapade, in the afternoon, the army prepared to move out. They were to cover the distance between the Alemannian and Burgundian camps by sunset, surround the enemy during the night and make a surprise attack at dawn – a copy, in fact, of the plan Raoulbrun had had three years before which had lead to Conrad's change of fortune.

The Alemannian cavalry and infantry were inspected by the Lord Gustavus before departing for the Burgundian lines. When he caught sight of Conrad, armoured and mounted, the general rode up to him. 'This is to be a lightning raid; I want only fit men to take part. You will remain behind with the others who are not yet completely recovered from their wounds.'

'But, my lord,' protested Conrad, dismayed, 'I *am* fully recovered. I want to fight.'

'You will obey my orders as you have sworn to do!' snapped the general. 'I am leaving you in command of the camp. Guard it well. We have wagons loaded with equipment here and months of supplies – including those we won from Ulric the Bold. In particular, keep a careful watch for that rebel; he has pledged himself to avenge the forays we made on his lands. Let no one into the stockade whilst we are gone.' Without further ado, the Lord Gustavus raised his arm and cried, 'Forward to victory!'

Conrad sat dejected, astride his horse, as his comrades rode by him. Many, including Ingram and Thorkell, gave him a sympathetic wave of the hand as they passed. When the last wagons, carrying the physician and his assistants, had disappeared from view, he made an effort to hide his disappointment and gave orders for the gates to be secured and sentries to be posted around the palisade. For a few hours, he rode slowly through the stockade finding some comfort from the fact that he had been entrusted with the command of the camp and planning what he would do if Ulric should launch a surprise attack. As the evening wore on, Conrad resigned himself to the fact that he was not going to be so lucky; there would be no glory for him, just a long night spent envying his friends who would be in the thick of the action by morning.

He dismounted and threw himself on the ground with his back against a tree. Soon he began to feel thoroughly disgruntled. His master had treated him unfairly. Did he think him a weakling? Of course he had the strength to fight and to fight well. Was his general implying that he had not fought well against the Burgundians? Did he think he had been wounded through his own negligence? Did he think he had no prowess as a warrior? Did he not value his skills in action? By the time Otto joined him, Conrad was in a very dark humour indeed.

The old man had been feeling his years of late and had been thankful to be left behind and spared another exertion. At any other time Conrad would have welcomed him warmly but so intent was he on indulging his self-pity that he barely returned Otto's greeting. Hurt by Conrad's coolness, the Axe-man said nothing for a while but then realizing and understanding how aggrieved the youth felt at being left behind, he attempted to divert his thoughts.

'Conrad, our lord has promised me that after this year's campaigning ends, I may retire from soldiering. He is to give me my own land close to the villa. Is that not good news, Conrad?'

The youth tried to reply with enthusiasm but he still found it impossible to keep his anger and frustration out of his voice. 'It is good news, Otto, but only what you deserve after all your years of service.'

'Just think,' mused the old man, 'me, a farmer! I never thought I would see the day when I should be grateful for such an offer. It is not in the nature of us Alemannians to toil in the fields for our rewards when we can win them so easily and gloriously in battle. But old age must have mellowed me for I am glad to exchange blood for sweat. Of course, I shall not cease to fight altogether: if ever our lord's estates are threatened, I shall defend them to the last breath in my body ...'

Conrad was saved the trouble of replying because at that moment he was hailed by a sentry. 'Wagons approaching!'

The youth leapt to his feet and climbed the wooden ladder at the side of the gates. Eight covered wagons were trundling towards the stockade, their gaily dressed occupants announcing their arrival as loudly as they could. Attracted by the unmistakable sound of female laughter, the soldiers rushed to the palisade and fought for every peep-hole that existed between the wooden stakes. They stood on one another's backs for a better view or clambered up the walls and clung precariously from the top. The wagons came to a halt before the entrance to the stockade and while the ladies flaunted themselves before the defenders, calling and waving to them, the leader of the party jumped down from his vehicle and walked up to the gates. Catching sight of Conrad, richly clad in hide and mail, he bowed low and addressed him.

'My lord, as you see we are a company of humble players

and entertainers. We crave your indulgence. We are journeying to the high pass over the mountains. It is almost dark and we have found no safe place to shelter for the night; we dare not travel further. I beg you to grant us your protection. I hear there are many robbers abroad. You would not want these defenceless young women to suffer at the hands of rough vagabonds. Let us rest inside your stockade. Our ladies will feel safe among such brave and gallant warriors.'

The brave and gallant warriors clamoured their agreement and implored Conrad to give his permission. There was only one dissenter – Otto. 'Do not listen to them, Conrad,' he pleaded. 'It may be a trick and, even if it is not, the Lord Gustavus would never allow them inside his camp: the Church denounces such people.'

Conrad was torn by indecision. He knew that Otto spoke the truth: the Lord Gustavus would never approve of entertainers. Yet would he leave women unprotected; out in the night to be preyed upon by evil men? Was that the action of a Christian? As Conrad deliberated, his eyes fell upon the young woman who sat in the nearest wagon. She was raven-haired and black-eyed; she had an alluring smile. Her master saw that she had captured the young man's attention and he surreptitiously beckoned her forward. She alighted and approached Conrad, gazing up at him seductively.

'May I present the Princess Griselda,' said the leader. 'We are travelling to the court of the King of the Longobards where she is a great favourite. She dances for His Majesty every night – is that not so, my dear?' The princess curtseyed low by way of acquiescence. Her master continued his wheedling. 'What a tragedy if any harm should befall this beautiful creature. She will dance for you as repayment for your protection; all my company will entertain you, my lord, to show our gratitude. We have jugglers, acrobats, musicians, singers and dancers, as well as fresh food and wine to share with you, our saviours.'

By this time, the Alemannian soldiers were pounding on

the palisade, threatening to force down the timbers from the inside. Conrad reasoned with himself: this was not the villa but a border stockade; it held no secrets which could be divulged to an enemy and there was no monastery or settlement nearby to which he could direct the company. Surely if he were here, the Lord Gustavus would make an exception and grant the request? Again Otto tried to intervene, only to be pushed aside by others, bawling and shouting, demanding that the players be allowed to enter. Some even ran to the gates and seemed about to unbar them – with or without leave. Conrad did not know what to do. He looked down at Otto and his hand went to the hilt of his sword. He half drew the weapon, hesitated then thrust it back into its scabbard. He could not kill his own men in such a cause. 'Open the gates,' he shouted. With a cheer, his command was obeyed; the soldiers ran out and joyfully led the wagons inside. Otto looked at Conrad, sighed, and walked slowly away.

The newcomers prepared a feast straightaway and as the Alemannians sat around the campfire, plied them with food and wine. Their leader treated Conrad like a king, sitting beside him, introducing the members of his company as they appeared, and refilling his cup whenever he drank from it. Conrad had never seen jugglers and acrobats before and was amazed at the feats the men could perform. But it was Princess Griselda – the greatest dancer in the world, her master claimed – who captivated him completely with her charms. The musicians played a melody, the like of which the youth had never heard before. Slowly, the young woman began to sway rhythmically before him, letting the firelight glow on the silky skin of her arms and neck. Conrad was enchanted and could not take his eyes from her. Gradually, the pace of the music increased and she began to whirl around the fire. Faster, faster went the music; faster, faster danced the girl. The earth seemed to be revolving with her skirts. Then, suddenly, through the haze Conrad saw shadows moving in the background: men climbing stealthily down from the covered wagons. He tried to get up, to call out a warning, but as he struggled to his feet, cup in hand, the vibrations inside his head erupted and he fell to the ground, muttering as he drifted into oblivion, 'The Trojan Horse.'

The rain pattering on his face made Conrad open his eyes to the cold light of dawn. Everywhere was shrouded in mist. He shivered and tried to raise himself from the damp ground. His head was throbbing relentlessly. He forced himself to look around. Beside him men were stirring, moaning as they awakened. Conrad stared at them stupefied and then slowly, memories of the previous night came back to him. Making an enormous effort he managed to struggle to his feet and stagger towards the stockade gates. To his horror they stood wide open. The tracks made by the wheels of many heavily-laden wagons were clearly visible on the muddy ground. Near to the entrance, scrawled in the dirt and not yet washed away by the rain, were the words, "Vengeance is mine".

'Ulric!' groaned Conrad. He turned, panic mounting inside him, and stumbled in the direction of the area set aside for the storage of the supply wagons. The place was completely empty. His head began to spin again and he lurched towards a tree for support. In so doing, he tripped over something lying in his path. He dropped to his knees beside it and waited for his vision to clear. It was Otto, lying in a pool of blood, his trusty axe still clasped in his hand. Shaking, and sobbing his friend's name, Conrad hugged the lifeless body to him. 'Why, why did I not listen to you?' he moaned. 'You have never failed me. Why did I not heed your warning? I have killed you just as surely as if I had struck the blow.'

Conrad was still crouched on the ground cradling the old

man's head in his arms when he became aware of another presence. Slowly he raised his tear-stained face and saw his master towering over him. The Lord Gustavus said nothing; he had no need for his look of cold disdain expressed all he felt. Heavy hands fell upon Conrad, tore off his mail shirt and leather tunic and ripped apart the back of his cloth undershirt. He was hauled to his feet and tied to the nearest tree. He made no protest; he was oblivious to all that was happening. Nothing penetrated his misery.

'My lord, I beg you to spare Conrad's life,' Ingram pleaded. 'He was weak from his wounds – you yourself forbade him to join the raid because of his weakness. He would never have allowed this to happen if he had been well.'

'Silence!' commanded the general. 'He neglected his duty as an officer. He knew – you all know – the penalty for such a heinous crime. He must pay with his life.' The Lord Gustavus looked towards the tree and the soldier waiting, whip poised, to carry out the sentence. He raised his hand and in a stony voice gave the command, 'Begin!'

Ingram ran from the scene and searched frantically for Thorkell. He found the skald anxiously questioning the other men who had been left behind to guard the encampment. He dragged him away saying, 'Thorkell, you must try to save Conrad. The Lord Gustavus will not listen to me.'

'I will try my best,' replied the skald as they hurried towards the crowd which had gathered to watch the execution. 'But from what I have learned our friend was the victim of his own kindly nature. Any other man, faced with a riot, would have killed a few of the demonstrators as an example and then ordered the rest to train their bows on the party trying to get into the stockade. Conrad could not bring himself to do either. To say to our master that Conrad could not kill his own men or leave unprotected women out in the night, would be no defence at all – just a sign of weakness. But one man has just told me something I may be able to turn to Conrad's advantage. If I choose my words carefully, I may be able to convince the Lord Gustavus that there is a similarity between this crime and his own past misdeeds. I know him to be a man so tormented that he speaks of his dark secrets in his sleep. If he thinks Conrad's transgression no different from his own, he may grant a reprieve.'

Thorkell elbowed his way to the front of the throng and threw himself at the feet of the Lord Gustavus. 'Master, I have learned that Conrad's downfall was brought about by a woman – a beautiful seductive woman. She bewitched him, my lord. Having no knowledge of women he was helpless, defenceless against her powers. Surely you must understand, master? Many men in the innocence of youth have been trapped by the guile of a woman; been unable to see their duty, blinded by her charms. And what are the consequences? For most, nothing more than a personal sense of shame at their own folly. Conrad's crime is no different from theirs but his folly has had tragic consequences. Is this not all the more reason that he should live? My lord, if you had suffered such a misfortune, if you had betrayed one who trusted you and thereby caused the death of one who loved you, would you want to be condemned to the fires of hell before you had made retribution? If you had erred in your youth, would you not beg for a chance to repent your sins and find redemption through honourable deeds?'

'Enough, Skald! You have said enough. He must be punished.'

'He will be, master. He will punish himself for the rest of his days. Show him clemency, my lord. Did Jesus Christ not say, "Blessed are the merciful; for they shall obtain mercy"?'

The general stared at Thorkell in silence for several moments; then he said, 'You are a persuasive man, Skald. So be it.' The Lord Gustavus looked towards the tree where Conrad hung limply, his back and shoulders a mass of bleeding weals. 'Cut him down!' he commanded. Then turning to Thorkell once more, he said quietly, 'But since he has failed to keep the conditions of the agreement I made with him, that agreement is invalid. He must return to the ranks from which he came and must suffer the punishment accorded to those ranks.' Addressing the guards who held Conrad, the Lord Gustavus called out, 'Take him to Carlo!'

As the general departed and Conrad was dragged away unconscious, Thorkell said to Ingram sorrowfully, 'I should not have pleaded for him: I have only prolonged his agony. He is as much a dead man in Carlo's Company as if he had remained here and been flogged to death.'

V

'The worst dishonour...'

When Conrad regained his senses, he found himself face down in the mud – and in agony. When he had been strung up to the tree he had not even heard the crack of the whip as it had lashed into his flesh; he had not felt the physical pain so great had been his mental pain. He had prayed only for death to release him from his anguish. Now he prayed for death again – to blot out the searing throbbing in his back and shoulders. Suddenly, his hair was grabbed and his head was jerked upwards so that it was close to the dirty, pock-marked, leering face of Carlo. Even in his wretchedness, he realized he had been condemned to a living death – and how appropriate that was. Otto had always feared he might be relegated to Carlo's Company – "the worst dishonour that could befall you" – and now as a punishment for killing that same friend, he had brought upon himself the very degradation that Otto had predicted.

Carlo, an ugly, stocky man, bald with blackened teeth, greeted Conrad mockingly. 'Welcome, nobleman, to my little band of criminals. What an honour it is. We have never had a member of the illustrious Companions in our company before.' He spat contemptuously on the ground. 'Our master must have decided that death is too good for you – that you must suffer first. Carlo gives you his word – suffer you will!'

The immediate problem for the whole camp was food: Ulric had not left a morsel anywhere. The cavalry was dispatched at once to search for the supply wagons and the entertainers, but no trace was found of either. The Lord Gustavus forbade any immediate reprisals against Ulric the Bold, not daring to risk further humiliation, but he ordered instead that the surrounding countryside, his own Alemannian territories as well as Burgundian ones, was to be scoured for any form of sustenance. Little was found since Raoulbrun had fed his army from them whilst he had been encamped near the border. He had since departed for his other estates, smarting from his most recent defeat suffered during the early morning raid by the Lord Gustavus, and taking any remaining food with him. The local Alemannians were hostile towards their own soldiers. It was too early for crops to have been harvested in any quantity and they endeavoured to hide what little they had from the requisitioning parties. For the most part, the soldiers contented themselves with running off the livestock. This led to daily invasions of the stockade by angry and embittered farmers. The Lord Gustavus had already sent to his other estates and those of his brother, the Lord Bardolph, for fresh supplies and eventually, he was forced to order that while these were awaited, the plundering must cease and the time be spent instead in trapping, hunting and fishing.

The years rolled backwards, or so it seemed to Conrad as once again he became a hunter and forager, but under the watchful eye of Carlo or one of the other guards, not the kindly eye of Otto. The weals on his back began to close although they were too deep and widespread for the scars ever to disappear. Inwardly he did not heal; his pain was as great as ever. He obeyed orders as though in a dream – or rather, a nightmare. He scarcely felt the kicks and blows of guards and fellow prisoners. He still prayed for death that he might escape his conscience. The fires of hell could not inflict worse agony than that which he endured from the burning anguish in his soul.

How could he have allowed conceit and hurt pride to overwhelm him? In retrospect, he had convinced himself that he had allowed the entertainers into the compound as a means of retaliation, to punish his lord for not permitting him to join in the assault on the Burgundian camp. As a result of this trivial and selfish desire he had betrayed all who trusted him. Remorse ate at him, gnawed at him night and day. He could find no respite from the torment of the voices within him – accusing and condemning. Sometimes he would make an effort to fight back by blaming others for his predicament: Tilly for setting him off on the road towards his dream, Otto for helping him further and the Lord Gustavus for allowing him to attain his ambition. He swore he hated them all but he knew he hated only himself.

By mid-summer it was rumoured that a new campaign was about to begin against the Raetians, the bellicose tribes who terrorised the high alp at that time of year. At last the preparations for the long march were completed and rumour became fact. Carlo's Company, as always, were sent ahead to draw any unexpected enemy fire during the journey; their guards, armed and ready, followed closely behind. Conrad, filthy and bedraggled, stumbled along with shoulders bowed and head down. He was once more an outcast, just as he had been in his early days at the villa. Then he had been a peasant among nobles; now he was regarded by his new companions as a noble, albeit a disgraced and fallen one, among peasants. Never before had a cavalryman and an officer been banished to their ranks but Conrad cared nothing for their opinions and made no attempt to explain that he had been condemned to share their punishment because he too was a peasant. He ignored their jeers and taunts and the coarse jokes they made about him. When they set upon him, as they frequently did, he made no effort to defend himself but waited passively for them to kill him. Carlo soon realized this and although he enjoyed watching the attacks, a sadistic smile on his face, he always stopped them before it was too late. At night, when the prisoners were chained together to prevent them from escaping, Carlo always ensured that Conrad slept close by him.

During the march to the mountains a minor incident, soon over, had momentous repercussions for Conrad. The men were resting in the shade of some trees and the guards passed round bread and water. Conrad refused his share. 'Eat, nobleman, or I'll ram it down your throat!' shouted the guard, threateningly. 'Carlo's orders!' Conrad slowly took the cup and sipped at it, handed it back and put the bread in his mouth. Satisfied, the guard moved on. As he chewed at the food half-heartedly, Conrad was grabbed from behind by two other prisoners and dragged into the undergrowth. He did not struggle and allowed them to beat him but the sound he made involuntarily when some of the bread lodged in his throat and he began to choke, alerted the guard and Carlo. They at once pulled his attackers off him.

'Still hoping someone will kill you and put you out of your misery, nobleman? Not so! Our lord has decreed that you shall live – for the moment. On your feet! We march!'

As Conrad got up he caught his torn undershirt on a bush, revealing momentarily a small section of Tilly's sash. The sun, glinting through the trees, flickered on the gold thread of the embroidery just long enough for the two prisoners who had attacked Conrad to see it and exchange glances. They whispered together, each assuring the other that what they had seen was a belt of gold. They made sure that they kept close by Conrad as the company left the tree-line behind. The climb towards the high alp became increasingly steeper and more difficult and, burdened by the heavy packs on their backs, the group soon became spread out.

Conrad, lost in his own tortured thoughts, did not see the two men hurry ahead and so he was taken completely by surprise when they waylaid him as he rounded a clump of rocks. They jumped upon him simultaneously, tore off his backpack and threw him to the ground. One man straddled his lower torso pulling at his clothing whilst the other, kneeling above his head, clamped one hand over his mouth and gripped his throat with the other.

'We know you have a belt of gold,' snarled the man fumbling at Conrad's shirt.

'Hurry up!' hissed his companion. 'Take it before the others come and see it.'

Someone was trying to steal Tilly's gift. At all costs he must not let that happen; it would be the final betrayal. Conrad lashed out with his feet and sent the man flying but although he tried, he could not disentangle himself from the powerful grip of the other attacker. He felt the pressure on his throat increase; he was choking; he could not breathe. This was what he had prayed for: an end to his torment. But in the moment of death a thought occurred to him that had never penetrated his wretchedness before: that once he was dead he would never have a chance to make amends for his wrongdoing. He must go on living until he had paid his debt to all those he had failed: until he had vindicated himself of dishonour. In desperation, Conrad strove again to throw off his assailant but the man retaliated by throwing the full weight of his body on top of Conrad. At the same time, he altered his grip so that he could throttle his victim with both hands. Unable to cry out, Conrad could hear the low croaking sounds coming from his crushed throat. His strength was failing; he was losing consciousness; he felt his life ebbing away. With animal cunning, he suddenly stopped struggling, gave a shudder and lay still. The ruse worked; the man relaxed his hold on Conrad's neck and raised himself off Conrad's body. In an instant, the youth took a deep breath, leapt up and hurled himself upon the strangler. The second man, still dazed from his heavy fall, attempted to intervene and the three fell to the ground locked in combat. They rolled off the narrow track and down the rocky hillside until they came to rest where the ground levelled out into a tiny plateau. Conrad was the first to regain his balance and he immediately grabbed a fallen tree branch as a weapon. His assailants did the same and hurled rocks and stones at him as well. In spite of being outnumbered Conrad fought fiercely and easily held his ground. His new-found will to live gave him a tremendous advantage. He was resolved to survive – by any means. When a chance came to trip one man he took it without hesitation and sent him, screaming, over the cliff. The second man rushed at the youth and tried to force him to follow. Conrad, exerting every muscle, managed to turn his assailant and push him nearer to the edge of the plateau. The pair struggled for some seconds until the man lost his footing and fell to join his comrade in the valley below.

Conrad, shaking, sweating and panting for breath, collapsed on the grass, overwhelmed by an immense feeling of gratitude to the little girl who had just saved his life and shown him a reason for wanting to go on living. Then he heard a low chuckling noise; he looked up and saw Carlo sprawled out on a rocky ledge, contentedly chewing on a blade of grass. The soldier stood up, grinned at Conrad, displaying his blackened teeth and called out, 'Now you are one of us, nobleman. Hurry up! You are keeping your comrades waiting.' Carlo gestured upwards with his hand and Conrad saw that all along the winding track above him men – prisoners and guards alike – were standing and watching him.

When they reached the high alp Conrad looked around at the cattle and the goats roaming the lush pastures and smiled to himself: he was in familiar territory. Herdsmen were everywhere; haymaking was in progress. He could have been on the alp above the Lord Bardolph's fortress – the scene was exactly the same. The sights, sounds and smells from his boyhood comforted him, shocked as he was by the fact that he had just killed two men and by the realization that no one appeared at all concerned about what he had done. The workers on the high alp looked up from their labours. They waved and cheered when they saw the soldiers, knowing that they had come to protect them from the robber hordes and were on their way to seek out the marauding tribesmen.

The ascent continued, Carlo's band of criminals following the course of a glacier until they reached the snowline. When a halt was called they found themselves standing unexpectedly on flat ground. The area was shaped like a bowl. In the centre was a small lake surrounded on three sides by cliffs – towering masses of bare rock. The silence was eerie. More Alemannians caught up with the spear-head and were affected in the same way by the desolate crags and bleak mountain peaks which seemed to be watching them and bearing down on them. The warriors looked around fearfully. Many crossed themselves and prayed to Jesus; a few, for good measure, prayed to Odin, Mars and the gods of their forefathers as well.

'Ever heard of the Raetians, nobleman?' asked Carlo.

'I have fought them,' Conrad replied calmly, his voice assuming a harsh rasping tone after the attempt to throttle him. 'They are warriors like any other; they just happen to inhabit a strange place.' His fellow-prisoners looked at him with a new-found fear and respect.

Suddenly, the thin air of the cirque echoed to the shrieks of the Raetians. Wild mountain men, clad in rough grey clothing, appeared from nowhere and fell upon the trespassers. Immediately, the Alemannians went into action, no longer stupefied by mysteries they did not understand. The disciplined troops beat off the attack; the Raetians, as one man, disappeared as suddenly as they had come and the eerie silence returned.

'Get used to it!' Carlo snarled, looking round at his bloodied band of criminals. 'There will be many more attacks like that over the coming weeks. Our orders are to pursue the Raetians into the heart of the mountains, destroy their settlements, drive off their cattle and seize their grain.'

'I am not venturing into those mountains,' one of the prisoners shouted. 'Everyone knows that the land of perpetual snow is the home of monsters.'

'He is right,' another prisoner agreed. 'I have met men who have seen them – hideous creatures.'

Carlo grinned and said in an ominous voice, 'Step forward any man who will not follow orders. I might as well kill you now and save on the rations.'

VI

The Wolf-man is born

The weather finally defeated the invaders but the fighting had become more sporadic and the outcome less profitable as time had passed. The Alemannians were not dressed for warfare amongst rugged mountains exposed to the elements and with autumn upon them they were forced by increasing cold to leave their enemies in peace. They descended to the alpine valley below, Carlo's Company bringing up the rear in case the Raetians followed and attacked to get back their grain. The serfs who had completed their appointed period of military duty were disbanded and sent home to their villages; the professional soldiers who had made service to the Lord Gustavus their life's work, were dispersed to their various winter quarters.

It was Sigurd who came to give Carlo his instructions and to get to the company commander he had to pass Conrad. The two exchanged glances but his former tutor did not speak to him or show that he knew him. Sigurd told Carlo that winter quarters for his criminals was to be an abandoned settlement of wattle and daub huts, inside a wooden stockade, which overlooked the Burgundian border. The company was charged with watching for any incursions by the enemy who had been known to make the most of any breaks in the winter weather to gain ground at the expense of the Alemannians.

Life for Conrad had come full circle. Once more he lived in a shack, much larger but very like the one he had built for Hulda and a forest, no different to the one above the Lord Bardolph's fortress, stretched to the gate of the compound. When the snows came and there was little chance of a Burgundian assault, Carlo stopped sending out patrols and even withdrew the sentries from the perimeter wall. He also ceased the nightly ritual of running a chain through the rings attached to every prisoner's ankle. The criminals had time on their hands but they did not use it to taunt Conrad. They had ceased their former habit as soon as he had killed his other tormentors single-handed. Conrad's reputation had been further enhanced by his subsequent actions during the campaign against the Raetians. So determined had he been to survive that he had attacked the mountain-men like a wild animal and had fought with equal ferocity for dead men's clothing and weapons. His own boots had been stolen from him while he lay unconscious after the flogging and he had been forced to bind rags around his bare feet. Since then he had found the culprit, beaten him senseless and taken back his boots. Such notorious acts ensured that he was left alone and he spent hours sitting apart from the other men silently indulging his boyhood pastime of woodcarving.

Conrad also had time once more to think: to mourn anew the death of Otto; to despair of what the future held for little Tilly without his protection; to ponder bitterly his own downfall. Again and again he went over the events of that fateful night when he had been left in charge of the camp. He reflected on his motives and his actions; on what should have been and what might have been. He saw the consequences of his behaviour with fresh eyes too. All that had concerned him at the time had been his responsibility for the death of his friend and the theft of the stores. He realized now that to the Lord Gustavus these were disasters of comparatively little importance when measured against the far greater catastrophe of Ulric the Bold's success. To have permitted his master's arch-enemy to wreak his revenge and score such a triumph was a crime of unforgivable magnitude. Conrad feared he could never atone for that sin.

As the months went by food became scarce. There was almost no wildlife to be found and though the men broke the ice on the nearby lake, they caught very few fish. The supplies Carlo had been issued with began to run out; what was left was strictly rationed and an armed guard sat by the stores day and night. Conrad felt the pangs of hunger keenly since he had the appetite of a growing youth. One night he tried to divert his thoughts from food by recalling the winters he had spent with Hulda in their forest refuge. He fell asleep thinking fondly of the old woman; soon he began to dream. He imagined he was walking through deep snow in a vast forest. In front of him was a crooked tree; he thought it must at some time have been struck by lightening. Sitting in the fork of the tree was an old crone. As he peered at her he realized that it was Hulda. She did not say a word to him but pointed with a gnarled finger at the ground. Where she pointed the snow melted, exposing a plant with succulent roots. Then a mist descended and engulfed Hulda; he saw her no more.

Conrad awoke with a start in the early hours of the morning while it was still dark. The dream was vivid in his mind and he lay motionless for a while, recalling the details and cursing himself for forgetting that there would be a supply of food, however difficult to find, under the snow. He got up and crept quietly out of the hut, taking care not to awaken the other inmates. He shivered in the chill air; moonlight filled the stockade. As he trod on the hard icy snow his feet made a loud crunching sound. He paused, certain someone would hear. Nothing stirred: the guards were all soundly asleep indoors. He hurried through the gate and entered the gloomy forest. The frost had killed much of the vegetation and in places, where it had drifted, the snow was very deep. But there were some areas around the bases of the trees, in spots which had thick intertwining branches overhead providing some shelter, where mosses and grasses still grew. Conrad crawled around in the freezing snow trying to dig with broken twigs and branches but the ground was so hard that his improvised implements kept snapping. His woodcarving knife might have helped but all weapons, even a whittling knife, were kept by the guards until needed. He sat back on his heels and looked upwards in despair. The moon on that clear crisp night seemed to be playing tricks on him, moving the shadows of the branches above him this way and that until suddenly he fancied he saw a crooked tree like the one in his dream. He scrambled over to it and began to dig at the base of it with his bare fingers. Soon they were burning and their tips became so numb that they lost all sensitivity. Driven by hunger and the conviction that he would eventually find a plant like the one Hulda had revealed to him, he pressed on and at last his persistence was rewarded. He gnawed ravenously at the roots and prodded the earth for more. When he decided that he dared not be away from the stockade any longer, he carefully buried the fragments he had discarded. He must not share his discovery with anyone else – vegetation was too scarce. It could mean the difference between life and death to him and he had already accepted that his quest for survival meant total dedication and total selfishness.

When he reached the safety of the hut once more, Conrad thanked God and Hulda for showing him a way to stave off starvation. He had long since forgotten Hulda's names for the plants he had just eaten but he did remember that she had set great store by them, claiming they had the power to produce strength and stamina. Every morning from then on he contrived to leave the compound, find and devour his secret repast and return before the rest of the company was awake. Sometimes he searched in vain and found almost no edible vegetation at all but on other occasions, he enjoyed a miniature feast and from the beginning of these excursions he fancied he felt stronger.

Spring was late in coming that year. Even the wolves were crazy with hunger and had been known to run, howling, around the outside of the palisade trying to find a way in.

Whenever the weather permitted, Carlo dispatched hunting parties further and further from the settlement in a desperate effort to find food. Conrad, who had soon earned a reputation as the best forager, was always included and he never failed to keep a wary eye open for wolf packs. On one particular day, he had seen and heard nothing but as he and two other prisoners were inspecting traps they had set previously, the guard behind them let out a strangled scream. Turning round, Conrad saw a huge wolf upon the man's back. The savage animal was sinking his vicious teeth again and again into the guard's shoulder. Without hesitation, Conrad rushed to the man's aid. He got behind the wolf and put one arm around the beast's neck and the other under its body. Summoning all his might, he wrenched the clawing, struggling, snarling predator off its victim. Then he threw it against the trunk of a tree with such force that the wolf was stunned. Seizing the beast's head, he crashed it repeatedly against the bark until the animal was dead. Conrad straightened, gasping for breath, expecting to hear the rest of the pack thudding through the trees towards him. All was quiet: this giant of a specimen must have become, for some reason, a lone hunter.

Conrad sighed with relief and knelt down beside the guard. He had been very badly mauled but he was still alive. Conrad called to the other two prisoners to help him. On receiving no response he looked round and saw that they were gone. Undeterred, he bound the injured man's wounds with strips from his undershirt and balanced him head first over one shoulder, his arm steadying and gripping the guard's legs. With his free hand he dragged his heavy kill by its hind-quarters. Thus, some time later, Conrad made a spectacular entry into the stockade, covered in blood and leaving two crimson trails in the snow – one from the man and one from the wolf. Criminals and guards alike stared, amazed; even Carlo stood open-mouthed in astonishment as Conrad deposited the guard and the wolf's body at his feet.

'The meat is for all but I claim the head and the skin. It was my kill,' said Conrad sternly.

'How did you kill it?' asked Carlo.

'With my bare hands,' Conrad replied. He stooped and lifted the guard up in his arms and carried him inside the hut. His whole being was aglow with exultation: he had taken his first small step along the road towards redemption.

Conrad finished sewing the wounded guard's torn flesh back into place; then, watched by the curious stares of his fellow prisoners, he went around the walls of the hut collecting cobwebs and mouldy dust into a bowl which he had already lined with moss. When he returned, Carlo was standing over the injured guard. 'You are wasting your time, nobleman,' he muttered. 'No man could recover from wounds so deep and terrible.'

'He will recover,' Conrad replied quietly as he spread the cobweb impregnated moss over the unconscious man's wounds and bound them. Then he said, 'I must go into the forest. I need to brew a potion for him to drink.'

'Then go, nobleman,' Carlo replied. Conrad at once picked up a bag and left the hut. One of the guards protested and suggested that he should go with the prisoner. 'Why bother?' was Carlo's response. 'He had his chance to escape and he did not take it. He will be back.'

The group of prisoners and guards were continuing to watch the wounded man when a spider scuttled out from underneath the dressings. One of the guards voiced the fear of all the shocked onlookers when he exclaimed, 'It is witchcraft!'

'What does it matter?' said Carlo in a lazy drawl. 'He is a dead man anyway.'

Carlo was sitting outside the hut when he saw Conrad approaching. When the youth was close enough he threw the wolf's skin, head attached, onto the ground in front of him. 'Here is your prize, nobleman,' he said, grinning.

Conrad picked up the skin, looked at it with satisfaction and threw it over his back so that the wolf's head was on top of his own. Then he looked at Carlo and said menacingly, 'Do not call me "nobleman" ever again.'

'So what should I call you?' asked Carlo, laughing. 'Perhaps you should be known as "wolf-man".'

VII

The saga begins

When the army re-formed for the start of the spring offensive and it was time to report the events of the winter to Sigurd, Carlo took the injured guard with him. Thanks to Conrad's ministrations the man had recovered from his terrible wounds and he generously recounted the details of his rescuer's amazing battle with the wolf. Sigurd was sufficiently impressed to send the guard to his master's military historian – Thorkell – for him to record the amazing feat for posterity. The skald was delighted to interrogate the man and as a result, composed a new song, *The Saga of the Wolf-man.*

When Conrad had first demanded that he be allowed to keep the wolf's skin he had had in mind that it would be a means of keeping warm: a mantle around his shoulders to cover his threadbare rags. But he also knew from his classical studies that the standard-bearer of a Roman legion would have worn an animal skin, with the head on top of his own, to strike fear into the heart of the enemy and, before long, Conrad found that the wearing of the wolf-skin helped to restore a little of his self-respect since it was a symbol of his strength and courage.

The wolf-skin, however, elicited some sad thoughts too: Conrad reflected ruefully that it was a year almost to the day since he had donned another special cloak, the one issued to him when he had become a Companion in Arms. How happy he had been that spring morning when he had ridden out of the villa gates behind the Lord Gustavus, a member of his master's noble guard; yet how soon he had thrown away his dream. His only comfort was in the thought that no one would recognise him as the proud youth of a year ago. To be recognised by his former comrades would only add to his sense of shame and to this end he had deliberately set out to make himself indistinguishable from the rest of Carlo's criminals. He had done nothing to improve his dirty appearance and he had allowed his hair to grow long; he had the beginnings of a beard. During the long winter months he had become much taller and more broad-shouldered. With the wolf-skin to complete his disguise, he was certain that none of his former friends would know him.

Conrad was wrong: neither Ingram nor Thorkell was fooled and although they dared not approach him openly for fear of incurring the Lord Gustavus's wrath, they both found ways to let him know they had not disowned him. During the very first battle that year, in the thick of the fighting, he heard a voice cry out a warning, 'Conrad – behind you!' He spun round to see a rider bearing down on him, sword drawn and poised to strike him. As he leapt aside, Ingram galloped past and killed his would-be assailant with one blow. After that, Conrad kept a watch for his friend and was able to return the favour and go to Ingram's rescue when he was unseated and disarmed in a later conflict. He caught his friend's horse in mid-flight and protected him against all attackers whilst he remounted and then, with a flick of his foot, he retrieved Ingram's sword and threw it back to him. Thorkell too, made it clear that he knew the identity of the man in the wolf-skin and whenever Conrad chanced to pass him entertaining his audience around the campfire Thorkell would grin at him and begin to sing his new song.

As the months passed Conrad proved that he was developing quite extraordinary physical powers. On one occasion, the column was moving down a hillside when there was a sudden landslide. Boulders blocked their path and one man was trapped underneath. No one could help until Conrad arrived on the scene. He lifted the heavy weight off the soldier single-handedly, cleared the path of other boulders and carried the heavily built man down the hillside. Soon he had many remarkable feats of strength to his credit and Thorkell added more verses to his song. Conrad attributed his ever-increasing powers to the fact that he was still secretly devouring the roots which Hulda had valued. As a youth still growing, he had a voracious appetite and since Carlo had never bothered to resume chaining him at night, he continued to creep away whilst others slept to search for edible plants. One night he was so hungry that he began his search too close to the perimeter of the entrenched encampment. He was on his hands and knees, the wolf-skin on his back and the wolf's head on top of his own head, and bent close to the ground gnawing at the roots. Two sentries saw what they thought was a wolf scavenging some distance ahead of them. When the "wolf" suddenly stood upright and they saw in the moonlight that it was the Wolf-man, they were petrified.

The very next night when Conrad and the other criminals were being marched to their allotted sleeping area, Thorkell shouted above the heads of his listeners, 'Yes, I will sing to you of the man whose blood was mingled with the blood of the giant wolf when they were locked in mortal combat; of the man who when he had slain the terrible beast emerged half man, half wolf – a man of magical powers and monstrous strength ...'

By the onset of winter and the cessation of hostilities almost no one, apart from his special friends, remembered Conrad's real name or how he had come to be a member of Carlo's criminals. He was spoken of and addressed as "the Wolf-man" and was renowned only for his heroic deeds. He was no longer an outcast; he had earned the grudging respect of his fellows in Carlo's Company but by his own choice, he continued to live like an outcast, speaking to no one unless absolutely necessary and living apart from his comrades as much as possible.

That winter, Carlo's Company was sent to garrison another fortified border settlement situated a few miles from a town. Carlo had friends in the town and after a while, having assured himself that the other guards could cope with the prisoners in his absence, he went to visit them. He returned unexpectedly the next day saying that there was a plague in the town and that many people had died. The news was greeted with horror.

'You may have already caught the plague,' said Conrad. 'Everyone should move out of this hut.'

'There is nothing wrong with me,' Carlo protested but the fear was plain to see in his eyes.

'The Wolf-man is always right,' muttered one prisoner.

'I will remain with you,' Conrad proposed. 'If you are still in good health after a few days it will be safe for the others to return.'

'Not afraid of catching the plague, Wolf-man?' asked Carlo.

'I have encountered the plague before, when I was young, and never caught it,' replied Conrad calmly.

'Then do as he says,' Carlo ordered, looking at the frightened men. 'Make yourselves some shelter against the stockade walls.'

Four days later Carlo died. The guards and their prisoners were huddled outside the wooden barracks when Conrad emerged wearily and shut the door behind him. 'I could not save him,' he announced sadly. 'Do not enter; leave him and I will bury him when I have rested.' He walked across the compound and lay down, exhausted, against the palisade and was asleep within seconds. He awoke hours later choking on smoke. He propped himself up on his elbow and looked around him in alarm. He found the barracks had been set alight; flames still flickered in some places and the remainder of the building was smouldering. The guards were huddled together in a corner, arguing fiercely.

One of the prisoners, seeing Conrad sitting up, hurried over and explained excitedly, 'We have burnt the barracks to the ground with the body and the plague inside it!'

Getting to his feet, Conrad asked anxiously, 'Where have you put the stores that were in the lean-to on the far side of the barracks?'

Conrad had his answer when the man's eyes widened in horror. At once the youth rushed over to the guards, wrenching an axe from the belt of one of them. As one man they stopped talking and looked at him fearfully as he stood over them, the weapon in his hand. 'This is no time to argue over who should succeed Carlo. You have just burnt the food which was meant to last us all winter. It is too late to get to the villa for more supplies. We have two days – three at most – to build ourselves a shelter and to find food. After that we shall be snowed in.'

'We can take timbers from the stockade to build a shelter,' said one of the guards sheepishly.

Conrad's tone was scornful as he replied, 'And let the wolves in?'

The next two days saw intense activity as Conrad ordered the entire company into the forest. There he chose those who were not so strong to hunt and trap wildlife and showed them what roots and plants were safe to eat and where to find them. His more muscular comrades he instructed to chop down trees, working in pairs, and felled many himself on his own. The fruits of everyone's labours were dragged inside the stockade and there Conrad directed the building of the barracks; the chopping of firewood and its storage inside; the plucking or skinning of wildlife and its preservation, together with edible roots, between layers of snow in a specially constructed enclosure just outside the barracks. They were then ready to face the winter – however harsh it might be.

Next Conrad organised the rota for patrols and sentry duty and no one dared to dispute his decisions. When the blizzards came the men remained warm inside their shelter but whenever the skies were clear, Conrad would order his comrades outside and they would clear the deep snow between the barracks and the gate to form a small parade ground. There he would direct them in wrestling and unarmed combat; in better shield-wall drills; in more accurate use of the bow and arrow and sling and rock; in more adept movements with shield, spear, knife and axe. Carlo had never bothered with formal exercise or weapon training and at first there was resentment in the eyes of some of the prisoners and guards. Conrad did not waste time on lengthy persuasive arguments but contented himself with making the brief statement, 'Men who are fit and well-trained live longer.'

When the weather confined the men to their barracks they were no longer lethargic and despairing. Meat would be roasting on a spit in the central fireplace and the skins of the animals they had hunted would be stretched out on wooden frames to dry. Some groups would be noisy, playing gambling games with stones or competing in target practice with small throwing arrows, whilst other groups would be quietly fashioning clothing from animal skins. Many of the men now wore a roughly made leather shirt. Conrad never joined any of the groups; he would sit alone for hours with small scraps of hide spread out on the floor in front of him. He would be elsewhere: back in the Long Hall at the villa remembering the mathematics taught him by the monks and the knowledge gleaned from the military engineers and, using sticks of charred wood from the fire, he would pass the time designing small war-engines.

Once the icicles which adorned the watch tower began to melt and drip onto the sentries it was time to rejoin the main forces.

Conrad, grown even taller and more muscular and with hair and beard longer, watched from a distance as the guards reported Carlo's death to Sigurd and related the events of the winter months. When they returned they told Conrad that he must go forward as the commander wished to speak to him. Sigurd too had never been under any illusion as to the identity of the Wolf-man and addressed him by his real name. 'It seems, Master Conrad, you have acquitted yourself so well during the winter that both prisoners and guards want you to continue as their leader. They also request that they be known from now on as the Wolf-man's Company. I must, of course, seek authorisation for such matters but how say you?'

'I should be honoured to lead them, Master Sigurd. But if the authorisation were to be forthcoming, I also have a request. Since the company's death rate is so high and therefore wasteful, I wish to be given access to materials and a forge so that I may fashion small portable machines to aid escape from rear-guard actions and the like.'

'I shall pass on your request,' replied Sigurd curtly.

VIII

The legend grows

All the requests were granted: the Wolf-man was confirmed as the new company commander; his men were to be known as the Wolf-men; he was allowed any materials and equipment he desired. Although he concealed his true feelings well, Conrad was secretly overjoyed at this unexpected turn of events. He had never thought that there was the slightest possibility that he would be given any official position of authority ever again. He had no doubt that the Lord Gustavus must have been consulted and must have given his permission. That he had done so astounded and mystified Conrad but it gave him hope that his master had, to some extent at least, forgiven him his transgression. What was beyond question was the fact that he had, for whatever reason, been given another chance. He vowed he would make no more mistakes; he would not fail his master or his friends a second time.

Conrad set about his new task with a determination and energy that had to be seen to be believed. His aim was to remove the stigma which had been associated with Carlo's Company and make it a company that any man would be proud to join. Now that he had the mandate, he began by instigating an even more intensive programme of training for his fellow criminals. It was his intention that they should attain the same high standards of discipline and physical fitness that he had experienced at the villa's military school.

The skills which Roderic had taught him had not been forgotten either and Conrad made it a priority to turn the drawings he had made during the winter months into reality. The many hours of hard labour at the furnace and the blacksmith's bench produced the small portable war-engines he had envisaged and by the time the fighting began in earnest, the Wolf-men were ready. They were still used as before to test the enemy's strength, to draw his fire and to cover the safe retreat of others, but although they continued to be deployed as expendable, the outcome was now very different: they were no longer sacrificed. When leading the column in order to spring any trap, as soon as they were ambushed they would kneel together, covering themselves with their shields, and the enemy's arrows and spears would bounce harmlessly off them. At the same time, Conrad would signal with a wolf-like howl to those men he had trained in the art of tracking and scouting. They would have been following the column on either side, parallel but at a distance, camouflaged under nets of leaves and bracken, and would fall upon the enemy with wolf-like cries. The men under the shields would jump up and join in the fray and the ambushers would find themselves ambushed.

The machines which Conrad had devised all had one thing in common: they could do the work of many men and give a misleading impression to the enemy as to the size of the opposition. Conrad made his inventions as light in weight as possible so that a man could carry one on his back. When the Wolf-men covered the retreat of their forces, some of the men would fire arrows at the enemy whilst others of their comrades would operate machines that propelled stones and incendiary materials which set fire to the undergrowth. Once Conrad had seen the main column disappear to safety, he would make his wolf's howl signal to his men. At once, they would shoulder their portable catapults, but as they retreated they would use their flaming torches to light ropes connected to the firing mechanisms of other small devices concealed previously behind rocks or in bushes. When the ropes burnt through, arrows would be released, thirty at a time, by delayed action if necessary. By varying the length of the trailing ropes, the Wolf-men could ensure that a hail of missiles at intervals would keep their antagonists under cover long enough for them to make their escape.

The same result was obtained in mountainous regions by the employment of a much simpler device: Conrad made specially tapered metal rods which he would place in strategic positions prior to the commencement of an attack. If it then became necessary for the main forces to withdraw and for the Wolf-men, as usual, to cover that withdrawal, Conrad would be able to buy his men precious time so that they too could escape, by operating the crowbars as levers to cause landslides, effectively preventing the Alemannians from being pursued. All these devices enabled the Wolf-men to extricate themselves safely from dangerous situations on many occasions. Such attention to detail and careful advance preparation resulted in Conrad achieving another of his ambitions: his company soon had the lowest instead of the highest death rate of any group in the Alemannian army.

Another benefit was that Conrad's efforts to save his men's lives naturally endeared him to them and earned him their loyalty more than any displays of rhetoric could have done. Once he was in command no prisoner ever attempted to escape – a point which Conrad made to Sigurd when the summer campaigns ended and he went to fetch his orders for the winter months. 'My men are loyal warriors; they should no longer wear shackles around their ankles. I request that they cease to be regarded as criminals or to be treated as criminals.'

'You and your men, by your conduct this summer, have already erased all stigmas. You are no longer regarded as prisoners; you may remove the shackles,' Sigurd replied. 'So successful have your exploits been that many young men want to join your company. They seem to think it will assure them fame and glory,' Sigurd added with a wry smile. 'This will be permitted so long as your company earns its keep by engaging in more special missions. Whenever it is deemed appropriate, you will make raids into enemy territory, attack supply lines and destroy military store-houses. You will act as decoys to lure the enemy to a particular spot, create diversions so that an adversary divides his forces, attack in such a way that our foe thinks he is facing a much larger force. What do you say to such plans?'

Conrad considered for a moment before replying, 'The Wolf-men would feel honoured to be awarded such distinction, but for such tasks they should be properly attired.'

'Leather garments have already been allocated to them,' Sigurd replied. 'Mark them however you wish. You may also draw armour and weapons for them as you think appropriate.'

The eager volunteers swelled the numbers under Conrad's command to one hundred. They became one hundred dedicated expertly-trained warriors who were feared by their many enemies as a formidable invincible strike force. Conrad was certain that the idea to utilise the Wolf-men's skills further must have come from the Lord Gustavus himself. Conrad was uniquely suited to be the leader of a special task force since he was able to make full use of his exceptional education and combine it with his inherent ingenuity and ability. He became as adept at laying ambushes as Hannibal; as skilled at deceiving and misleading the enemy as Alexander; as excellent at seizing opportunities as Julius Caesar. He could assess a situation quickly and accurately; make decisions immediately and correctly. His men had absolute confidence in him and obeyed him without question. His fine personal example was infectious: in battle he was calm and courageous whatever the situation and he inspired his followers to perform deeds they would never have thought possible. In a remarkably short time he had transformed a company of criminals into a company of heroes.

Conrad laid down a strict code of conduct based on the

lessons he had learned in his youth. He had a reverence for life that was almost unique for his time and it embraced the lives of his foes as well as the lives of his own people. His first priority was always the safety of his own men and he would do nothing to jeopardize that, but whenever possible he tried to devise methods whereby he could carry out his orders successfully with maximum speed and the minimum of casualties – to the enemy as well. He was true also to his boyhood vow, made after he had witnessed the fall of the Burgundian town, that he would show mercy and compassion to his vanquished foe. He was not a general in name but in his small world among his select body of men, his word was law and he wielded as much power as the general he tried to emulate – Alexander the Great. Like his hero, he had the capacity to feel sympathy for those he had defeated and he would allow no wanton butchery by his troops. In the years that he led the Wolf-men it could never be claimed that his company was guilty of committing atrocities or of deliberate massacre. He remembered too what it was like to starve and he would never permit his soldiers to terrorize the peasant population. When he made raids into enemy territory he would achieve his military objective and then order his men to return to their own lines without pausing to rape and pillage on the way. When asked by Sigurd to explain this unusual policy, he justified it by claiming that he had no wish to alienate the ordinary people. 'I prefer to leave a feeling of goodwill rather than vengeance in my wake,' he asserted, 'in the hope that one day those same people might be needed as friends rather than foes.'

Much of Conrad's thinking, especially his regard for the value of life, was influenced by his childhood love of the countryside. Even as a man he welcomed any opportunity, however short, to escape the chaos of the battlefield for the peace of the fields and forests. He was happiest of all when he could wander among the trees; it did not matter whether he was in the mountains above the snowline where only the conifers, the hardy pines and the firs grew, or on the lower slopes and plains among the maples, the oaks and the beeches, the trees brought comfort to his tortured soul. However much his fortunes changed, Nature's round never changed and he found solace in her constancy. For that reason he looked forward to the rare brief moments of peace when there was no employment for him as an infantryman and he worked instead as a serf on the Lord Gustavus's estates. Then he would bend under the plough and toil in the fields in contentment.

It was on one such occasion that Conrad learned something which gave him much satisfaction. He was clearing a ditch by the roadside, only a few miles from the villa where he had spent his privileged youth, when he saw a rider coming along the road. The man was well-dressed and rode a fine horse. He was exceptionally well-built but with spindly legs; it was unmistakably Roderic. As he drew alongside Conrad, a peasant hailed him from the other side of the road and he looked towards the old man as he doffed his hat respectfully and said, 'Good morning, Master Blacksmith.' Roderic returned the greeting and rode on without glancing in Conrad's direction. The knowledge that Roderic at least had attained his dream and succeeded his adoptive father as master pleased Conrad very much. He only wished he had the consolation of knowing that little Tilly had also found happiness.

Most of the time there was little respite from fighting and therefore little time for Conrad to grieve over Tilly and Otto, or to dwell on his misdeeds and speculate on what might have been. His stream of ingenious ideas seemed inexhaustible and he developed more and more miniature war-engines and devices to increase the might of the Wolf-men. It became commonplace for his one hundred warriors to be able to keep the enemy fully occupied on one front while the rest of the Alemannian army either surrounded them from the rear or, even more audaciously, attacked and overran one of their refuges many miles away. He borrowed many stratagems from the past which he had learned at the villa and in particular, made frequent use of the tricks of Belisarius, the celebrated general of the Eastern Roman Empire who was the master of military deception. On one such occasion, Conrad unwittingly contributed a momentous verse to Thorkell's saga.

Sigurd had come to Conrad at dusk one evening when the Alemannians were entrenched in low hills; the enemy camp could be seen in the distance. 'This engagement is to be brought to a speedy end,' Sigurd had said. 'Your Wolf-men are to deceive the enemy into thinking that our whole army is still camped here but during the night our main force will skirt round and behind them. At dawn you will engage them from the front whilst we attack from the rear.'

As soon as Sigurd had departed, Conrad had called two of his men over to him and had given them their orders. 'You are to take most of our men with you and collect dry twigs and bracken. You are to light fires all over the hillside to deceive the enemy into thinking our whole army is camped here. Hurry now!'

One of the men hesitated and, unusually for a Wolf-man, questioned the instruction. 'But will camp fires fool them?'

'Yes!' replied Conrad sharply. 'It is a trick of Belisarius.'

'Who is Belisarius?' asked the man. 'I do not know him.'

Conrad half-smiled as he replied, 'No, you would not know him: he died more than a hundred years ago.' The two men looked at Conrad in surprise. He misunderstood their reaction and thought that they needed further reassurance that the ruse would work. 'The enemy *will* be fooled,' he declared emphatically. 'I *know* that the trick always worked for Belisarius. Go tell the others.'

The two men scuttled away and were soon in a huddle with their comrades. 'So we had better do as he says,' said one of the men fearfully. 'I, for one, am not going to argue with him.'

'Nor am I,' asserted the other man, 'He told us so himself: he has lived for hundreds of years.'

The Wolf-men scattered and the order was carried out even more speedily than usual. A few hours later they fought as heroically as ever and the battle was soon over. Afterwards, Sigurd came to speak to Conrad and as they walked together, the fires the Wolf-men had lit could still be seen smouldering all over the low hills in the distance.

'Your company has done well; our losses were minimal,' Sigurd said and then he added, smiling, 'Have you heard the latest verse of the skald's most popular song? It seems that the Wolf-man is also immortal.'

The Wolf-men were not always engaged in independent exploits; they spent much of their time as part of the regular infantry although they stood out, clad as they were in hide with byrnies and a tabard with a wolf's head emblazoned on the front. When a standard battle-array was called for they formed the front ranks of the shield-wall and when the required formation was a "swine-array", Conrad held the honour which Otto had always wished for him: he formed the "snout" and led the entire army into battle as champion-of-champions. At first they would march but when they got closer to the enemy lines, Conrad would break into a run, calling to his men with a loud wolf-howl. They would take up the same battle cry and run with him in formation. The sight and sound would strike fear into the enemy infantry and many would abandon their shields and weapons and run. No other duty gave him greater pleasure. He felt he was making amends to his old comrade in the one way that Otto would have appreciated and he prayed that he might see him and be proud of him.

The enemy could see him and he was a truly horrendous sight. No Roman standard-bearer in his animal skin had struck more fear into the most belligerent of adversaries than Conrad.

His stature had increased until, when he reached his full height, he was the tallest man in the Lord Gustavus's army. The wolf's head, crowning his own, made him appear even taller – a giant in fact. Over the years his hair and beard had grown longer and more unkempt and he had never once trimmed either. He no longer adopted such measures to hide his identity but instead regarded his hideous appearance as a constant and deliberate reminder of his shame and an ever-present warning against the dangers of conceit. Since he continued to live a solitary life and, like his master, calling no man his friend, it was not surprising that the strange tales about him grew – even amongst his enemies. Thorkell's song of how he had slain the wolf had spread far and wide and there were many who agreed that the famous encounter had produced a creature of superhuman powers. The Burgundians accepted this myth enthusiastically, particularly after a few of their number had seen him on all fours rooting in the undergrowth for his favourite vegetation. After that episode they were convinced he was half-beast, half-man and many of them would throw down their arms and run at the very sight of him, preferring to chance Raoulbrun's wrath rather than face the Wolf-man.

Neither Raoulbrun nor the Lord Gustavus's most formidable enemy, Ulric the Bold, ever came face to face with him but they had often heard his terrifying wolf's howl – his bloodcurdling battle cry. They had seen him too, towering above his men, the wolf's head seeming to merge with his own head. Both of them, secretly, had some sympathy with their soldiers' reluctance to confront him; fearless warriors though they were, they too were as susceptible to the myths, superstitions and rumours as their cohorts. They too felt the same chill whenever they saw him in the distance – an instinctive sensation that they were in the presence of something supernatural.

But there were others who reacted quite differently to the Wolf-man's fame: those who yearned for fame themselves and hoped to achieve it by claiming, 'I slew the Wolf-man'. Often a formal request would be sent to the Alemannian camp by an adversary, asking that the Wolf-man be allowed to meet his champion-of-champions. Conrad fought these duals with pride, knowing he was fighting for the honour of all Alemannians. He was never beaten. Sometimes he was challenged unofficially, even on rare occasions by one of his own tribesmen. He knew that in his phenomenal strength he had been given a rare gift and he must not abuse it. His code of conduct, therefore, forbade him to fight anyone who was demonstrably not his equal. If his challenger was a champion himself Conrad accepted although even then, he tried only to disable the man rather than to kill him, but if his opponent was a young warrior demanding a contest to prove his manhood, Conrad would disarm him, break his weapons with his bare hands to prove his superior might, and urge the youth not to value his life so lightly.

Thus fame brought Conrad many additional problems and responsibilities but in one respect he welcomed it: because it enabled him to repay Thorkell for risking his life to steal Raoulbrun's sword to cure his wound with its life-stone. Conrad knew that his daring adventures had provided Thorkell with the legendary hero he had longed for; as a result the skald's predictions made so often in jest, had come true – Conrad was indeed the subject of Thorkell's greatest and most popular composition. Whenever he passed a campfire where Thorkell was seated, the audience seemed to be clamouring for *The Saga of the Wolf-man*. The song grew longer every year as Thorkell added new verses to celebrate each bold escapade. There was no wonder it was such a favourite: it was a song to delight any warrior, a song of might and valour and the pursuit of honour and glory. Conrad had been forced to discourage all Thorkell's attempts to meet him secretly, knowing how much their master would disapprove, so it comforted him to think that by his deeds he had pleased his friend. The skald was one person he had not failed; he never ceased to regret that he had failed the Lord Gustavus.

The passage of time did nothing to heal the pain that Conrad felt at being rejected by his master; he feared he would have to pay the penalty for his wrongdoing forever. When he had first been appointed commander of the Wolf-men, he had hoped he might be able to win back his general's favour. His expectations had been raised even higher after he had begun to work on his inventions: no request for materials or equipment was ever refused and Conrad had seen this as a sign of his master's approval. He was to be disappointed. He had been invincible in battle and had carried out every mission successfully but the Lord Gustavus had never once sent for him or acknowledged him in any way. He despaired of ever finding a means of redeeming himself in his master's eyes. Yet Conrad could not help but marvel at the situation in which he found himself: had he made no mistake and remained a Companion in Arms, all he could have hoped for at his age would have been to remain a cavalryman and a junior officer. By committing the unpardonable sin of allowing Ulric the Bold to outwit him and being reduced to the lowest rank possible, he now held a position of authority which gave him total freedom of action within the confines of his orders and allowed him to make full use of his talents, his training and his experience. He knew that many men must envy him and he swore that if he could only find a way to breach his master's inexorable attitude towards him, he would be content.

At last, Conrad's wish was fulfilled. At the height of a battle, he chanced to look up and see that the Lord Gustavus was in danger. He and his aides were being attacked as they stood on a hillside overlooking the battlefield. Conrad called to some of his men and together they rushed to their general's defence. They were out-numbered by the would-be assassins but Conrad was undaunted. All that mattered was that he had the chance he had prayed for to make retribution. He fought proudly alongside his master, shoulder to shoulder, repelling every onslaught but as the last assailant was driven off he sank to the ground, bleeding from many wounds.

Thorkell came closer to where Conrad lay on a bed, deathly white and still, bloodstained cloths over his wounds. Tilly's sash was still around his waist and the skald bent over and touched it lightly. 'Well, my friend,' he whispered, 'I'm glad to see my little gift was not wasted.' A sound behind him made Thorkell turn around. He saw that the Lord Gustavus had entered the tent.

The general looked down at the bed and was silent for a few moments but then he said quietly, 'Skald, I want you to compose a final verse to *The Saga of the Wolf-man.*'

'Yes, my lord,' Thorkell replied. 'I shall sing that the Wolf-man forfeited his immortality in exchange for the life of his chieftain; that he died with honour and glory, a valiant warrior's death upon the battlefield.'

As Thorkell was speaking, Ingram entered. He approached the bed and looked sadly down at the still figure. 'My lord,' he said, 'I beg the honour of leading the Wolf-men.'

'Your request is granted,' replied the Lord Gustavus.

PART FOUR

I

Return to the mountain fortress

The court was in session inside the Lord Bardolph's mountain fortress; the Great Hall was crammed with people. Seated at the table at the far end of the chamber was the chieftain himself, the Lady Matilda at his right hand. Father Almeric sat close by, laboriously recording the proceedings and, behind him were the Lady Adela and the Lady Gertrude.

Gareth the Bailiff held the floor. 'The next dispute, my lord, concerns grazing rights,' he explained. 'One of your tenants has accused another of taking more cattle to graze on the pastureland of the high alp than he could reasonably expect to be able to feed during the winter. Shall I call the witnesses, sire?'

The Lady Matilda leaned forward in her chair and looked at her father in eager anticipation. Bardolph nodded and replied, 'Call the witnesses, Master Bailiff; the Lady Matilda will question them.' He slumped back in his chair, noting the satisfied smile on his daughter's face as she began her interrogation.

'This is a most serious matter and if proved, is a crime against our entire community.' The crowd murmured its agreement and pressed forward, anxious not to miss a word of the argument. Bardolph smiled to himself: these farming disputes gave Matilda much pleasure. He himself found court days increasingly tiresome and he made the bailiff hear all cases beforehand and deal with the minor ones himself. Gareth, of course, was quite capable of dealing with all cases himself but Matilda would not hear of such a thing. She enjoyed court days and questioned everyone with enthusiasm; in fact she carried out all her duties with enthusiasm. She would make a good leader when the time came. She was everything he could have wished for in a successor: proud, strong and single-minded. His only regret was that she would not marry. He had told her many times that she needed a husband to lead her armies into battle.

'Nonsense, Father, I shall lead them myself,' she had always insisted. 'Send me to my Uncle Gustavus's military school that I may be properly trained.' Bardolph hated to refuse Matilda any request but on that one matter he had stood firm against all her entreaties. 'Why should I not be trained?' she had argued. 'In Thorkell the Skald's homeland there are many women champions as well versed in the martial arts as any man. The shield-maidens are famous for their courage and prowess.'

'Curses upon that skald,' Bardolph had raged repeatedly. 'I forbid you to listen to his tales. You are not a Norsewoman and I will not have you risk your life in such a way. Your duty is to stay alive to rule our peoples; it is for others to face the danger of the battlefield on your behalf. If you would only choose a husband – one to take command when your Uncle Gustavus is gone ...' But Matilda would not choose a husband though he had paraded many suitors before her since she was thirteen years old. Bardolph knew he could have forced a marriage upon her but he had not even tried. Matilda meant so much to him; he could not see her unhappy. He had to admit also, that none of the contenders for her hand had been truly worthy of his beloved child. Nevertheless, the problem was becoming more urgent and he was beginning to feel his years. How old was his Matilda? He feared she must be twenty two years old. Such an age to be unwed: she should have had at least six children around her by now. What was the answer? Bardolph's thoughts were interrupted as his daughter gently shook his arm.

'Do you agree with my decision, Father?' Tilly asked in a

whisper. 'I find the charges proved. The man keeps six head of cattle over and above those which he can provide with fodder during the winter months. I judge that these six should be slaughtered immediately, before they can eat more precious grass, and the meat taken to your storehouses.'

Bardolph addressed the accused man. 'I concur with the Lady Matilda's judgment and, as a punishment for abusing the right to graze, I stipulate that ...' Bardolph was saved the trouble of thinking of a suitable penalty: at that moment a guard flung open the main doors at the far end of the chamber.

The man announced in a loud voice, 'The Lord Gustavus approaches!'

Immediately, Bardolph's lethargy vanished. 'The court is at an end,' he declared. 'Gareth the Bailiff will deal with any remaining cases. Make way for the Lord Gustavus!'

Hastily, the guards pushed back the crowd and made a passageway for the general. As he strode into the Great Hall followed by a number of his Companions, Bardolph got to his feet with renewed vigour, left the table and came forward to greet his visitors. The two brothers embraced warmly. Bardolph led the Lord Gustavus back towards the table; there the general bent and kissed the hand of the Lady Matilda who seemed as delighted as her father at his arrival.

'What is this,' demanded Bardolph in jest, 'late summer and you have ceased campaigning already? Have you accumulated such a vast amount of plunder you cannot store any more?'

The Lord Gustavus shook his head. 'It is true I have brought you some gifts but they are of minor importance.' A chair was brought and set at the table. When the general had seated himself he continued, 'I shall waste no time in telling you the purpose of my visit. I know you have been troubled on a very grave matter; I have felt for some years that I had the solution to the problem but there were reasons why I had to bide my time. I waited almost too long; death nearly robbed me of my plan.'

'You speak in riddles, my lord,' said Tilly. She had only half-listened to what her uncle had been saying: her attention had been captured by the stranger standing at the head of her uncle's followers and she had been unable to take her eyes off him. 'And you have forgotten to introduce the new member of your Companions to us.'

'No, my lady,' replied the Lord Gustavus, 'I have not forgotten. This man is not a new Companion. I have trained him from boyhood and know him as well as I know myself. The purpose of my visit is to introduce him to you.' The general paused and stood up. He spoke slowly and clearly that none should mistake his meaning. 'I have chosen this man to succeed me as warlord of our tribes and, to prove to you all the trust I have in him, I have also made him my heir, bequeathing to him my estates and my name.' He looked down at his brother and niece. 'My Lord Bardolph, my Lady Matilda, I present to you, Gustavus the Younger.'

A hush fell over the entire gathering. Bardolph was stunned. His first thought was that his saintly brother was, after all, as human as any other man – this must be his natural son. Then he reasoned that the two men bore little resemblance to one another: they were alike only in height and military bearing. Bardolph got to his feet, stretched out his hand and said, 'If you have satisfied my brother's exacting standards you must be a remarkable man indeed. I accept the decision. Welcome, Gustavus the Younger.'

'Thank you, my lord,' replied Conrad, stepping forward and taking the hand that was offered. 'You have my word that I will serve your interests, and those of the Lady Matilda, as faithfully as the Lord Gustavus has done.'

Tilly offered her hand also and as Conrad stooped to kiss it he met her penetrating gaze reluctantly. He saw at once that the face framed becomingly by her head-dress, was very beautiful. He looked quickly away. A beautiful woman had been at the centre of his downfall; he had vowed he would never be the victim of a woman's charms again. He was saved from further embarrassment by the Lord Bardolph who suggested that he and the Lord Gustavus should talk with him privately in his room. Conrad accepted gratefully.

When the men had departed, Tilly and the ladies hurried upstairs to share the announcement with the Lady Isolda. 'And he is so handsome, Mother,' said Tilly enthusiastically, concluding her story.

'He is even taller than the Lord Gustavus,' added Lady Gertrude, 'and his eyes – I have never seen a man with such clear blue eyes!'

'Blue eyes are hardly a necessary requirement for a warlord,' snapped Lady Adela. 'I noticed his broad muscular shoulders – much more useful!'

Tilly laughed. 'Do not quarrel, ladies. I agree with both of you. He has fine eyes and fine shoulders – in fact he is the perfect warrior – a mighty giant!' They discussed the newcomer happily until they were interrupted by a knock on the door. Bertha opened it and cheerfully ushered in the Lord Bardolph and the Lord Gustavus.

'My lord,' cried Lady Isolda to her brother-in-law. 'I am so pleased to see you.'

'And I am happy to find you so well, my lady,' said the general with a smile. 'I have brought you some fine tapestries and silks but,' he indicated the walls, all hung with colourful decorations, 'it seems you have no room for them.'

'I thank you,' answered Lady Isolda, 'and I assure you there is always a place for your gifts. I am a fortunate woman to have two such generous and thoughtful men as you and my dear husband.' She smiled fondly at Bardolph as he sat down beside her bed.

'We merely seek to bring some pleasure into your life,' Bardolph replied. 'I only wish I could persuade you to let me have you carried down to the Great Hall to share the entertainments there.' The Lady Isolda shook her head sadly. Bardolph understood: for years the room had been his wife's prison but it had also become her sanctuary which she was now too afraid to leave. He changed the subject. 'Have you no questions to ask our brother, my dear, concerning his momentous news?'

The Lady Isolda raised her face again; there was gratitude in her eyes for her husband. Tilly saw the glance. It pleased her that her parents had found such harmony. They were both beginning to look old, their hair streaked with grey, but as time went by they seemed to find more and more pleasure in one another's company. They were very precious to her.

The Lady Isolda's laughter broke Tilly's daydream as she answered, 'Of course I have questions – many questions!'

'And so do I,' said Tilly, joining in the conversation. 'Why have you never brought this young man to visit us before, my lord?'

'He has been fully occupied learning his profession,' replied her uncle.

'But you have never even mentioned him before,' chided Lady Isolda gently, 'yet you knew how concerned we were about who would succeed you when you retire from fighting.'

'Retire, my lady!' Gustavus was amused at the suggestion. 'I shall never retire but one day I shall die – I pray that it will be in battle. As for why I have never mentioned him, I had to assure myself beyond any doubt that my choice was the correct one. When this man was little more than a boy, he was guilty of a transgression – a sin of youth. It was the manner in which he rose above his subsequent remorse; the way he overcame his adversity and turned disaster to triumph that made me hope I might, at last, have found a man worthy to be my successor. I have tried and tested him many, many times since and never once found him wanting. He has powers of endurance beyond belief; ingenuity which borders upon genius; strength of mind and body found only in a supreme champion. He is the youngest commander I have ever had and by far the best. He inspires more confidence in his men than any general I have ever encountered. His courage, loyalty and integrity are beyond reproach. In his personal life he follows a moral code as strict as my own – in fact, we are very alike.'

Tilly had scarcely been able to contain herself during her uncle's glowing tribute. As soon as he paused she demanded, 'But, my lord, does your paragon have a wife?'

The Lord Gustavus made no attempt to hide his annoyance at the interruption or the irrelevance of the inquiry. 'A wife, of course he does not have a wife! Gustavus the Younger has lived his life as I have lived mine: a celibate life among warriors.'

'Then,' announced Tilly decisively, 'I shall take him as a husband.'

II

A predicament

There was silence. Everyone stared at Tilly in disbelief. 'Why are you astounded? Have you not all been urging me for years to marry a man capable of leading my armies?' she protested. 'If your heir is unused to female company, dear uncle, I may find him boring at first but I have no doubt that I can mould him to my liking in time.'

The Lord Gustavus remained speechless; the Lady Isolda did not. 'But we know nothing about him. What about his family, Gustavus?'

The general recovered his voice with an effort. 'He has no family, my lady. He was orphaned as a small child. I must confess that I found this an advantage when assessing his value to me. Had I known his father I might have been tempted to take my feelings for him into account; as it is, I have judged the man solely on his own merits.'

They argued for some time, discussing every implication at length until at last it was agreed by everyone that the Lord Gustavus's heir would be an excellent match for the Lady Matilda – everyone that is, except Conrad!

When Conrad was summoned to Bardolph's room and told the fate proposed for him, he too was at a loss for words at first. Regaining his composure, he replied politely but firmly, 'I am honoured, my lord, but I am not free to marry: I have been lawfully betrothed since boyhood.'

Bardolph turned on his brother. 'You made no mention of a betrothal.'

'I knew nothing of it,' answered the Lord Gustavus, adding, 'although it explains many mysteries.'

'Who is this woman?' snapped Bardolph. 'What is her name? Who are her family? I will gladly pay any fine they demand – and the Church too – to free you from this bond. My daughter's happiness is at stake.'

'I thank you, my lord,' replied Conrad, unperturbed, 'but I do not want to be freed from my promise. I do not know where my lady is – I have not seen her since she was a child – but I intend to search for her until I find her.'

'A child!' exclaimed Bardolph. 'She could be dead by now, or wed to another, thinking you were dead.'

'Those thoughts have tortured me for years, my lord, but I must know the truth. I owe her so much; I cannot break my oath to her. She is the only wife I desire.'

Bardolph retraced his steps to his wife's room and as he did so he reflected that he had heard those same words before – from his brother Gustavus's lips. It all came back to him: his father, King Theodoric, had made peace with the Burgundians and his own marriage had been a result; Gustavus had wanted to wed one of his mother's ladies; the king had forbidden it, saying he must save himself for a political union; Gustavus had sworn he would have no other lady but the one of his choice. The arguments had been long and bitter; eventually, his brother had declared he would not stagnate in a country where there were no wars to fight and he had left home to seek adventure and fortune abroad. By the time word had been received that he was returning to claim his bride, King Theodoric was long dead. Their mother, Queen Clothilda, had known what to do. 'We must send the girl away quickly – marry her off to some distant relative,' she had decided. The plan had failed because the young woman had contracted a fever and died on her journey to meet her new husband. Gustavus had reacted strangely to the news: he had blamed himself and not his family for the death of his beloved. Bardolph could not quite remember why this was but he thought his brother had been troubled by the fact that he had delayed his return by lingering too long at some fallen town. The reason was of no consequence now: it had all happened so long ago. What concerned Bardolph was the fact that his brother had been true to his word even after death had absolved him from it – he would take no other wife. Queen Clothilda, always astute and forthright, had commented, 'That girl was fortunate. Gustavus would have made an even worse husband than you, Bardolph! As it is, we have given your brother the very excuse he wanted to lead precisely the kind of martyred life he will most relish.' Perhaps her perception had been correct; however, he had to accept that the young man was very like Gustavus in manner and principles. He feared that Matilda would lose the husband of her choice whatever the outcome of the search for his betrothed.

Bardolph entered the room with trepidation. His announcement was received as he had feared: all the ladies were shocked and disappointed but Tilly was inconsolable. Her father realized that she had been thwarted over few things in her life and he could see she had convinced herself that Gustavus the Younger was all she had ever truly wanted. She had rejected so many suitors he could understand that to be rejected herself was an experience she could not accept. He tried his best to comfort her as did her mother, the ladies and Father Almeric – all to no avail.

'I forbid each one of you to speak of this matter outside this room,' Bardolph commanded, anxious to spare his daughter further mortification. 'I shall return to my room and send for Gareth the Bailiff. I am certain he will find a solution to this problem.'

Bardolph, red-faced, paced the floor rubbing his throbbing thigh as he raged at the bailiff. Gareth was not responding with his customary assuredness and this was not the reaction he had come to expect from his most competent of servants.

'But you say that even the young man does not know where to look, sire,' protested Gareth.

'You will find her, Bailiff, before he does,' Bardolph insisted. 'And if she and her family cannot be bribed, kill her!'

'My lord, please ...'

'I do not care how you achieve this – I do not want to know – but he *will* marry the Lady Matilda. She has rejected every suitor I have paraded in front of her but this young man she has chosen herself. Go see to it, Bailiff!'

When Gareth left Bardolph's room, a worried expression on his face, he found Thorkell nearby sitting on a trestle at the end of the Great Hall, swinging his legs and grinning at him. 'My, my, what a furrowed brow and troubled look you have, my friend,' exclaimed the skald.

'I have always managed to solve my master's problems up to now,' answered Gareth with a sigh, 'but I fear I cannot solve this one.'

'And the problem, doubtless, is how to persuade Gustavus the Younger to wed the Lady Matilda,' said Thorkell, archly.

'Who told you that?' demanded the bailiff. 'The few who know have been sworn to secrecy.'

Thorkell, acting out the role of a player, replied with a flourish of upturned palms. 'I am a skald; I know everything. It is my business to know everything.' Then he added with a roguish glint in his eyes, '*You* cannot solve that particular problem but *I* can.'

Gareth looked at the skald keenly. 'Do you mean that you know where to find this man's betrothed?'

Thorkell nodded. 'And I have a plan, but for that plan to

work, you must persuade our Lady Matilda and her reluctant suitor to journey to your home.'

'But why? His betrothed cannot possibly be at my home.'

'Have patience, my friend. Indulge me in this and you will be rewarded with the solution to your problem – and with your master's undying gratitude.'

Gareth hurried to the Lady Isolda's room where Tilly had flung herself across her mother's bed, sobbing as though her heart was broken. Eventually, the bailiff managed to persuade the distraught young woman to stop crying long enough to listen to what he had to say. 'My lady, the Lord Bardolph has acquainted me with the predicament that has presented itself regarding your proposed marriage. Might I suggest, Lady Matilda, that your father's crowded fortress is not the best place to settle a problem of this nature. In the past when you have been distressed, you have told me that the calm atmosphere of my home has charmed away your troubles. Perhaps it might have the same effect on Gustavus the Younger.'

'Of course!' exclaimed Tilly, sitting up immediately and giving Gareth her full attention. 'How right you are – but then you are always right, Master Bailiff.' Tilly's good-humour had returned in an instant. 'We shall leave first thing in the morning; when we ride home to this fortress once more, he shall be mine.'

III

Secrets revealed

The party set out early for Gareth's house, flanked by armed guards. At first, Tilly rode beside Conrad but he had so little to say to her that she soon tired of him. She reined in her horse, dismounted, drew herself up to her full height – she had grown into a tall and slender young woman – and with a disdainful glance at Conrad, joined her ladies in the covered wagon. Thorkell, assessing the situation, immediately left the men and rode alongside the vehicle so that he could entertain the passengers. Shortly afterwards, Tilly could be heard laughing.

Gareth took the opportunity to speak with Conrad. 'It is an onerous task you have been bequeathed, my lord,' he began. 'We live in violent and turbulent times.'

'I agree, Master Bailiff,' replied Conrad, 'but I pray that it will not always be so. I have seen enough carnage and bloodshed over the years to know there must be a better way to settle our disputes. War should be regarded as a last resort.'

Gareth looked at Conrad sharply. 'Those are strange words for a man who will one day be our warlord.'

Conrad smiled. 'Have no fear: I do not intend to allow our lands to be overrun by our enemies. I shall see to it that our army is as well-trained and well-equipped as it is possible to be. It shall be our deterrent: a warning to all aggressors not to trifle with the Alemannians. And there will be plenty, driven by greed, who will try. No one – I repeat, no one – shall take our freedom or our lands from us whilst I live. But, Master Bailiff, while I defend our right to protect what is ours, I also recognise the right of others to protect what is lawfully theirs. I do not hold with Raoulbrun's attempts to encroach upon our territory, but nor can I sympathise with our attacks upon his possessions – unless, of course, he uses them to launch attacks upon us. There have been times in the past when Alemannians and Burgundians have existed side by side in harmony. There has been much intermarriage – even the Lady Matilda is half-Burgundian. The only real difference between our two peoples is in language. We should accept one another as brothers and live and work together in peace.'

Gareth looked mystified but said nothing; he merely nodded his head at intervals and allowed Conrad to continue without interruption. 'I tell you, Master Bailiff, I abhor the long-standing dispute with Ulric the Bold even more. I cannot condone any situation which forces Alemannian to take up arms against Alemannian. The matter must be settled – and quickly. When I was a boy, my dream was to be a soldier and ride with the Lord Gustavus. Now that that dream is a reality it has been replaced by another: my dream now is to unite our warring tribes. Look around you, Master Gareth; see all the mountains. This land we share with the Burgundians is in itself a natural fortress. If we were to join forces, Alemannian with Burgundian and, provided we remained strong and vigilant, we could easily repel the Franks and any other invaders, however belligerent. Our country would become a haven, a quiet refuge in a harsh world, and an example to all of how to live with one's neighbour for the common good.'

'Those are brave sentiments, my lord, and ones with which I agree – in principle,' said Gareth. 'They show you to be an enlightened man but, I fear, a man born long before his time. Peace would not be welcomed by the young warriors: they dream, as you did, of fame and glory. And you would be hard-pressed to support an army, merely as a deterrent, without the spoils of war. Such concepts would certainly not be well-received by either the Lord Gustavus or the Lord Bardolph –

nor, for that matter, by the Lady Matilda. She has been brought up to regard aggression as the natural way of life. You might persuade her to treat with the Burgundians – it has always pained her to have to call her mother's family enemies – but to be certain of bringing your policies as a whole into force, you would need more power than that of a warlord – you would need the power of a king. Such power is within your grasp, my lord. You have only to marry the Lady Matilda and I am certain that in the course of time, when you have settled the question of the succession with Ulric the Bold as you say you intend to do, the chieftains would elect you as their king by common consent.'

'No, Master Bailiff,' stated Conrad emphatically, 'I have no wish to gain power in such a way and, as I have already told the Lord Bardolph, I am not free to wed the Lady Matilda.'

'I understand, my lord,' continued Gareth, 'but I wished merely to point out that if your dream of a country united in peace were sufficiently important to you, there might be a way for you to make it come true. For the time being, I would advise you to reveal your thoughts to no one else and, I must confess, I am surprised that you should reveal them to me – a stranger.'

'You are not a stranger to me, Master Bailiff,' replied Conrad with a laugh. 'I have confided in you because I know you to be a just and reasonable man and one whom I would expect to share my views. I have always trusted you and always shall.'

'My lord, you have me at a disadvantage,' protested Gareth. 'As far as I know, I have never seen you before in my life.'

'Indeed you have but I was a boy when we last met,' explained Conrad. 'I welcomed this chance to visit your home because I wished to speak to you of those days. I was known then as Conrad the Goatherd. I believe, Master Bailiff, that you are the only man who can help me to find my betrothed. Her name was Tilly; she was but a child herself – a servant at the fortress. It was she who taught me to read and write and to speak the language of the Burgundians. Without that knowledge, I should never have reached my present position. I must find her – and Hulda too, the old woman with whom I lived. You, yourself, promised to take care of her. I beg you to remember, Master Bailiff.'

Gareth, whose astonishment had increased as the conversation had progressed, replied in a low voice, 'I do remember but it would not be wise to speak further at present. We shall talk again at my house. The Lady Matilda seems annoyed that you have paid her so little attention. The journey is almost over; I suggest we ride alongside the wagon for the short time that is left.'

'Very well,' agreed Conrad, 'but will you help me in my search?'

'You have my word,' answered Gareth.

Tilly greeted the two men peevishly. 'Well, my lord, you appear to have no difficulty in finding topics of conversation with the bailiff.'

'Master Gareth and I have much in common,' replied Conrad politely.

'And you conclude you have nothing in common with me!' retorted Tilly.

'I am not accustomed to the company of ladies. I know nothing of the intricacies of embroidery or tapestry-making. You would find me a poor companion, my lady.'

'Embroidery!' snorted Tilly. 'Tapestry-making! Do you imagine that is all that interests me? My lord, you exasperate me more with every hour that passes.' Conrad looked away, unable to think of any acceptable words of appeasement. Tilly suddenly pulled the cord which tied back the curtain on that side of the wagon. The material was at once released and provided a partition between her and Conrad. 'I cannot think why I want that man!' she hissed, her cheeks flushed with rage.

'Could it be because he does not want you?' inquired Lady Adela quietly.

Gareth, embarrassed at the incident, saw with relief that his house had come into view. He addressed Conrad. 'I hope, my lord, that you will like my home. It is an old Roman villa but of course not as grand as the Lord Gustavus's villa and very, very small by comparison. I was riding through this district one day, many years ago, on my master's business when I came across a statue growing, or so it seemed, out of a bush. I was intrigued and dismounted to investigate. I found the statue was at the centre of a paved courtyard and around it were the floors of several rooms. I discovered marble columns too, some still standing but overgrown with brambles and creepers, others lying on their sides hidden in the undergrowth. The Lord Bardolph most generously allowed me to rebuild the villa. I like to think that the Roman who once lived in it might have been employed as I am – as an administrator.'

Gareth made sure his speech lasted long enough for him and his guests to reach the entrance to his house. His wife came out to greet them. She was a pretty woman, gentle in her manner; Conrad felt at ease with her. Tilly also was happy to see her hostess and she seemed to cast aside her ill-temper as soon as she alighted from the wagon. When the formal introductions had been completed she asked, 'Where is your son?'

'He is playing in Grandmother's room, my lady,' replied Gareth's wife.

'Come, my lord,' Tilly commanded, 'you must meet the rest of Gareth's family.'

Gareth's wife ushered Lady Adela and Lady Gertrude away whilst Gareth led Conrad, Tilly and Thorkell across the inner courtyard. Conrad gazed around him at the marble and the mosaics; he was reminded of the lectures he had attended in the Lord Gustavus's magnificent apartments. They entered a room with flowers growing around the door; the scent filled the air.

Tilly smiled at Conrad and pointed to the child playing contentedly on the floor. 'And here, my lord, you see Gareth's pride and joy.' The child looked round and seeing Tilly, he immediately got to his feet and rushed happily into her arms to be hugged. Once more Tilly looked towards Conrad. 'My lord, did you not hear me? This is Gareth's son.' Conrad did not reply: he stood transfixed, staring across the room. 'What ails you?' cried Tilly in alarm.

Again, Conrad did not reply, but suddenly he rushed past Tilly to where an old woman sat on the far side of the room. He fell to his knees and cried, 'Hulda! Hulda! Do you not know me? It is Conrad.' Recognition dawned in the old woman's eyes and tears of joy began to trickle down her wrinkled cheeks. Tilly, the significance of what she was witnessing dawning upon her, was so shocked that she was momentarily paralysed. Gareth, seeing her distress, went over to her and gently took his child from her embrace. Tilly ran out into the courtyard, distraught; Thorkell, with a nod to the bailiff, followed her. Conrad did not even notice them leave – he had eyes only for Hulda as he embraced her. He turned to Gareth and said, his voice full of emotion, 'How can I ever thank you? Not only have you taken care of Hulda as you promised, you have made her one of your family.'

'Mistress Hulda brought to my household her gift of healing,' answered the bailiff. 'From the very first day that she came here she used it generously. My wife was an invalid: she suffered from an affliction which robbed her of her strength. She could barely walk or stand; some days she could not lift her head from her bed. Through years of loving care, Mistress Hulda restored her strength, so much so that five years ago our greatest wish came true – we had a son. To be given the title, "grandmother", is small reward for all that Mistress Hulda has given me.'

'Nevertheless, I owe you a debt of gratitude I can never repay,' Conrad maintained.

Gareth smiled and picking up his son in his arms said, 'I shall leave you. You must have much to discuss.'

Outside in the courtyard Tilly, white-faced and shaking, confronted Thorkell. 'You knew his true identity,' she accused. 'Why did you not tell me?'

'It was better that you found out for yourself,' replied Thorkell gently.

'And Gareth? He must have known too since Grandmother is Hulda and she has lived here for years. How many more knew? Every one must have been laughing at me,' said Tilly bitterly.

'No, little one,' said the skald kindly. 'It is true that Gareth knew about your meetings as children but, when your uncle made his announcement at the fortress, he did not know that Gustavus the Younger was Conrad. I was the only person who knew that. I shall never divulge your secret to anyone and nor will Gareth. We both adore you – as you well know – and have done since you were a tiny child. We will do everything in our power to protect you. You have nothing to fear, my little shield-maiden.'

'That was what you used to call me when I was a child,' said Tilly, ruefully. 'God is punishing me now for still behaving like a child – a spoilt child – is he not, Thorkell?'

'No,' the skald replied. 'He is a kind and forgiving god.'

'Oh, Thorkell,' wailed Tilly, throwing her arms about the skald and sobbing against his chest, 'what am I going to do? I loved Conrad as a child and I want him now as a husband. You have always been my friend; tell me what to do.'

Thorkell looked down at the tear-stained face and

wondered how many times over the years he had been called upon to come to her rescue. He had never failed her. 'It seems to me that the answer is a simple one,' he said affectionately. 'Conrad wants Tilly – let him have her. Trust me, little one and do as I say. All will be well, I promise.'

That night Conrad had great difficulty in getting to sleep. He had spent hours talking to Hulda and the excitement was still upon him. He was in a light slumber and dreaming when a sound awakened him. At once he was fully alert. He sat up and thought he saw someone standing in the darkness by the door. 'Who is there?' he called. The shadow moved and by the light of the moon shining through the window, he could see the figure of a woman with long flowing hair.

The woman put a finger to her lips and whispered, 'Hush, Conrad – it is Tilly.'

Immediately, Conrad was on his feet and beside the apparition. 'Tilly,' he cried incredulously, 'is it you – are you real?'

'See, I wear the betrothal gift you gave me around my neck.' Tilly held out the carved wooden pendant for him to touch.

'My little Tilly, it *is* really you,' exclaimed Conrad. 'So Master Gareth has cared for you too. How much I owe that good man. But I cannot see you – let me attend the light.'

'No, No!' Tilly protested in a low voice. 'No one must know I am here.' She had her back to the window so that the moon's soft glow formed a halo around her head.

Conrad stroked her hair tenderly and said, 'They will all know about you tomorrow when I tell them that I have found my betrothed. You gave me the gift of learning; now I enjoy the fruits of that gift and you shall enjoy them too. I can buy your freedom and build you a fine house as I promised.'

'You also promised to claim your betrothed as your wife,' murmured Tilly.

'That I shall do, little Tilly,' answered Conrad. 'You are my wife; you have always been my wife and I will have no other.'

When Conrad awoke next morning, the first thing he did was give thanks to God for answering his prayers. A sense of gratitude overwhelmed him. Could any man be more blessed than he? He had the esteem of his revered master; he had position, authority and wealth; best of all, he had his beloved to share it with him. What more could he ever want? As he tied Tilly's sash around his waist, he thought of how his fortunes had changed since the day she had given it to him. The gift had been lying near his head when Conrad had recovered consciousness after the last battle; it had been the first thing he had seen when he had opened his eyes. Then a familiar voice had said, 'Welcome back, Master Conrad.' He had turned his head slightly and seen a smiling Sigurd sitting beside his bed keeping vigil. He had found himself in the Lord Gustavus's tent, his long hair, beard and dirty clothes gone and the sash, washed and restored almost to its original glory, by his side. In the days that had followed he had felt that the sight of it, the memories which it had invoked, the promises which it had recalled, had given him the strength to recover from his grievous wounds.

He dressed hurriedly and went in search of Tilly. He found her with the Lady Adela and the Lady Gertrude. She had her back to him but he knew her from her long golden hair. He went up to her and took her arm, saying as he did so, 'Lady Adela, Lady Gertrude, you are the first to share my good news.'

As he spoke, Tilly turned round and faced him. 'My lord,' she began, 'I have just told the ladies that you and I are reconciled.'

The smile left Conrad's face. 'Lady Matilda,' he stammered. 'My apologies – I thought you were someone else.'

Tilly leant forward and whispered in his ear. 'You seemed in no doubt who I was last night, Conrad.'

Instantly, Conrad concluded that yet again he had allowed himself to be ensnared by a cunning woman. Somehow, the Lady Matilda had learned about Tilly and had used the information to compromise him into marriage. His face reddened as anger welled up inside him.

Tilly sensed the change in his mood and at once took his arm and propelled him outside to the inner courtyard saying, 'Let us walk in the garden, my lord.'

Thorkell and Gareth, unbeknown to the couple, had been only a few paces away when the encounter had taken place. They watched as the pair walked together and the skald observed, 'She will soon convince him – and herself – that she had no other choice but to deceive him all those years ago; that she rejected all other suitors because she was waiting for him; that she knew instinctively who he was. See, now she is bringing forth her deadliest weapon: her dazzling smile. It will transport him back through the years to the meadows and forests of their childhood. He will see again the shining eyes and eager expressions he knew so well; his misgivings will vanish. He will be defenceless against that radiant smile – just as we have always been.'

The skald and the bailiff smiled at one another as Conrad and Tilly left the courtyard and rejoined the ladies, their joy plain to see. Sadly, that joy was short-lived because a few minutes later a messenger arrived with orders for Conrad and Thorkell. Ulric the Bold was threatening one of Bardolph's towns; they must leave at once. The lovers bid each other a fond farewell and went their separate ways – Conrad to war and Tilly to her fortress.

Bardolph showed no surprise when Gareth told him that a solution had been found to the problem of Gustavus the Younger and his betrothed. As expected, he did not inquire how such a miracle had been achieved – he employed the bailiff to perform miracles. Tilly spent her time making plans for her wedding, her happiness clouded only by the fear that Conrad might be injured in the fighting with Ulric's tribesmen.

One morning, Tilly and Bardolph were sitting together in the Great Hall. She was chattering like a child, cheerfully discussing her future and he was listening indulgently, sipping his wine. Soon his cup was empty and the man standing behind his chair leaned forward and refilled it. When he had done so the servant walked away carrying the wine-jug with him. Bardolph drank only once from the fresh cup. Moments later he struggled to his feet, his face contorted in agony. He clawed at his throat and fell writhing across the table; then he was still. Tilly flung herself across him and tried to rouse him. Gareth was the first to come to her aid. He picked up the cup and smelt the contents. Immediately, he ordered the servants to carry the Lord Bardolph to his room. Tilly, crying and trembling uncontrollably, made to follow. Gareth stopped her. 'No!' she protested. 'I must be with him.'

The bailiff's grip tightened. 'You must put aside your grief,' he said earnestly. 'You cannot help your father now except by carrying out his wishes. This is the moment he has prepared you for. What you do and say at this time will set the seal, not only on your fate, but that of your descendants. You must be brave.'

'I understand,' whispered Tilly.

Gareth led her firmly back to the table. The chamber was in uproar; Bardolph's henchmen were crowding forward to see what had happened and were clamouring to be told. The bailiff banged on the table for silence. 'The Lord Bardolph has been murdered – poisoned!' he announced. Again chaos broke out and Gareth called for order once more. 'Our chieftain is dead – long live our chieftain!' Seizing a spear held by a guard, he raised it aloft in salutation and cried, 'Hail, Matilda!' Still calling her name, he banged the spear handle repeatedly on the table so that the metal dishes clanged together. Others, slowly at first, took up his chant until the Great Hall was filled with their shouts and the clashing of their weapons on shields as the tribesmen acknowledged their new leader as custom decreed, by assent of arms.

When the noise had subsided, Gareth and the guard lifted Tilly onto the table and ashen-faced, she made her first speech as tribal chieftain. Her voice was steady as she said, 'I thank you – I thank you all for the years of loyal service you have given to my beloved father. I thank you too for the allegiance you have just shown me. I swear by Almighty God that I will not fail you and, with His help, will be a strong and just leader.' She paused and bowed her head briefly in prayer. When she raised it again her eyes were blazing with fury. 'First, my father's murder must be avenged!' Her followers yelled their agreement. 'Let no man rest till the assassin has been found. I have no doubt that he was in the pay of Ulric the Bold. Send word to the Lord Gustavus. Let the warning bell be rung and the people called into the fortress. Make ready for an attack by Ulric the Bold!'

IV

The trap is set

As the bell above the chapel sounded, people left their fields and their villages and crammed the road to the fortress. In the panic and confusion, Ulric's men were able to mingle with the crowd and enter the gates undetected. Once inside, with the element of surprise in their favour and assisted by the uproar coming from the frightened throng, they were able to mount the steps to the battlements unheard and to overcome the sentries on the perimeter wall with scarcely a struggle. Next they swarmed into the Great Hall where Bardolph's personal band of followers were still mourning the man they had known as a comrade as well as a chieftain. These men too were caught off guard, quite unprepared for the early timing and the suddenness of the attack. Although they put up a good fight, they too were soon Ulric's captives.

Tilly and the ladies were upstairs comforting the Lady Isolda when the door suddenly opened and a man walked into the room. 'Who are you?' Tilly demanded, leaping from her mother's bed, her eyes red and swollen from weeping.

The intruder bowed and said, 'I regret that our first meeting, face to face, should be under such distressing circumstances, my lady. I am your uncle come to offer you and your mother my condolences.'

'Ulric the Bold! You are Ulric the Bold!' cried Tilly. 'Who told you the news? How did you get here so quickly? Were you waiting outside the gates while the murderer you hired killed my father?'

Ulric was unmoved by the passion in her voice. 'You are distraught, my lady. You know not what you say. I come only to console and defend you.'

'You are not welcome,' said the Lady Isolda in a harsh voice. 'You have made numerous attempts on my husband's life over the years and now you have succeeded. I wonder you dare to show your face here.'

'My mother speaks the truth,' asserted Tilly. 'I shall call the guards.' She rushed to the door only to find the way barred by armed men she did not recognise.

'You forget, ladies,' continued Ulric, a wry smile on his thin lips, 'that this treacherous deed has robbed me of a brother. It is my duty to protect his widow and daughter against his enemies. This I mean to do. My soldiers at this moment are preparing to withstand a siege.'

Tilly ran to the window and recoiled in horror when she saw that Ulric's men were on the battlements and on guard outside the kitchen door. '*You* are our enemy!' she shouted. 'But you have made a mistake: you did not get here soon enough. I have already sent a messenger to the Lord Gustavus.'

'I watched him depart, my lady,' replied Ulric quietly, 'and I sent my own men after him to make quite sure he reached his destination safely. I shall leave you now, ladies, to continue your lament for your loss. When I return, perhaps I shall find you more amenable to my kind suggestions for your future welfare.' Ulric bowed again and swept from the room, the gloating satisfaction plain to see in his eyes.

As the door closed behind him, the ladies looked at one another despairingly. 'What can we do?' cried Tilly. 'Ulric has captured us and the fortress and he obviously intends to ambush our soldiers as they return. My first act as our chieftain was exactly what Ulric wanted – I have lured our people to certain death.'

'You had no choice, Lady Matilda, but to send for the Lord Gustavus,' said Lady Adela brusquely.

Lady Gertrude nodded her agreement and added, 'There was no one else you could have asked for help.'

'There is one other person,' said Lady Isolda slowly. 'We could ask my father.'

The ladies all looked at the Lady Isolda in astonishment. 'But why would he help us?' asked Tilly.

Bertha the Nurse looked up, hope suddenly in her eyes. 'Because you are half-Burgundian and his granddaughter,' she replied.

'Precisely,' said Lady Isolda, 'but how do we send word to him? Ulric will have ordered his men to let no one leave the fortress.'

Depair descended upon the gathering once more until Lady Adela announced, 'I have the answer – Brother Thomas! He brought fruits from the monastery earlier and as is his custom, he lingered to eat with Father Almeric. When our Lord Bardolph was so cruelly poisoned, I saw him enter our lord's room with Father Almeric. They will have returned to the chapel by now. I will tell the guards on the door that I must go to the chapel to pray. Brother Thomas will think of a way to get out of the fortress, I am sure.'

'But will he dare to seek out Raoulbrun the Burgundian and plead with him for our deliverance?' asked Lady Gertrude.

'You should have more faith in the courage of others, cousin,' said Lady Adela tersely.

Brother Thomas drove his wagon towards the gates and called out cheerily to Ulric's men. 'Sentries, let me through. I must go back to the monastery for another load of vegetables and fruit now that there are so many more mouths to feed.'

'We have orders to let no one leave,' one man called out.

'What harm can it do to let one old monk go?' Brother

Thomas argued. 'No one is hiding in my cart. See for yourself – it is empty. Ah, no!' he cried out, laughing, 'It is not quite empty: there are some apples in one corner. Would you like them? Come down and fetch them.'

The sentry climbed down from the parapet and collected the apples. Some of his comrades had heard what Brother Thomas had said, and they walked along the battlements towards the gates. The sentry threw them some of the apples and they all began biting into them. 'Yes, Brother, they are nice and juicy. You can go and fetch some more,' the sentry decided. Then he called out to his fellow guards, 'Open the gates! Lower the drawbridge! Let him through.'

As the monk drove his horse and cart out of the fortress he waved to the men on the battlements and called out, 'God be with you, my sons.'

Ulric called to one of his vassals, 'Hedwig, bring the man to me.' He then went into Bardolph's room at the back of the Great Hall and sat down at a small table. Hedwig entered soon after with the servant who had administered the poisoned wine to his master.

'You have done well,' said Ulric, 'and here is the gold I promised you.' The man stretched out his hand towards the small bag but Ulric pulled it back out of reach. 'But first, answer my questions. I am here because of your information; I must be certain that you were in no way mistaken.'

'My lord, it is as I told your spy,' stated the servant. 'The Lady Matilda plans to wed this warlord whom the Lord Gustavus has made his heir.'

'Was the match forced upon her by her father?'

'No, my lord, the Lady Matilda made the choice herself. The day after the Lord Gustavus arrived here and introduced his successor, the Lady Matilda took the young man to visit the bailiff's home. She must have made her decision there. She returned the following day – alone. Gustavus the Younger had been recalled to the battlefield. It was then that she informed her father that she had chosen her consort. I was not present at that meeting, of course, but I know that ever since, when she has been in the Great Hall, she has spoken of nothing else but her new love.'

'You are sure there has been no formal announcement of the marriage: no betrothal ceremony or exchange of gifts?'

'I am certain, my lord. There has been no opportunity. The young man was only in the fortress for one day and the Lady Matilda had not chosen him then.'

'And you think she is fond of him?'

'My lord, she is besotted by him!'

'Good,' said Ulric, fingering the scar which stood out pale against his swarthy cheek. 'Nothing could suit my purpose better. Here, take your reward.' He threw the bag of coins at the informer, adding, 'Get out of here before your fellows realize you are the traitor.'

Ulric turned to Hedwig as the man departed. 'The day I have prayed for has dawned, Hedwig. Everything works in my favour. Soon my father and my sainted and most revered mother will rest in peace. I shall have avenged them at last.'

'It will be a fitting end to all your endeavours, my lord,' agreed Hedwig. 'Within a few days you will rule over all the lands and all the peoples of your father, King Theodoric.'

'So it shall be. Now fetch the Lady Matilda.'

In the few minutes it took Hedwig to obey the command, Ulric sat drumming his fingers on the table, his thoughts far in the future, and a smile of smug satisfaction on his face. He then dismissed Hedwig, saying to Tilly, 'We shall talk alone, my lady.'

'I have nothing to say to you – save that I hate and despise you,' retorted Tilly. 'How dare you occupy my father's room? How dare you sit in his chair?'

There was contempt in Tilly's eyes as Ulric got up and

caught hold of her arms. 'I do not wish to quarrel with you, my lady; I hope you will see reason. I am the rightful king of all Alemannians; it would be better for you and your people if you accept that fact here and now. I am not a cruel man by nature and I would rather take what is rightfully mine by lawful and peaceful means than by bloodshed. If you do not wish your followers to die needlessly, you will do as I ask. Matilda, put an end to this incessant fighting; unite our tribes – by marrying me.'

For a moment, Tilly was so astounded by the unexpected proposal that she was struck dumb. Then she shrieked, 'Marry you? Never!'

'Why not, Matilda?' Ulric's strong hands were on Tilly's shoulders now, shaking her. 'I am a childless widower – that fact is indisputable – and you, it is well-known, have refused all suitors. There would be no more killings; our tribes would be as one and the succession would be assured by our heirs.'

'No! No! Never!' protested Tilly, fearlessly. She beat her fists on Ulric's chest and in the subsequent struggle they both fell onto Bardolph's bed.

Ulric laughed scornfully at her feeble attempts to escape him; with one hand he pulled off her headdress. 'It is said that you have beautiful golden hair, my lady – such a pity to hide it. How I shall enjoy stroking these silken locks.'

'Do not touch me!' snarled Tilly. 'I shall never submit to you!'

Ulric put his face close to hers and hissed menacingly, 'Make no mistake, my lady, you are no match for a warrior of my strength. I shall do with you as I please.' Tilly, unable to free her hands, suddenly darted her head forward and bit Ulric on the cheek. He drew back with shock and instinctively raised his hand to strike her. Then he stopped himself saying, 'No, my lady, you make me forget my carefully laid plans. This was not part of my design: I *will* have you, but lawfully. That is what matters to me most: that our union shall be seen to be lawful.'

He stood up and pulled Tilly to her feet. He wiped away the blood which trickled down his face and commented, 'A spirited full-blooded wife will be an added bonus.'

'Are you deaf or mad?' snapped Tilly. 'Have I not told you I will never be your wife? I am ...' Tilly hesitated and did not finish her words.

'You are what, my lady?' inquired Ulric with a sneer.

'I am ..., appalled by your suggestion,' announced Tilly, hurriedly. 'I loathe you! You are repulsive, repugnant to me – an odious creature!'

Ulric's expression contorted into an ugly leer. 'This I promise you, my lady,' he said in sinister tones, 'before very long you will go down on your knees and beg me to take you as my wife.' With a stony tight-lipped expression on his face, he marched Tilly in silence to the door and handed her over to Hedwig who was waiting outside. 'You know what to do,' he said, indicating Tilly. Then he addressed Gareth, who was standing a short distance away. 'Come in, Bailiff. I would speak with you now.'

Tilly, still glaring defiantly, was escorted by Hedwig. In the Great Hall, her dishevelled appearance was greeted by Ulric's men with lewd derision. As he passed her, Gareth patted her arm sympathetically. He stood calmly before Ulric's chair and could not resist a slight smile when he noticed the bleeding teeth-marks on the conqueror's face.

'I have heard good reports of you, Master Bailiff,' Ulric began. 'You are renowned as an excellent administrator. I wish your people no harm – in fact, I regard them as my people, which they rightfully are. Tell them that provided they cause no trouble and make no attempt to overcome my soldiers, they will not be injured. I do not want bloodshed. I am here to bring our conflict to a peaceful end through union with the Lady Matilda. I am a widower; she is unmarried and has never been promised to anyone. Is that not so, Master Bailiff?'

Gareth, though shaken by what Ulric had just told him, managed to reply in even tones, 'It is so, my lord.'

'Then it is a fitting solution. You will arrange the wedding as soon as possible.'

'But, my lord,' protested Gareth, 'the Lady Matilda's father was murdered only hours ago.'

'That matter has been taken care of,' stated Ulric the Bold. 'My men have already apprehended the assassin; he confessed under torture and was summarily executed. I have arranged for the Lord Bardolph's body to be buried at dusk in a warrior's grave with full tribal honours. The marriage ceremony I leave to you.'

'But such unseemly haste, my lord, when the lady is in mourning,' argued Gareth.

'I agree with you that it would be proper to wait,' said Ulric, 'but the Lady Matilda is a young woman alone. She faces many dangers, many enemies. The sooner she has the protection of a husband, the better. You, of course, would continue in your present powerful position after the marriage, except that your authority – and your rewards – would be increased once our tribes are united. Do we understand one another, Master Bailiff?'

'We do, my lord,' Gareth replied. 'And I shall attend to the arrangements for your marriage at once,' he said, bowing as he made for the door.

Hedwig entered the room as the bailiff left. He waited until the door had closed before reporting, 'The lady has been secured, my lord.'

'Watch the Lady Matilda closely, Hedwig. She is a firebrand.'

'My lord, you must be on your guard even when you are wed,' ventured Hedwig. 'I fear she will not hesitate to kill you, given the opportunity.'

'I am aware of that,' replied Ulric, smiling sardonically, 'but to live under the threat of peril will only serve to increase my pleasure. And when I can tolerate it no longer – once she has furnished me with an heir, an undisputed successor to reinforce my claim to the leadership – she will no longer be indispensable. It is well-known that the Lady Isolda has poor health so what is more likely than that her daughter should inherit her mother's sickness – and die?

But that is all in the future, Hedwig. We have other more urgent matters to settle. I was encouraged by the fact that both the Lady Matilda and the bailiff were at pains to prevent me from knowing of the existence of Gustavus the Younger. That means they are expecting him to make a rescue attempt. If he does not arrive after all my preparations, I shall be bitterly disappointed. Remind the sentries not to be over-vigilant – I want no heroes ruining my plan. As for Gustavus the Elder, it may be another day before his forces reach this high alpine valley but whenever he comes, we shall be ready for him.'

'Indeed we shall, my lord,' agreed Hedwig. 'The rest of our army will be in position, waiting to ambush him, by sundown.'

'All my antagonists removed from the face of this earth within hours of each other,' said Ulric, gloatingly. 'How sweet the taste of revenge.'

V

Trickery abounds

'You are right, Conrad,' said Ingram. 'There are not many of Ulric's men in evidence on the battlements. His main contingent must be hidden elsewhere, waiting for the Lord Gustavus to be lured into the trap.'

Conrad, Ingram and Thorkell crawled back through the undergrowth the way they had come until they reached the shelter of the trees above the fortress. There, Ingram left the other two and went further into the forest to give instructions to his Wolf-men. Since only the Lord Gustavus, Sigurd, Ingram and Thorkell knew that Gustavus the Younger was a resurrection of the Wolf-man, Conrad had been careful never to let his former company members hear him speak. Ingram was the only one who had direct contact with them and so the legend of the heroic leader remained intact.

Ingram addressed his men. 'There is little doubt that Ulric the Bold's seizure of the Lord Bardolph's fortress is a stratagem. He hopes to tempt our master to rush carelessly to the Lady Matilda's aid so that he may catch him unawares and annihilate him. Obviously, he has forgotten about the existence of the Wolf-men or, as seems more likely, he has been misinformed and assumes that as a force we have been disbanded. He will regret that mistake!' The Wolf-men howled their agreeement. Then Ingram singled out some of his men. 'It will be your responsibility to locate the exact spots where Ulric's forces are hidden. Then you will make all haste to meet the Lord Gustavus and warn him. The rest of you will enter the fortress with me at the appointed hour. Our prime objective will be to secure the release of the Lady Matilda. That accomplished, we shall overcome Ulric's men and recapture the fortress. On the instructions of Gustavus the Younger, war-machines will not be used and you will stun and disable rather than kill Ulric's men.'

As Ingram made his way back to rejoin his two friends, he thought back to the conversation which had led to that final instruction. Conrad had said, 'Remember, I want no harm to come to our people. That is why I forbid you to use any portable war-engines – they fire their missiles indiscriminately. Even Ulric's men are Alemannians whom I hope one day will join us of their own free will. I want as little slaughter as possible.'

Ingram had smiled and shaken his head. 'My friend, you have changed little over the years.'

'But you will respect my wishes,' Conrad had insisted.

'I am a good soldier,' Ingram had assured him. 'I always obey orders.' The two men had clapped each other on the shoulder and laughed.

Once the three were together again, Ingram turned to Thorkell. 'It is time for you to depart. We must pray that the sentries on the gate do not recognise you.'

'It is the price of fame,' said the skald, jokingly. 'Even the enemy knows the face of such a valiant warrior-poet as me, but in this half-light and in these stinking rags, no one will suspect my true identity.'

'Take care, Thorkell,' said Conrad.

'Come, you beasts,' commanded Thorkell, 'and mind you obey me!' He marched out of the forest followed reluctantly by a herd of goats which had been contentedly grazing and needed to be urged into action by the hidden company. The skald, controlling his animals with difficulty, made for the entrance to the fortress where two guards watched his approach with interest.

'Who goes there?' yelled one sentry.

'I am the goatherd from the next valley,' answered Thorkell. 'Why are the gates closed? It is not quite sundown yet.'

'Enemies about!' the man replied.

'Is that true?' demanded the "goatherd", feigning alarm. 'When I went to my village it was deserted – no one there. An old beggar I met on the road told me the Lord Bardolph has been murdered and that everyone has taken refuge here because Ulric the Bold is coming.'

'He spoke the truth,' shouted the other sentry. 'The Lord Bardolph is dead and Ulric the Bold is coming to invade us.'

'Then let me in quickly,' cried Thorkell. 'I do not want Ulric's men to catch me or my goats.'

The two soldiers laughed heartily at their ruse as they let down the drawbridge over the ditch and opened the gates. As Thorkell passed them, one called out, 'Goatherd, mind you bring us some fresh milk for rescuing you!'

'And some goat's cheese,' yelled his comrade. 'We are very partial to goat's cheese.'

The two sentries watched in amusement as Thorkell drove his herd into the crowded bailey with much cursing. He turned and waved to them, uttering more profanities under his breath. They then resumed their guard duties so they did not see him abandon his charges and his disguise at the first opportunity, and run off to seek out the bailiff.

The skald made his way to that part of the old Roman wall which enjoyed the least illumination either from the moon or the lighted buildings: the part shrouded by the mountain. He stood in the shadows for a few moments counting the number of sentries stationed on that section of the battlements. There were six. He withdrew a little way and then approached the wall again, this time noisily, singing at the top of his voice.

'Who goes there?' called out the guard above him.

'Who goes there? Why, I go there,' replied Thorkell, deliberately slurring his words and hiccupping. 'I am Thorkell the Skald. Surely you have heard of me?'

'I have heard of you,' a second sentry called out. 'Come to entertain us, have you?'

'I might as well,' answered Thorkell woefully. 'I came here last week to entertain the Lord Bardolph but now he cannot hear me.' He pretended to sob; the men on the wall laughed.

'Never mind, Skald, come up here and sing us your songs. We need someone to ease our boredom.'

'Help me then,' said Thorkell, holding up his arms. The two men leant over the parapet and tried to pull him up; he managed to frustrate their efforts.

'Let him come up the steps,' suggested one man.

'In his drunken state and in this blackness, he would never find them,' laughed the other. He called to the next two sentries along the wall to come and help. All four managed to haul Thorkell onto the battlements.

'I thank you, gentlemen, I thank you. Please forgive me my state of depression,' he said mournfully, beginning to enjoy his play-acting, 'but I got to thinking as I supped my wine that now I have no master.'

'It may be,' said one of the soldiers, 'that our master would be glad to employ you. You could compose some fine poems about Ulric the Bold. We could tell you stories about him you would never believe.' His companions confirmed this and cheerfully began to relate some bawdy examples of their lord's prowess, on and off the battlefield.

'Thank you, thank you, my friends,' Thorkell enthused. 'Now I must reward you as I promised.' He began to sing, choosing subjects he knew would enthrall the listeners. After a few minutes, the remaining two sentries further along the battlements, joined their comrades. When all six were present, Thorkell changed his tune and, as pre-arranged with Ingram, began a loud rendition of *The Saga of the Wolf-man*. Thorkell's singing, together with the clapping and cheering of his audience, drowned the sound of the Wolf-men's grappling hooks as they bit into the top of the wall. The assault party swarmed into the fortress swiftly and silently then crouched in hiding whilst Thorkell disengaged himself from his new friends.

'Well done,' Conrad whispered to the skald. He felt more than the usual amount of satisfaction at the success of his plan. He had deliberately chosen a means of access to the fortress which would not only ensure no loss of life but also had many similarities to the trick Ulric had used to gain access to the Alemannian stockade. That defeat had never ceased to rankle and in all his years as the Wolf-man, he had been doubly careful in his encounters with Ulric's forces.

'Tell us what you have been able to find out,' said Ingram quietly.

'Bad news,' replied Thorkell. 'Ulric's plot is much more devious than we had suspected. The bailiff says he has hurt no one except the Lord Bardolph's murderer who he has executed. The garrison and the Lord Bardolph's henchmen have been locked in the barracks but none of them has been killed. Gareth believes Ulric genuinely wants to take over the tribes with the minimum of bloodshed.'

Ingram sighed. 'Are there no more ruthless generals left – but me?'

'Ulric *is* ruthless,' Thorkell maintained emphatically. 'He has devised a plan whereby he can achieve his ambition and gain all the power he desires – legally – as he calls it: he intends to wed the Lady Matilda!'

Conrad was horrified. 'Thank God we are here,' he gasped.

'He is a mad man,' concluded Ingram. 'He must know the Lady Matilda would never agree to such a thing.'

'The bailiff fears Ulric would shrink from nothing to make her agree,' said Thorkell. 'Her father was buried this evening

266

but she was not present. She is being held in the dormitory above the Great Hall with her ladies. No one has been allowed inside the room but servants who took food to the door saw her lying on her bed, bound and gagged.'

Conrad was incensed. 'If he has harmed her ...'

'We shall soon have her safe,' Ingram assured him.

'There is no time to be lost,' Conrad decided. 'Ingram, the two of us will go alone – less risk of detection.'

'You can get to the dormitory through the chapel,' said Thorkell. 'Do not use the main door: it may make a noise and betray you. There is another way into the chapel: a small side door into the priest's cell behind the altar.'

Ingram left Conrad and Thorkell still huddled together, whispering, and went to speak to his men, ordering them to remain where they were in hiding. 'Have the net ready for the Lady Matilda. When we return with her, the skald will resume his act to divert the sentries. As soon as we have lifted her safely over the wall we can complete our mission.'

Conrad and Ingram crept towards the inner wooden palisade, making use of every available bit of cover. The gates stood ajar invitingly; there were no soldiers guarding them. 'This is too easy,' whispered Ingram. 'I suspect a trap.'

'We have to take that chance: we have no choice,' said Conrad, urging his friend forward. They eased themselves inside, their backs flattened against the frame of the gate. They continued thus, edging themselves along the stockade in the darkness, making sure their bodies hugged the wooden stakes. Across the inner courtyard they could see sentries standing in front of the main entrance to the Great Hall; others were patrolling the outer walls of the building. Sounds of merriment were coming from inside the Great Hall itself where Ulric's followers were feasting noisily. As they cautiously neared the side of the compound where the chapel stood, they found more guards on duty at those doors also. They continued to creep silently along the palisade until they found themselves at the rear of the chapel. There were no guards in that vicinity although a number of horses, obviously belonging to Ulric's men, were tethered there at the back of the Great Hall and the kitchens. Stooping low so that the shadows concealed them, they hurried stealthily across the courtyard from the stockade wall to the chapel and quickly located the small door to Father Almeric's cell. The old man was snoring and did not stir as they entered the tiny room and crept past his cot. As they went into the chapel, Conrad looked up at the balcony. He had attended Mass only once in the place – the day the Lord Gustavus had presented him to the Lord Bardolph as his heir – but he remembered its design exactly. He could just make out the figure of a guard near the dormitory door.

'Stay here in case we were followed.' Conrad mouthed the words; Ingram nodded. He concealed himself behind the altar and watched as Conrad crept stealthily up the narrow staircase. When he judged that his friend was ready, he deliberately shook the altar causing the ornaments on it to rattle. The guard leant over the balcony rail to investigate the noise and Conrad stunned him with one blow of his hand on the back of the neck. The man collapsed silently onto the floor. Conrad listened for a few moments at the door of the upper room before warily opening it and peeping inside. One small light had been left burning and he could make out a bed with a trussed figure lying there. Two other beds stood in shadow against the opposite wall. He could hear steady breathing coming from the occupants. He tiptoed into the room and crossed to the bed standing alone. Gently he pulled away the cloth which covered the lower part of the sleeper's face. But then he drew his breath in sharply – he was looking into Lady Adela's face! Simultaneously, he leapt aside and drew his sword as he heard the beds behind him creak. One man sprang at him with sword drawn and tried to force him back against the wall. He saw out of the corner of his eye, four other soldiers emerge from the shadows at the other end of the long room and advance upon him. Conrad was undeterred by such odds – he had fought much larger numbers single-handed many times before – and he prepared to do battle.

Then a steely voice called out, 'Lay down your weapons or my sword pierces her heart.'

Conrad glanced to one side and saw that Ulric the Bold had gone straight to where Lady Adela lay bound upon the bed and, holding the hilt of his sword in both hands, had positioned the tip of the blade so that it was touching the centre of her chest. The lady herself, her eyes closed, was quietly praying. Conrad at once threw down his sword and unbuckled his sax. 'Now release the lady,' he said to Ulric.

'Not until you yield to my men and allow them to secure you,' replied Ulric coldly.

Lady Adela began to weep. 'I am so sorry, my lord, so sorry.'

The men approached Conrad and bound his arms behind his back; he did nothing to stop them. 'Now take away your sword,' he shouted.

Ulric complied and placed his sword back in its scabbard. He was elated. 'You are exactly what I expected, Gustavus the Younger and, you have acted exactly as I expected. I knew my brother would not attack this fortress while his niece was held prisoner inside. I knew he would send his favourite to rescue her and I knew that you, anxious to play the gallant hero and blinded by love, would throw caution to the winds. I was so sure you would come that I did not even keep watch for you; I merely baited the trap and waited.

You entered by the chapel so we shall not leave by that route in case you have other men waiting there. We shall leave by the kitchens instead. Hedwig, cover his head and body with cloths from the bed. We shall have to descend the staircase from this dormitory to the Great Hall to get to the kitchens and I do not want our prisoner to be recognised. I want as few people as possible to know what happens here tonight.'

Moments later the guards ushered a struggling hooded Conrad out of the far door of the dormitory followed by Ulric and Hedwig. They left behind them a weeping Lady Adela who began to cry for help. Ingram, concerned at the length of time Conrad had been in the dormitory, had climbed the chapel staircase to the balcony, stepped over the unconscious guard and listened at the door. As soon as he heard the lady's cries he rushed into the room. When she told him that Gustavus the Younger had been taken by Ulric, his henchman, Hedwig, and four guards, he was incredulous.

'He allowed himself to be beaten by a mere six men – a warrior of his stature? I heard no sounds of fighting – no clash of blades upon blades. I would have rushed in to join in the fray if I had heard such sounds. Are you telling me he yielded without a fight?'

Lady Adela nodded, tears in her eyes. 'He submitted to them because of me. Ulric held his sword against my heart and threatened to pierce it through if he did not yield.'

'Ah, now I understand,' said Ingram shaking his head. 'Yes, he would yield to them without a fight under such circumstances. Come, my lady, I shall escort you to the priest's cell; I suggest that you take refuge there till morning although I am certain you no longer have anything to fear from Ulric the Bold. As far as he is concerned you have served your purpose. Then I must return to my men and we must search the fortress for the Lady Matilda and Gustavus the Younger.'

Tilly was half-asleep and bewildered when two soldiers marched into her mother's room where she had been lying on the floor beside Lady Gertrude. They roughly pulled her to her feet and dragged her, protesting, towards the door. In spite of Lady Isolda's screams and the efforts of Bertha and Lady

Gertrude to stop them, the two men soon had Tilly captive. They marched her down the staircase, through the Great Hall and the kitchens and outside into the night air. Neither would answer her questions as they crossed the bailey and entered the blacksmith's shop. The lean-to was illuminated by the glow from the furnace as two other soldiers worked the bellows energetically to make the fire burn brightly again. Ulric and Hedwig were waiting for her.

'Why have you brought me here?' Tilly demanded icily.

'I wanted you to witness a little ritual,' replied Ulric. 'Come closer, my lady.'

Tilly suddenly noticed a limp and bleeding body hanging in chains from the far wall. She turned her head away from the dreadful spectacle and shouted at Ulric, 'You are a fiend! Cut that poor wretch down! You will not win me by torturing my people.'

'Perhaps you should take a look at him – he may be known to you.' Ulric obligingly jerked up his prey's sagging head by the hair. Tilly shrank from the battered face in horror. 'Look again,' insisted Ulric, grabbing her by the hair also. Reluctantly, she obeyed.

'Conrad!' she shrieked.

'Conrad – is that his real name?' Ulric's delight at Tilly's anguish was plain to see. 'Conrad, Gustavus the Younger – whatever he is called – had the presumption to think he could outwit me and save you.'

'Oh, Conrad, Conrad!' wept Tilly. At the sound of her voice Conrad opened his eyes. He tried to speak her name but no words came from his swollen lips.

'And you too thought you could deceive me, my lady,' Ulric continued. 'You did not mention your beloved to me lest I set a trap for him. But I already knew about him; in fact, it was the knowledge of your forthcoming marriage which precipitated my actions. I have enjoyed my contests with your uncle, Gustavus, but the time for intellectual games is over. Did you think I would allow you to wed such a man as this: a warlord whose victories would inspire men to follow him? Did you think I would suffer yet another contender for the leadership of our tribes? No, my lady, I mean to be king. Soon I shall have no rivals: Bardolph is already gone; Gustavus will join him tomorrow and this upstart I shall put to death, slowly and painfully, in your presence tonight.' Tilly sank to the floor, moaning, as Ulric asked his men, 'Are the irons hot?'

'Red hot, my lord,' replied Hedwig.

'Where shall we begin the mutilation?' Ulric paused. 'First, I think we shall put out his eyes.'

'No, No!' screamed Tilly. She clawed at Ulric in desperation but he threw her effortlessly against the wall. Two of the guards approached Conrad and stood one on either side of him, each holding a glowing rod in his hand. Tilly rushed at Ulric again, tearing at his clothes and pleading with him. Again he pushed her aside but as she fell to the ground he said slowly, 'It is within your power to stop this. You have only to give your consent to our marriage.'

Tilly, in despair, nodded her head. 'Anything, I will do anything but do not harm him further.'

Ulric was jubilant; with a triumphant leer on his face he pointed to the ground in front of Tilly. 'Go down on your knees and grovel. Beg me to take you as my wife.'

Conrad's chains rattled as he tried to find the strength to protest. 'No, no,' he muttered.

'Do it!' Ulric commanded ominously, grabbing hold of one of the guards and thrusting the poker nearer to Conrad's face.

Tilly gave a strangled cry and crawled on all fours to Ulric's feet. With her head bowed she whispered, 'I beg you to take me as your wife.'

'Louder!' snarled Ulric. 'Louder! And I want to see your face when you say it.' He wrenched Tilly's face upwards and she repeated dolefully, 'I beg you to take me as your wife.'

'Now swear that you will relinquish all claims to the

leadership and order your tribesmen to acknowledge me, your husband, as their king.'

'I swear it.'

'You have made me so happy, my lady. Never again shall any man dispute my right, or that of my issue, to be King of all Alemannians.' Ulric turned to Hedwig and ordered, 'Unchain him.'

Tilly, the immediate danger averted, stood up and confronted Ulric, her fear subsiding. 'You have not won until I speak my vows before the altar. That I will do only if Conrad is alive and free.'

'You must think me as big a fool as this man – your beloved,' scoffed Ulric. 'If I set him free you will have no reason to go through with the ceremony. No, my lady, he remains in my custody until after the wedding. Then and only then, when you are my wife, will I release him; you have my word on that.'

Tilly knew she was beaten. 'Very well,' she agreed resignedly, 'but I want Conrad taken back to the Great Hall and cared for by my physician.'

'I agree to your request.' Ulric bowed mockingly.

Tilly stepped nearer to him and looking at him intently, said with unmistakable menace in her voice, 'And if in the years to come I learn that you have harmed Conrad in any way, I swear by Almighty God that I will kill you with my own hands.'

VI

The shield-maiden

One by one the Wolf-men returned and reported to Ingram, Thorkell by his side, that they had found no trace of either the Lady Matilda or Gustavus the Younger. But the last man to return had a different story.

'I was searching the shacks built against the outer walls when I saw a light; it was coming from the forge. As I approached, Ulric and his henchman came out holding the Lady Matilda between them. Four soldiers followed and they were carrying someone on a litter. When they passed the spot where I was hiding, I saw the bloodied face of the man they were carrying. I am sure it was Gustavus the Younger.'

'Was he alive?' asked Thorkell anxiously.

'I could not tell; he was very still but they had left his face uncovered. If he had been dead they would not have been carrying him so carefully. I followed them and they went through the inner palisade towards the Great Hall. They did not go into the building by the main doors but crossed around to the side and entered through the kitchens – all of them, including the Lady Matilda.'

'You have done well,' Ingram told the man. Turning to Thorkell, he said, 'Now we know how Ulric intended to force the Lady Matilda to marry him. He is a very cunning and clever man.'

'Yes,' agreed Thorkell, 'he is very clever for a mere warrior but, is he clever enough to better a warrior-skald? I must leave you now, my friend. I am the only person who can roam about this fortress without arousing suspicion. I shall come back to you once I have found out what Ulric plots next – and once I have devised a way to foil his plans! Where shall I find you? It will be daylight soon. You must find somewhere safer to hide or your warriors' attire with the wolf's head emblazoned on your tabards will betray you to Ulric's men.'

'Ulric is unlikely to return to the vicinity of the forge,' Ingram decided. 'We shall conceal ourselves there in the shacks built against the battlements. Once it is morning and the villagers who sought refuge in the fortress awake, the area will be teeming with people. They will keep us from discovery, I am certain. We shall stay hidden until you return. Godspeed, Thorkell!'

Ulric the Bold sat in Bardolph's chair behind the trestle at the far end of the Great Hall with Hedwig seated beside him. The physician stood nervously in front of them.

'I am told that you are a Burgundian,' said Ulric, 'and that you came here many years ago in the Lady Isolda's retinue. Is that not so?'

'It is so, my lord,' replied the physician.

'Then you owe no allegiance to anyone save her,' Ulric stated. The man did not reply; Ulric continued. 'I have promised the Lady Matilda that I will release Gustavus the Younger. I must keep my word and you shall be the instrument whereby he is released – from his mortal coil! I shall permit my bride to visit him at midday so that she may assure herself that you have done everything possible for his welfare. After she leaves you will administer this potion to him.' Ulric handed the physician a phial; he took it with a trembling hand.

'My lord, all will know that I have done the deed.'

'That is my intention,' said Ulric. 'It would distress my lady to think that I had murdered her loved one. But you have nothing to fear: I shall arrange for you to make your escape while everyone is in the chapel witnessing the marriage ceremony.'

'I regret, my lord,' stammered the physician, 'that I cannot do what you ask.'

'It appears that you misunderstand me.' Ulric paused to give his next words greater emphasis. 'It is his life or yours and that of your family. At this very moment, my men are removing your wife and daughters to a place of safe-keeping. They will be my hostages.'

For a few moments, the physician seemed to struggle with his conscience then he said, 'I see I have no alternative but to do your bidding. I insist, therefore, that you have a cart with my family in it placed in the courtyard outside, ready and waiting for me, after I have killed Gustavus the Younger.'

'It shall be done,' replied Ulric. 'Now you may return to the sickbed and your ailing charge.' When the physician had disappeared through the door to what had been Bardolph's bedchamber, Ulric turned to Hedwig. 'Arrange for the cart as I have agreed and instruct the sentries to open the gates and lower the drawbridge as it approaches. Such action should allay any suspicians the occupants might have. Tell the sentries also to have their bows ready strung and when the cart comes within range, to see to it that not one member of the physician's family survives to tell the tale.'

Tilly, her face a picture of abject misery, leant on Gareth's arm and gazed at Conrad's bruised and battered face as he lay in her father's bed. The physician who sat beside him said gently, 'He is only sleeping, my lady. Sleep is a great healer; he will recover.'

Ulric, standing in the doorway, was in no mood for delay. 'Make haste, my lady. It is time.'

Tilly bent over Conrad and kissed him tenderly on the forehead. As she straightened, tears fell onto her wedding gown. She took the bailiff's arm again and slowly left the room, pausing in the doorway for one last glance at the man she loved. Ulric hesitated too, looked back as Tilly and Gareth passed him and nodded at the physician. The man got up and pressed a phial to his patient's lips. As the liquid went into Conrad's mouth he shuddered. Ulric smiled and abruptly departed to join the wedding procession. He caught up with Tilly and Gareth as they were leaving the Great Hall. Positioning himself on the other side of his bride, he entered the chapel with her. The congregation was packed tightly together: Ulric had ordered that as many servants and villagers as possible must be crammed into the building as witnessses.

'Try to look a little happier, my lady,' he urged Tilly as they approached the altar. 'This is your wedding day.' Their path was lined by Ulric's soldiers, all facing towards the congregation, watching for any troublemakers.

Father Almeric came forward and in a sad feeble voice began the service. Tilly could not look at him; she kept her head bowed until Gareth squeezed her hand. At first, she thought he was only trying to comfort her but then she sensed urgency in his action: he was trying to tell her something. She looked up and saw that Father Almeric had an assistant – a monk. Next moment, the man raised his cowl slightly and winked at her. It was Thorkell. Hope suddenly welled up inside her and she began to tremble. Ulric, misunderstanding her reaction, shouted at Father Almeric. 'Speak faster, old man!'

'The Lord God's business cannot be hurried,' replied the priest with dignity. He continued at his previous slow pace for several more minutes while Ulric's exasperation increased; then he paused as though waiting for something.

The silence was suddenly broken by a voice which seemed to come from the very rafters of the building. 'I forbid this marriage: it is unlawful!'

The congregation looked around in astonishment. Then an

old servant chanced to look up at the balcony. 'It is the Lady Isolda,' he gasped. Many other retainers – those who had worked at the fortress long enough to remember their dead master's wife before she had been bedridden – echoed his words. They bowed their heads and murmured their respects.

Ulric followed their gaze and, seeing the Lady Isolda, glowered at her in fury. 'What are you saying, my lady?' he demanded.

The Lady Isolda, physically supported on either side by the Lady Adela and the Lady Gertrude, stated imperiously, 'My daughter was betrothed as a child; gifts were exchanged. In accordance with tribal law and in the eyes of the Church, she is legally bound to another.'

'You lie!' shrieked Ulric. He darted towards the staircase only to find his way barred by the old dependants. The soldiers moved to protect Ulric and were themselves surrounded.

'This is the moment,' Gareth whispered to Tilly. 'All has been arranged.' He pushed her towards Thorkell who grabbed her hand and pulled her behind the altar and through Father Almeric's cell into the courtyard. There a cart was waiting with the physician and his wife on the front seat and two girls seated in the back of the vehicle.

'Get in quickly,' urged Thorkell. 'The bailiff cannot hold Ulric prisoner for long.'

Tilly was about to protest when she saw that Conrad was lying on the floor of the wagon. 'He is alive,' the physician assured her. 'I beg you to hurry, my lady.'

Tilly lay down beside Conrad and Thorkell hastily covered them both with skins and furs. As the skald hurried away, tearing off his monk's habit as he ran, the physician urged the cart forward around the chapel, across the courtyard and throught the gates of the inner stockade. By the time it reached the outer bailey, Ulric's soldiers burst through the locked chapel doors, but Thorkell and some of the Wolf-men were already on the roof of the building waiting for them. They dropped the net which had been intended to aid Tilly's escape, carefully over the yelling mob and slid from the building. Leaving behind a struggling mass of entangled bodies in the chapel doorway, they raced across to the gates and closed them behind them. They hauled carts and every other heavy object available against the woodwork to form a barricade to delay Ulric's men further. Within moments, the guards had freed themselves from the netting, raced to the palisade and were hammering on the inner gates trying to push them open. Thorkell and the Wolf-men lent their weight to the barricade in an attempt to counter these efforts; they also knocked back any of Ulric's men who managed to scale the stockade. The few villagers left in the bailey, who had been unable to get into the chapel, ran to help them. Their actions went unnoticed by the sentries on the outer battlements. They also ignored the uproar coming from the inner courtyard: their attention was captured entirely by the sounds of a battle being fought in the distance. The eyes of every one of them were focused down the valley towards the plain.

Meanwhile, the wagon driven by the physician had made its way through the bailey, its progress hindered by the many grazing animals, towards the Roman wall. The noise of the trundling wheels caused the sentries to turn round. Suddenly, remembering their orders they rushed to open the gates and lower the drawbridge but as they made to raise their bows to shoot, they were pounced upon by Wolf-men. Throughout the entire length of the battlements, Ulric's men were taken by surprise. So engrossed had they been straining to ascertain the outcome of the distant battle, they had not heard the Wolf-men creeping up on them.

Ingram called out from the parapet in jubilation, 'The fortress is ours!' He dashed down the battlement steps and came running towards the cart. The physician brought it to a halt, turned in his seat and helped by his daughters, uncovered his passengers. Tilly sat up, tears of joy in her eyes. Conrad lay beside her, still dazed, but now his eyes were open. Sobbing with relief, Tilly threw her arms around him. 'Is Conrad safe?' Ingram asked anxiously as he reached the wagon.

'Thanks to you all, he is,' replied Tilly.

'I have been giving him potions every few hours to keep him in a deep sleep,' explained the physician, addressing Tilly. 'That way Ulric would think he was very ill and close to death. The liquid I gave him after you had visited him, my lady, to say farewell, was not the poison Ulric had given me but a bitter-tasting mixture to lift him out of his stupor. It takes some time to work – the body has to absorb its properties – but soon he will recover his senses and be well again.'

As the physician spoke, Conrad began to stir. He struggled to sit up and look around. When he saw Tilly beside him, his first thought was concern for her. 'The last thing I remember is Ulric forcing you to agree to marry him. Tell me you did not …'

'My mother stopped the marriage,' Tilly assured him. 'Her ladies must have carried her to the chapel balcony and she announced that I had been legally betrothed as a child.'

'It was Thorkell's idea,' said Ingram, interrupting. 'We needed a diversion to enable us to get the Lady Matilda, and you, away to safety. It worked just as the skald said it would – the chapel was in uproar.'

Conrad turned to Tilly and took her in his arms. He pushed away her ornamental headdress, already askew from when she lay concealed under the covers in the cart, and kissed the top of her head. 'Thank God you are still mine,' he murmured. Then other considerations took over and he demanded, 'Where is Ulric now?'

Ingram replied quickly. 'The plan was for Gareth the Bailiff and the servants to detain Ulric and his men inside the chapel for as long as they could and for Thorkell, with some of the Wolf-men, to hold them inside the palisade until I and the rest of the Wolf-men had re-taken the fortress. That we have done, so now I shall go with my men to the stockade.'

'I am coming with you,' Conrad announced as he climbed unsteadily out of the wagon.

'Oh! No!' cried Tilly in alarm. 'Where are you going?'

'Many people have made sacrifices for me today, my little Tilly, not least you. Now I must do my part.'

'But Conrad,' Tilly protested, 'you are still weak from your tortures.'

'I shall soon recover,' he assured her. Quickly, he addressed the physician. 'Take the Lady Matilda and your family to safety: the fighting is not over yet. I must seek out Ulric.'

Without further ado, Ingram and Conrad ran towards the inner stockade as the physician turned the cart away from the gates. At that moment, Ulric's men succeeded in forcing aside the barrier of obstructions. Ulric, together with as many of his warriors as he had been able to muster, galloped at speed into the bailey, scattering people and animals. Before Ingram's men could close the main gates Ulric and his followers, bending low over their horses' necks to avoid the hail of arrows which met them, were through them and over the drawbridge, headed for the battleground.

Thorkell was furious: he seemed to think he alone was responsible for Ulric's escape. 'You did well to detain him for so long,' said Conrad, 'and I owe you much already. You have saved my life not twice, but three times now.' When Thorkell looked puzzled, Conrad added, 'Ingram told me only recently that it was you who persuaded the Lord Gustavus into a stay of execution.'

For a moment, the skald looked almost bashful; but he quickly recovered and added flippantly, 'Only a fool lets his chance of fame and fortune slip through his fingers.'

More people came surging out of the courtyard; this time it was the servants and the villagers who had bravely tackled Ulric inside the chapel. Many were brandishing the legs of benches which they had used as improvised weapons and several appeared injured. Conrad sighted the bailiff – he too appeared to be cut about the head – but contented himself with a wave of salute. He knew he must be indebted to many people for his salvation and Tilly's, but this was not the time to express his gratitude.

Ingram rode up with horses and borrowed weapons – a sword and a shield apiece – for Conrad and Thorkell and as they mounted he told them that the garrison had been released. 'Those men will take over the fortress thus releasing the Wolfmen for the battlefield. Bardolph's nobles had been imprisoned with the garrison and they have volunteered to come with us.'

Moments later, Conrad, Ingram and Thorkell led the Wolfmen from the fortress closely followed by Bardolph's henchmen, intent upon the most important hunting expedition of their lives. Tilly, who watched them go, was not rewarded with one single wave or backward glance. She stood beside Gareth in the bailey – she had refused to go with the physician and his family – as the riders disappeared from sight.

'Oh, Gareth, he should not have gone,' she cried as they walked together towards the inner palisade. 'He must be so weak; he will surely die.'

'No, my lady, he is a warrior. He will have recovered quickly from countless beatings and woundings over the years,' the bailiff assured her. 'We feared your betrothed would have regained his strength by this morning and that, recklessly, he would once more have come to your aid. That is another reason why the physician deliberately induced a state of deep sleep in him, lest you both be killed. The skald's plan was designed to minimize the amount of danger you would be in and to prevent loss of life on both sides if at all possible. Thorkell knew that was what Gustavus the Younger would wish.'

Before Gareth could continue with his reassurances, the noise of a commotion coming from the battlements made them stop and turn around. Men were running to their appointed stations and the garrison commander was shouting his instructions. 'Raise the drawbridge! Shut the gates! The Burgundians are coming! Prepare for an attack!'

Tilly was aghast. 'Brother Thomas must have persuaded my grandfather to come to my rescue. I must stop our soldiers from shooting him.' She began to run towards the Roman wall, but she was hampered by the hundreds of villagers and servants who, screaming in panic, were trying to get back into the haven they had just left: the inner stockade. 'The Burgundians come as friends not foe! Do not fire on them!' she yelled again and again. But her words were lost as the pandemonium increased.

Gareth caught up with Tilly and grabbed her arm. 'Stop, my lady, it will do no good. Raoulbrun has no way of knowing that we have re-taken the fortress. He will think that the soldiers on the battlements belong to Ulric and he will order his army to fire on them.'

'Oh, Gareth, what have I done? What have I done?' Tilly wailed. 'They will kill each other and all because of me.'

'You must go back to the inner palisade. It is your duty as chieftain to stay alive,' said Gareth earnestly. Then, seeing how distraught she was, he added kindly, 'I will seek out the garrison commander and get him to stop his men from firing their arrows. Go, my lady. Take refuge inside the stockade.'

Tilly watched as the bailiff pushed his way through the throng. 'But who will get Raoulbrun to stop *his* men from firing *their* arrows?' she whispered to herself. She looked around her in despair, overwhelmed at the thought of the needless slaughter which could shortly ensue. Suddenly, she had the answer. 'I will!' she shouted out loud.

A soldier, who had been reeling his horse around in the crowd ahead of her, heard her cry and immediately rode to her side. He dismounted and placed his hands around her tiny waist and lifted her effortlessly onto the horse. 'The garrison commander has ordered that I take you to the safety of the stockade, my lady. I have been searching for you for several minutes. We must hurry before the Burgundian missiles start to land inside the bailey.'

The man made to jump up behind Tilly but she thwarted his efforts by instantly changing her position so that she was straddling the horse; placing her feet in either stirrup. 'Give me your shield!' she demanded.

'My lady?' inquired the man, puzzled. 'I shall protect you.'

'I order you to give me the shield which is slung across your back,' she said harshly. Reluctantly, the man obeyed, disentangling himself from his shield and passing it up to Tilly. Without hesitation, she put her right forearm through the leather arm-strap on the underside of the shield and clasped the fingers of her right hand firmly around the metal bar which formed the hand-grip. Holding the reins high in her left hand she then urged the horse forward, digging her heels into his sides.

When the stallion moved forward, the soldier realized what was in her mind. 'No, my lady! Stop! You will be killed!' he called out.

Tilly did not stop until she neared the Roman wall. Then she shouted, 'Open the gates! Lower the drawbridge!' When the sentries hesitated, she repeated her instructions. 'I am your chieftain. You are sworn to obey me. I order you to open the gates and lower the drawbridge!'

Gareth and the garrison commander, talking together on the battlements, were astounded to hear the clanking of the chains as the drawbridge was lowered. They rushed along the parapet towards the gates and were in time to see Tilly gallop out onto the drawbridge before it was fully lowered. She made the horse jump as they reached the edge and easily cleared the ditch; then headed down the meadowland towards the advancing Burgundian army. Everywhere arrows intersected the air: from both the Alemannians on the battlements and the Burgundians on the meadowland. The stallion reared up, startled by the constant hissing noise as the missiles crisscrossed past him from all directions. Tilly managed to hang on, gripping the animal with her knees, talking to him soothingly and leaning forward so that she could hold the shield over his head as well as her own. The hail of arrows seemed to increase in intensity but most glanced harmlessly off the shield. Some, however, became embedded in the tough leather of the outer cover. Others had been discharged from their bows with such power that Tilly did not have the strength to deflect them properly and the shield tilted under the force of their impact. When these arrows fell from the rim they scraped her upper back, her left shoulder and her left arm. The sharp edges of the metal piles penetrated the delicate silk material of her wedding dress and grazed her flesh. Soon those sections of her gown were in tatters and its pale pastel colour turned to bright crimson. Undeterred she pressed on, skirts billowing and long golden tressess fanning out behind her, galloping towards the unmistakable figure of Raoulbrun the Burgundian. The hailstorm of arrows coming from the direction of the fortress petered out as the garrison commander's cry of 'Cease firing!' was at last heard by his men. Now Tilly was close enough for Brother Thomas to recognize her. At once he raced ahead until his mount was alongside Raoulbrun's and he could call out to the general that this was not a champion come to challenge him but his granddaughter come to welcome him.

The bailiff and the garrison commander watched with relief as the Burgundian archers lowered their bows and as Brother Thomas introduced the Lady Matilda to Raoulbrun the Burgundian. Minutes later, the two men stood on the parapet as Tilly, bloodied but triumphant, eyes shining, face aglow, raised her shield on high in salute – arrows still embedded in it – as she rode at the head of the Burgundian army and led them over the drawbridge into her fortress. All her tribesmen on the battlements cheered and clashed their weapons as she passed through the gates. 'How sorry Thorkell the Skald will be when he learns that he has missed such a spectacle – such a moment of glory,' said Gareth, smiling. 'But I am certain that will not prevent him from composing a most rousing song in tribute to our very own heroic shield-maiden.'

VII

'To the victor, the spoils'

The wind in Conrad's bruised and swollen face helped to revive him as he galloped towards the sounds of battle. He could feel it blowing away the last vestiges of the sleep-inducing potions the physician had given him. By the time he arrived at the battlefield – at a bend in the valley just out of sight of the mountain fortress – he had regained his senses fully. The Lord Gustavus saw the reinforcements arrive and raised his sword in acknowledgement. Conrad rode over to him. 'The Lady Matilda is safe, my lord. The Wolf-men took back the fortress and it is in the safe hands of its garrison once more. Where is Ulric the Bold?'

'I have not seen him,' replied the Lord Gustavus. 'If I had, I would have killed him for what he has done.'

The two men could talk no more; they were soon separated in the fray. The battle raged, a confusion of individual contests. Ulric had been denied the grand tactics he had planned: the Wolf-men had discovered his positions in time and had informed their general.

Suddenly, Sigurd ran up to Conrad. 'Come quickly! The Lord Gustavus is mortally wounded. He challenged Ulric the Bold in the name of the Lord Bardolph.'

When they reached the scene, the Lord Gustavus was lying on the ground supported by his Companions and Thorkell. Conrad knelt beside him. 'He was too strong for me – too young,' he murmured. 'I should have challenged him years ago.'

'Save your strength, my lord,' urged Conrad, clasping his master's hand. 'We have sent for the physician.'

'Too late,' whispered the general. 'Remember, to the victor, the spoils. You must be the victor ...' Then with his last breath he gasped, 'You are my chosen son – avenge me ...' His final words were lost in a sigh but there was no mistaking his meaning.

Conrad, his voice full of emotion, promised, 'I will avenge you, my lord; I swear it.' He remained head bowed in silent lament until the chanting of the chaplain roused him. He took his dead lord's hand to his lips in a gesture of farewell then reluctantly relinquished his grasp. As he got to his feet he announced, 'I must find Ulric the Bold'.

'He rode off up the valley, my lord,' replied Sigurd. 'He called to his men to follow, saying there would be another day, but few heard him.'

At once Conrad shouted above the uproar, 'Let the horns sound for battle to cease!' The notes filled the air and gradually the fighting ended and stillness descended upon the combatants. 'Ulric the Bold has deserted the field of battle,' announced Conrad in a loud voice. 'The Lord Gustavus is dead. Lay down your arms. I go to challenge Ulric to single combat. Let our conflict be settled now and forever by the outcome of this dual.'

Thorkell brought Conrad a horse and he had already mounted it when Ingram came running up. 'The Lady Matilda was right: you are not strong enough to face Ulric yet. It is only weeks since you almost died of your wounds and last night's injuries will have weakened you further. Let me go in your place.'

'Thank you, Ingram, but no,' replied Conrad solemnly. 'It is for me to go – and to go alone.'

Ingram was about to protest further but Thorkell stopped him. 'It is pointless to argue. Conrad is right: he alone must avenge Gustavus the Elder and, above all, he alone must settle the matter of the Alemannian succession.'

With the good wishes of his friends ringing in his ears, Conrad rode back the way he had come until he was within sight of the fortress. As he crossed the open pastureland he saw Ulric disappearing into the trees above him at the very spot where he and Tilly had enjoyed many meetings when they were children. Urging his mount forward, he gave chase. As the climb became steeper he abandoned his horse and pursued his enemy on foot. Soon Conrad had left the darkness of the forest behind and had emerged into the bright sunlight of the open alp. Here were the favourite haunts of his boyhood. Now he knew where Ulric was going: he was making for the high pass over into the next alpine valley. Conrad increased his pace, determined to head him off. Eventually his plan succeeded and he leapt out in front of a startled Ulric. Brandishing his drawn sword, his shield at the ready, he declared in steely tones, 'I challenge you in the name of the Lord Gustavus. Prepare to defend yourself!'

'Ever the hero,' replied Ulric sarcastically as he dragged his shield from his shoulder and drew his sword from its scabbard.

The two warriors circled one another warily. Conrad had never come face to face with Ulric in battle before. As he watched his adversary he felt his rage increase, welling up inside him until he felt he would burst. This man had caused him so much suffering over the years: he had murdered the Lord Bardolph; he had killed the Lord Gustavus; he had terrorized Tilly and would have condemned her to a life of misery. Conrad had never felt such hatred for anyone as he felt for Ulric at that moment. Then he cautioned himself: he must not allow himself to become inflamed. When his emotions were roused he made mistakes – disastrous mistakes. How else had Ulric been able to outwit him – twice? How else had he come to be wounded so badly by Raoulbrun, and by the would-be assassins of the Lord Gustavus? He must remain calm; he must forget that he was facing his arch-enemy in a fight to the death; that the outcome of this dual would set the seal upon Tilly's fate; that it would decide who should be the ruler of all the

Alemannian tribes. Instead, he must pretend that the man he was facing was just another champion come to challenge him.

The combatants sprang together delivering the first strokes. The rocks resounded to the clang of metal on metal, of sword blade on iron rimmed shield. Conrad's pain disappeared; his injuries of the previous night were forgotten. Ulric proved a tough and vicious opponent. They exchanged blow for blow and slowly their contest brought them down the mountainside till they were just above the treeline again. There catastrophe awaited Conrad: he fell backwards over a tree root and his sword fell from his grasp. In an instant, Ulric had seized the weapon and flung it high in the air. It vanished from sight into a ravine. Conrad regained his footing and bounded back inside the forest, desperately searching for something he could use in his defence. He grabbed a fallen branch and used it as a weapon just as he had years before when the prisoners had attacked him to steal Tilly's sash. But this time it proved a useless deterrent: Ulric slashed at the branch repeatedly with his sword until the sharp blade had reduced it to a mere stump in Conrad's hand.

Certain of triumph, Ulric rushed at him yelling, 'I have you at last!' Only his shield saved Conrad: he used it not just to protect himself and to intercept Ulric's blows but, as Otto had taught him first when he was a boy, as a weapon to inflict injury upon his opponent. As he deflected his enemy's sword away from him, he jammed the iron rim of his shield into Ulric's ribs and the bronze boss into his face. When Ulric staggered backwards from the force of the attack, Conrad hooked his foot behind the torturer's calf and sent him sprawling to the ground. At that moment, a ray of sunlight through the trees glinted on something in the distance. The glimmer caught Conrad's eye and made him look up, beyond the prostrate figure of his adversary. He knew at once what it was that was shining; beckoning him like a beacon. It was an axe stuck in a tree where it had been abandoned by a frightened woodcutter when he had heard the warning bell sound in the fortress below. Ulric was struggling to get up. Conrad hesitated; then remembering that he still held the remains of the branch in his hand, he threw the stump at Ulric's head with all his might, stunning him. Seizing his opportunity, his spirits soaring, Conrad dashed through the trees and grabbed the axe. With his face upturned to the sky he called out, 'Forgive me Otto and help me now!'

Ulric scrambled to his feet, blood trickling from the wound to his temple, and hurled himself headlong after Conrad. The fight began all over again but from the start Conrad had the advantage. He had recovered his strength after his last battle as the Wolf-man but not the supernatural might he had known previously – that had deserted him. But as soon as he took the axe in his hand, even though it was not the Frankish throwing axe which he had been accustomed to, he felt his former legendary powers returning, flooding his body like a river. He felt inspired: as though he had to show Otto that all the hours he had spent in training him had not been wasted but had been for this one purpose. He felt that once more he was the mighty invincible warrior, the leader of the "swine-array", the champion-of-champions. Instinctively, he threw back his head, adopting his famous wolf's howl and descended upon his enemy like some raging avenging angel.

Ulric had heard that battle cry many times over the years and though he had never faced the creature himself but had only spied him in the distance, many of his warriors had described the fearsome sight to him. He saw the blazing eyes and heard the chilling howls. He was stunned as realization dawned upon him. 'Now I know who you are,' he gasped. 'You are the Wolf-man!' Suddenly, it seemed to Ulric that the warrior rushing towards him was not Gustavus the Younger but a giant with a wolf's head. He fought back courageously but he sensed that the axe was no ordinary weapon to his antagonist. He became weaker as this monster became stronger. He could no longer take the blows on his shield; rather the shield seemed to grow heavier, dragging his forearm downwards. With his guard lowered and his means of defence gone, gashes appeared on his arms and chest as the axe found its mark. He was convinced that, without an iota of doubt, he was facing the immortal superhuman being of the saga – facing his nemesis and facing his doom.

Conrad brought years of skill to bear knowing that a lifetime of learning and experience would culminate in that moment when he would strike the fatal blow. At last that moment came and summoning all his might he sent Ulric the Bold to his death.

With his foe lifeless at his feet, Conrad fell to his knees and gave thanks – to God, to Otto and to the Lord Gustavus – for his deliverance. Then he threw Ulric's dead body over his shoulder in the same manner that he had carried the wounded guard and, grasping the handle of the axe in his other hand, he dragged the weapon along the ground just as he had the huge wolf. Thus he strode down through the forest and emerged from the trees like the legendary hero of the saga. The sight which greeted him stopped him in his tracks. He saw below him the massed armies of Gustavus, Ulric and Raoulbrun, watching and waiting in silence for the outcome of the duel. There too were the servants of the fortress and the villagers; in front of them stood Thorkell, Ingram, Sigurd and Gareth. Tilly was there with her ladies and her mother. The Lady Isolda, seated upon a litter, had her father, Raoulbrun the Burgundian, beside her and Father Almeric and Brother Thomas.

For a few moments Conrad surveyed the momentous scene, a gathering he had not dared to hope for so soon: Alemannians and Burgundians standing side by side in harmony. Could his dream become a reality? Could these warring tribes unite and live together as neighbours for the common good? Only the years ahead would provide the answers. Then he let Ulric's limp form slip from his shoulder and roll down the slope towards the onlookers. Taking his axe in both hands he held it high above his head in triumph. Tilly, a girl once more, hoisted her skirts and raced up the hillside towards him. As she reached him, he cast aside the axe, caught her in his arms and swung her joyfully into the air. A roar came from the assembled crowd below and with one accord all the warriors clashed their weapons against their shields and raised them in salute to the victor.